I0736619

THE THING
IN YELLOW

THE THING IN *Yellow*

D.T. NEAL

NOSETOUCH PRESS

CHICAGO · PITTSBURGH · MMXXIII

THE THING IN YELLOW
© 2023 by D.T. Neal
All Rights Reserved.

ISBN-13: 978-1-944286-33-0
Paperback Edition

Published by Nosetouch Press
www.nosetouchpress.com

For more information, contact Nosetouch Press:
info@nosetouchpress.com

Cataloging-in-Publication Data

Names: Neal, D.T., author.
Title: The Thing in Yellow
Description: Chicago, IL : Nosetouch Press [2023]
Identifiers: ISBN: 9781944286330 (paperback)
Subjects: LCSH: Horror tales—Fiction. |
Occult—Fiction. | Supernatural—Fiction. |
GSAFD: Horror fiction. | BISAC: FICTION / Horror |
FICTION / Occult & Supernatural.

Cover & Interior Designed by Christine M. Scott
www.clevercrow.com

For Christine,
WITH ALL OF HER
GRAND DESIGNS…

TABLE OF CONTENTS

The Yellow Journalist

Yellow: Featuring sensational or
scandalous items or ordinary news
sensationally distorted (yellow journalism).

Yellow journalism. Such an insult to the profession. Some might say I'm a yellow journalist, but it's just because of what I've been studying.

You want to judge the health of a nation, look to its journalists. They're the canaries in the coalmine. Yeah, canary yellow, right? Caught that, did you? But, seriously, truth is always a dangerous thing, and a journalist, I mean, a *good* one, has to chase the truth wherever it takes them. That's the story the journalist covers. You have to follow the story to its end, wherever it takes you. That's the danger, the dance, the dedication to the profession.

A journalist is a detective more than anything else. Did you know that? It's true. We sniff out stories and find leads and we chase them down. We learn by asking questions, by sticking our noses into other people's business, by snooping.

And people hate journalists for it. I'm saying if you're a good journalist, a hard-hitting one, people will come to hate and fear you. Find me a well-loved journalist, and I'll tell you that you've got somebody who likes being seen as a journalist but isn't practicing so much journalism. It's a real problem—celebrity journalists? You see them out there? No journalist worth their salt (ha) is a celebrity.

Or more to the point, a journalist who values their celebrity more than their journalism isn't going to remain a journalist for long. Sooner or later, they sell their soul for celebrity, and that becomes more important to them than the journalism they were doing before they got famous. Here's the equation, the simple math:

$$\text{Celebrity} \neq \text{Journalism}$$

I know what you're thinking—but maybe a high-profile celebrity journalist can uncover truth because they have access to other high-profile people. Wrong answer! Nope. Their specialty is puff pieces and public relations, not journalism. Having a couple of celebrities chatting each other up isn't journalism:

$$\text{Puff Pieces} \neq \text{Journalism}$$
$$\text{Public Relations} \neq \text{Journalism}$$

I'm not famous; I'm not even infamous. But I am definitely hated, if not feared. If a journalist becomes feared, they eventually end up dead, if they're up against some really nasty things. It's how I might end up, to be honest.

Heh, to be honest. What a phrase that is. To be honest, I might end up dead. Lying would've been so much easier. Safer, even. Maybe?

That's the thing—a good journalist exposes the bad guys, and the bad guys always tend to be powerful. That's a fact. I didn't make it up, it didn't start with me. It goes something like this:

Powerful, privileged bad guy(s) → hate(s) journalists who expose them

Goes back to the canary in the coalmine. You watch what happens to journalists in a society, and you can pretty much figure out what's going on in that society. Or, at the very least, you can gauge the overall health of a society by the condition of its journalists. If you live in a country where journalists get murdered a lot, then you're definitely in a scary place, a nasty place, an evil place.

That word doesn't get thrown out nearly enough these days. Journalists hate the word "evil"—it's too laden with emotion, right? They want to appear objective and cool-headed. You lob out an "evil" in an article, your editor's going to spike it, or demand that you rewrite it. They're going to think there's something wrong with you if you think in terms of good and evil as a journalist. Take this story for example:

AREA MAN MURDERED BY EVIL COSMIC HORROR CULT

Chicago (AP)—Local author and journalist, Elliott Burke (35), was found dead in his apartment Friday night, having been strangled by members of an evil cult known only as the Order of the King. This group had been hunting Mr. Burke for the better part of three years, after he had accidentally uncovered the secret meeting place of the Order and its association with the King in Yellow.

Mr. Burke had, on more than one occasion, threatened to expose the membership of the Order of the King, only to be on the receiving end of escalating retaliation undertaken by the fanatical members of the cult.

I mean, no editor's going to let that stand, so they'll have the writer recast the story as follows:

AREA MAN FOUND DEAD

Chicago (AP)—Local author and journalist, Elliott Burke (35), was found dead in his apartment Friday night, apparently attacked by unknown assailants in a possible home invasion gone wrong. Mr. Burke was known for his aggressive and adversarial journalistic style, and authorities believe he may have antagonized some criminal elements with one of his exposés.

Mr. Burke, a known conspiracy theorist, had, on more than one occasion, threatened to expose private citizens he believed were involved in what he referred to as "[A] massive occult conspiracy with members throughout the country and the world."

Burke's efforts have drawn the attention of law enforcement authorities in the past.

See how they can just scrub out the offending parts and make it seem like I'm the problem? Anyway, the point I was trying to make is that journalists run from the word "evil"—even when they're writing about evil things, they try to steer clear of it because it's too emotional, and maybe too subjective.

That's what it really comes down to, right? Subjectivity versus objectivity. Journalists are always really worried about appearing objective, even in situations where simple objectivity is going to get you hanged in your apartment by evil cultists.

Do I sound obsessed? Is that what you're thinking? Look, I have *seen* them. The Order of the King is real. They sent me a letter—how old-school is that? An actual letter. A yellow envelope, addressed to me by someone using an admittedly beautiful calligraphic script. Of course, I opened it. I'm a journalist. It's what I do—I open letters, I read them, and I comment on them:

Dear Mr. Burke—

We strongly urge you to refrain from your provocations regarding *The Thing in Yellow*. While we understand you take your work very seriously, it is against your interests to continue along this particular path you are continuing to explore. We are gravely concerned about your conduct in this matter.

To that end, the Order is willing to negotiate with you on an appropriate sum to dissuade you from pursuing your current course of action. We will be in touch with you soon and look forward to you making the correct decision.

Also, we would advise you to avoid contacting law enforcement about these matters, as we have allies and confederates within this community, and it will not go well for you if you opt to do this.

~The Order of the King

I ask you what you would do if you got something like that delivered to your door. And that's it—that yellow envelope was slipped under my door! Which means that the Order actually got into my apartment building, came to my door, and slid that envelope under my door.

There's an implicit threat in delivering something that way. They're basically saying "We know where you live, and we can come see you any time we like, and there's nothing you can do about it."

As it happens, I wasn't home. I was chasing down some missing persons reports tied to the Yellow King. That's the thing about this—it's all tied together. This Order of the King is out there, and I don't know who they are, but they're clearly disciples of the King in Yellow. That's how he operates. He plays with his pawns, his bishops and knights.

It's tied to the play, *The King in Yellow*—people read it and they go crazy. I mean, who doesn't know this by now? Something foul within it, the second act, it just makes people lose their minds. Maybe it's a spell, like a curse, I don't know. But it affects everyone who reads it.

And now you're wondering if I read it, aren't you?

Of course, I read it.

I'm a journalist.

What kind of journalist would I be if I didn't read the infamously cursed play? I mean, sheesh. I'm not a "road less traveled" kind of guy. If I were in the Garden of Eden, I'd take a bite out of the Forbidden Fruit and then ask for seconds. That's just how I roll.

So, yes, when confronted with a cursed play, I'm naturally going to read it. Part of me wants to just explain it to you, Gentle Reader, so you can understand what it's all about. Wouldn't that be what a good journalist would do?

But here's the thing: I know it's what the King wants me to do. Crazy, right? How crazy is that? I mean, if I laid it all out for you, then you'd go crazy, too. Or you'd fall under his spell. Maybe they're the same thing.

That's what *The Thing in Yellow* is all about. I mean, it's laying out just what we're dealing with, here. It's a warning, a clarion call, showing people how dangerous this King and his thing really is. And it's why the Order is going after me. They know what I'm trying to do, they're trying to stop me.

It's not that hard to do. I'm just one person. I'm just a guy. It's so easy. I think the CIA has a manual about it, a kind of how-to for death squads, like how far somebody has to be thrown off a building for it to be guaranteed fatal. I think it's like 75 feet for a reliable fatality. Makes you wonder how they came up with that number, doesn't it? Practice makes perfect, I guess.

Then you just make it look like a suicide. I'm telling you this: if I ever take a header off a building, it's because the Order of the King did it. If you find me hanging in my apartment, it's the Order of the King that put me there. If I die of a drug overdose, it's because the Order of the King administered it. Or they jabbed me with some nerve agent or poison.

If I die of anything but old age, it's because the Order of the King went after me. I'm not suicidal, okay? That's for the record. And I try to take care of myself, I try to stay healthy, so if I just drop dead for no good reason, it's because *they* killed me. Make no mistake.

And you're probably saying, "Elliott, you're just one guy, like you said. Why would this secret society even care enough about you to do anything? You're just being paranoid."

It's not paranoia if they're actually trying to get you. And the Order of the King is trying to get me because they know that if *The Thing in Yellow* gets out there, enough people will be warned away from the King in Yellow, or at least they'll be prepared. They'll know what to look for, and they can steer clear of it. That alone is useful. It's like being aware of handwashing as a means of avoiding getting sick during a pandemic. Here's what you need to look out for:

- The Yellow Sign: Avoid this

- The King in Yellow (entity): Definitely avoid him

- *The King in Yellow* (play): Don't read it. Duh!*

- Pallid Mask (band): Don't buy their (literally) damned music‡

- Yellow King merch: Don't buy it ⁑

- The Order of the King: Avoid them at all costs†

- Black Star Distillery: Avoid them, don't buy their merch, don't drink their drinks; they are definitely in on it

- Anybody named "Cassilda" or "Camilla": Be *very* careful around them

- Anybody who talks about the Hyades, Aldebaran, the Lake of Hali, Hastur, black stars, or especially Carcosa: Watch out for them!

- Anybody who gets any kind of King in Yellow related tattoo: Look out! They're either in on it, or they're already insane, or they're going to go insane and do something horrible, probably to you, when you least expect it

- Anybody who loves the play, *Equus,* way, way too much: Keep an eye on them‡

*Disclaimer: I know I sound like a hypocrite here because I'm warning you away from it after having read it myself, but trust me, it's for your own self-protection. You'll thank me for it later.

‡ Seriously, don't support them. Those pop culture parasites have been pimping the King out to audiences for like 30 years. Literally everything they do is tied to pushing the King on the unwary, the innocent and naïve, and the unprepared. In fact, they're a refinement on the original concept of the cursed play-as-delivery system. What's more insidious than music? It's like putting sugar around a cyanide capsule. I even tried to find out the identities of the band members, but they're like an empty set. They could be anybody, and I think the King wants it that way.

⁑This is another insidious thing they're doing. I can't fully verify that the Order of the King is behind this, but anybody selling King in Yellow merchandise is part of the conspiracy. It's intended to raise awareness of the King and subvert people without them realizing that they're being subverted.

†You're wondering how you'd even spot a member of the Order of the King. And you're right—like all good secret societies, they try not to stand out. But you can spot them if you know what to look for. First off, they *love* the color yellow, so look for their use of it to accessorize or even be a featured part of their wardrobe. And they love to talk about the King in Yellow, whether the play, or the entity, or the Yellow Sign. I mean, they can't stop. It's symptomatic of their fractured, buckling mental state. Any Yel-

low Sign bling like rings, brooches, stick pins, lapel pins, walking sticks, etc. Watch out!

‡I can't entirely vouch for this as it relates to the King in Yellow, but *Equus* is a two-act play, and, you know, *The King in Yellow* is a two-act play, and there are thematic crosscurrents between them, although the former isn't cursed, as far as I know. And while there may not be a 1:1 correlation, anybody who likes *Equus* way too much, or says it's their favorite play, or talks about it too much, they're at least very weird, and/or are at high risk of being susceptible to the temptations presented by the Yellow King. They're also very likely to have *The King in Yellow* on their bookshelves, which would put you at risk of exposure to the cursed play if you're not careful. They might even be a member of the Order of the King, so watch out.

There are probably other warning signs, but I'm trying to provide a baseline sort of punch list, so you can be aware. I mean, anybody who likes the color yellow a little too much, that seems really suspect to me, just on general principles. Yellow is a messed-up color.

Oh, sure, you're going to talk to me about bananas and lemons and some varieties of pears, and, I don't know, yellow cake and yellow peppers and yellow apples, and stuff like that. Yeah, yeah, I know. Those are all great.

But have you really thought about the historical associations of yellow? I mean, the Yellow King digs it for a reason. Have you thought about that, Gentle Reader? Look it up, you'll see what I'm talking about.

Hold on, somebody's at the door. Probably the building superintendent. I was complaining about somebody leaving the back door propped again. Who does that in the city, I swear? It's crazy. You just have to be vigilant, you know what I'm saying? On guard all the time, at all times. They get you when you least suspect it.

In the meantime, definitely read *The Thing in Yellow*. I think you'll find a lot of useful information in it to help you, you know, stay on guard. It's like a vaccine for your brain, an inoculation against insanity.

Just remember that the King is everywhere, and, you know, the Order of the King, well, they're just plain crazy. Every last one of them.

Don't go anywhere; I'll be right back!

ONE

It had been Elizabeth's idea, and only after she'd started calling herself Erzabet. The six of us—Daniel, Sarah, Andrew, Jess, Christopher, and Liz—had been slaving at the Hali Street Theater. Liz and Christopher were brother and sister, and had come into more than a little money, and had purchased the old Chicago theater about five years earlier.

We'd run a host of small one- to three-act plays, ranging from comedies to ribald farces and even a few horror performances.

We all acted in them. Our troupe was small and tightly knit—Christopher was the wannabe playwright, while Liz, Jess and Sarah vied for the female leads. There was a semi-gracious agreement between them, where they'd take turns taking leads. Between Daniel and myself, we'd basically flip for it, with Christopher as the inevitable wild card. He'd insert himself into a performance when he felt it would raise his profile enough to merit it.

Daniel and I had other jobs, of course, as did the other ladies. Only Liz and Christopher lived and breathed at the Hali Street Theater. But we all pitched in for set design work, and, at least until Liz became Erzabet, we had a pretty good routine.

Liz had this lioness face, what I call a catface, round, inscrutable. And, as if aware of her catlike countenance, Liz gave herself a mane of hair that she colored copper. Her mane framed her face, her big green-grey eyes and Slavic pout-mouth. Petite but well-figured, Liz ruled the Hali Street Theater with Christopher, who was prone to wearing faux fur coats and tweed trousers. Christopher had a colossal nose and sandbag eyes that gave him a mole-like bearing. The odd features played well onstage, however, under big lights and deep shadows. And Christopher was tall, with golden baritone tonsils that could shake the timbers of the Hali Street Theater.

Liz and Christopher ruled our troupe, while the rest of us were part of their court. Sarah was tall and refused to wear the glasses she needed to wear, which gave her a near-sighted, doe-eyed presentation onstage that made her the model of theatrically winsome innocence. Her long limbs and slender fingers made her seem like a marionette, and the ballet she danced with her long blond hair was itself hypnotic, tying her ponytail with the flourish of a born upstager.

Daniel was our resident lion tamer, a twee theater brat who had taken it upon himself to be Liz's confidante and lickspittle. He'd come from New York, had a degree of cachet that only someone from there could possess. The youngest and most handsome of our ranks, he managed to convey the dusty-haired bearing of a tourist who was trying to fit in without appearing to. His dark brown eyes played perfectly with Sarah's own guileless blues.

Jess was the actorly assassin, the black-haired villainess who wore her shellacked bangs whenever she was offstage, and chain-smoked with incendiary enthusiasm. She wore silver rings on every finger except her middle digits, which she used to punctuate her sentences. Her eyes were another flavor of blue from Sarah's, trending toward melting glacial ice.

And there was me, fit and neither as tall as Christopher nor as smoothly gregarious as Daniel. I was the Hali Street Theater's Everyman, entrusted to take the roles that came to me, and to do my part without exceeding it. Unlike the others, I knew my place, and my place was at the bottom of the theatrical ladder. As such, my work was more often confined to production work, making sure everything went off without a hitch.

A small theater, we wore many hats, some of them stacked atop each other, sometimes interchangeable.

So, when Liz came in, brandishing *The King in Yellow* and demanding that we stage the impossible play, it was something close to business as usual.

It was Daniel who spoke first, with the degree of contempt for which only he could fully muster.

"That thing? No one's ever staged it, Liz," Daniel said, sniffing. We were all lounging backstage, waiting for Christopher to emerge.

"First off, call me 'Erzabet' henceforth, Daniel." Liz said. "I'm Erzabet forevermore."

Jess scoffed and glanced at me, rolled her eyes.

"Um, okay, *Erzabet*," Daniel said, with sarcastic emphasis. "It's a banned play. Why in the hell would you want to perform it?"

Little Liz stalked between us, wearing black leggings and a shocking pink bodysuit which she'd topped with a grey pullover.

"I've already talked it over with Christopher," Liz said. "It's what we're doing."

"It's only two acts," Daniel said. "Two acts."

"Correct," Liz said. "And we'll make it ours."

"I heard it's cursed," Jess said, popping some nicotine gum into her mouth, tossing the wrapper into a nearby basket. "That everybody who reads it goes insane."

"Everybody's *already* insane," Liz said. "Can you imagine?"

She handed out scripts, which everybody took.

we moved inexorably from the seemingly innocuous first act, toward the inevitably apocalyptic second.

My movements remained mechanical, compelled by rehearsal, pulling both suns out of the Lake of Hali, and only in the moment realizing that our theater bore the same name, and wondering if that was by coincidence or design.

I decided in that moment that it was by design, and that Christopher himself was the grand architect, having tainted Liz with the forbidden play, knowing that she would herself not fail to deliver it to a willing audience. In that moment, I felt that it had been Christopher's deep design all along, and that the acquisition of the theater itself had been part of his intent. That everything before then had been building for this terrible present.

Lost in my thoughts, I didn't yet see Christopher approach behind me, dressed as the Stranger, dressed in his tattered yellow, bearing the Pallid Mask like a talisman over his face, while Cassilda and Camilla danced around each other on the ghostly stage, with set-designed attendees rising in the background at my nimble hands, the mocked-up mimicry of a masquerade, a party well-attended by shadowy bodies that Jess and I had cut with jigsaws, while Daniel had managed to wrangle himself a little part as one of the partygoers, doing business upstage to create the semblance of attendance. The illusion was complete.

"The moments," Christopher whispered to me. "The moments, Drew. Drawn breaths, fabled fortunes lost in the articulated eternity of the here and now. Simply perfect. I have lived for this all my life, this moment. Tonight. This night."

"Go get'em," I said, choking it out, as the Stranger took the stage, towering and tattered, noticed by Camilla, who was no longer Sarah, not anymore. There was only Camilla, looking upon the Stranger with her big eyes, while proud and forlorn Cassilda turned, and the Stranger strode toward center stage.

"Camilla: You, sir, should unmask.
Stranger: Indeed?
Cassilda: Indeed it's time. We have all laid aside disguise but you.
Stranger: I wear no mask.
Camilla: (Terrified, aside to Cassilda.) No mask? No mask!"

And yet, in the staging of it, Christopher carried that mask that was no mask, and the maddening juxtaposition of it carried me off, while Cassilda cried out, arms outraised, as I'd seen Liz perform it that first time, as she ran through dim Carcosa, crying out to the lengthening shadows.

"Cassilda: Not upon us, oh, king! Not upon us!"

I dropped the curtain before the startled crowd, while Jess bathed them in darkness, and someone (I think it was Daniel) played the taped music that took us in the direction of the second act.

Meanwhile, Liz and Sarah and Christopher panted backstage, already spent, but determined to carry on. I no longer recognized them as my friends, but saw only the apparitions they'd become, consumed by the fateful play.

"Magnificent," Liz whispered, spellbound, her eyes aflame as she gazed at me like I was somehow the ghost, and not her.

"Yes," Christopher said, grabbing some water to drink, while Sarah paced around, clutching herself, and Daniel looked on, having put on another costume, his face contorted in one of wounded aggravation at having been denied the part of the Stranger.

Christopher brandished the Pallid Mask as he walked over to me, giving me a stage whisper.

"Marvelous work, Drew," he said. "The stage has been set, it looked divine. On to the second act."

FIVE

It was F. Scott Fitzgerald who said that there were no second acts in American life, in an essay he wrote called "My Lost City." He had said "I once thought that there were no second acts in American lives…."

But on that night, at the Hali Street Theater, I saw that second act blaze to life onstage, as I hoisted the black stars I'd cut with my own hands, a veritable constellation of them in the winding path of the Hyades, beneath the golden glow of the twin stars that illuminated Carcosa.

I saw the audience struck mad by the performance of the play, in their writhing and wailing, while the players, onstage, were as captive as the rest to the macabre performance—towering Christopher, caterwauling Liz, and hapless Sarah, whirling like a dervish, in a mesmerizing cacophony, while Daniel played the tapes and I pulled forth champagne bottles I'd decanted for the occasion, having filled them with kerosene and handkerchiefs.

Jess, herself, had wrapped chains on the doors to the theater, having abandoned her post in the lighting array. She'd wound chains around the old doors and bound them in brass locks she'd shoplifted from a hardware store, while I lit bottle after bottle of kerosene and hurled it onstage and off, watching the bottles crack and shatter, spilling great plumes of fire that caught everything they touched.

Christopher's tatters went ablaze in moments, and he dove offstage and ran into the audience, shrieking as he went, while I tossed more bottles after him, watching them tumble and break and explode in fireballs.

The audience laughed and screamed at once, tearing at each other as they fought to flee the flames, while I hurled a bottle at the curtains, watching the fire ride up them.

Of Cassilda and Camilla, I can't say, for by then, the smoke from the growing fire was too great to see clearly, and I only tossed one bottle over my shoulder as I ran from that place, the fire cutting off my path behind me, while I ran out the back, and into the alley Jess and I had occupied before the performance. I worked my way to the street, like I was in a stupor, horrified and delighted at what I had done.

I saw Jess at the entrance, gasping, a cigarette perched on her lip as she staggered out, and, seeing me, she began laughing. We shared an undulating cackle that blended with the enveloping blaze we left behind, arm in arm, while sirens rose over the sounds of muffled screams.

Gilding Lily

Lily Caryatid walked with grace, confidence, and poise in the studio, moving back and forth in front of her audience of three.

They were the Count Nikolai von Herzog, a broad-shouldered, uniformed cavalryman with dueling scars on his cheeks. He played them up with cavalier golden sideburns he let run wild down his temples, like an invading army, and played with a gallant white scarf he wore around his neck. There was Marina Tasset, black-haired beauty and courtesan-lover of von Herzog, resplendent in a billowingly revealing gown of red. And there was Lily's creator, Benjamin Goselein, sculptor and erstwhile alchemist, dark-haired and darker-eyed.

And there was Lily, golden beauty, metallic and marvelous, cast to perfection by Goselein's unparalleled and heretofore unrevealed technique that had earned him accolades across the Empire. She had the delicate features of a great and youthful beauty, cast in the lustrous bronze Goselein had used, with a body that rivaled that of Venus, herself, if the Goddess of Love had been a ballerina. Lily's eyes were blankly beautiful, a pair of handpicked blue jewels.

"She's a wonder, Goselein," von Herzog said, smirking at the young and dizzingly talented sculptor who ran a steady hand through his brown hair, his eyes only on Lily. "The Emperor will not believe his ancient eyes. What a wondrous age we find ourselves within."

The mention of the Emperor broke Lily's spell on Goselein, who looked over at von Herzog with a grimace.

"She's not for the Emperor," Benjamin said simply, without affectation.

"Nonsense," von Herzog said. "She's perfect. She'll win me a proper place at Court."

"I think she's terrible," Marina said. "So very cold. Why would you make such a thing, Mr. Goselein?"

Von Herzog looked at his cherished Marina and laughed heartily.

"Why, because he can, my dear. Look at his hands. He's an artist's artist, hands steadier than a surgeon's, yet alloyed with a fool's madcap abandon. That toy automaton he's created will impress the Emperor, and will give us an army of metal men. Can you imagine that? An army of metal men, clanking their way across a battlefield toward victory against the Mohammedans?"

The courtesan smiled beautifully, her bare shoulders like alabaster over the red gown she wore like a flower. She bore a stunning gold necklace that was itself bearing an emerald pendant. The pendant was a gift from von Herzog, one of many such gifts.

"I should think that would be a dreadful sight, Nikolai," Marina said. "Would your sculptor create mechanical horses, too? A mechanical cavalry? Everyone clanking and clashing."

Goselein shook his head, noting that Lily had stopped her promenade, and had turned to listen to the conversation, while the sculptor fidgeted with a valise, wherein he'd placed the designs that had created Lily.

"I am an artist, not an industrialist," Benjamin said. "Empire or not, I have no interest in sharing my techniques with ham-handed, bourgeois businessmen."

Von Herzog thought that was hilarious, clapped the sculptor on the back.

"Nonsense, Goselein," von Herzog said. "Every man has his price. Artists especially. For what is an artist without a patron? Penniless. Hopeless. Listless. Lifeless."

Lily watched the conversation with unblinking eyes, her gaze a disarming thing, like that of a statue. She did not breathe, and what clockwork movements animated her offered only the slightest whirring within, only barely discernible over the crackle of the fire in the fireplace.

"She is a work of art," Benjamin said.

"I commissioned you to create her. Ergo, she is mine to do with as I see fit," von Herzog said. "And you have wildly exceeded my expectations, Goselein."

The courtesan could sense the whiff of umbrage in the Count's tone, and moved to smooth things over.

"We simply must celebrate his success," Marina said, pouring some red wine into gilded goblets. She held a cup out for both of the men, while Lily observed.

"Yes, yes, of course," von Herzog said, taking a goblet. "To your success, Goselein."

"To Lily," Benjamin said, taking the offered cup and raising it to his creation.

"To Lily," Marina echoed, and they all took drinks. "I ask you, Mister Goselein: does she understand us?"

"Completely," Benjamin said.

"She's a golem," von Herzog said. "Don't let the Inquisition hear of this. Can you imagine what they'd do to you, Goselein?"

The sculptor shook his head and drank deep of his cup. Lily simply observed, then held out an elegant arm, gesturing gracefully for a goblet. Delighted, Marina grabbed another and made as if to pour wine into it, then held it out for Lily to take.

It was a momentary tableau, the automaton and the courtesan, a moment not lost to Benjamin, whose well-trained artist's brain locked that image away for future use.

He'd make a sculpture one day, the two of them posed that way, like mirrors of each other, like sisters.

Lily took the proffered goblet and gazed into it in a clockwork pantomime, only to pour out the empty goblet with a turn of her beautiful wrist, emptying it of its emptiness on the Safavid Persian rug.

"I don't think she likes the vintage," von Herzog said, slapping his knee, his saber swaying at his hip as he did so.

"Whatever would possess you to make such a thing as this, Mister Goselein?" Marina asked, watching Lily with a certain degree of feminine bemusement, bordering on envy and contempt. As a courtesan, she had seen far too much of the world to be taken aback by anything, but she also took a degree of delight in the novelty of the encounter.

Benjamin looked into the big brown eyes of the courtesan and sighed. "Why, I think you may have been something of my inspiration, Miss Tasset."

"I am singularly honored to have been your muse," Marina said. Von Herzog, who could never countenance a conversation not being dominated by him, rode in hard on a string of wine-soaked syllables.

"I would daresay that my lovely Marina is an inspiration for all men of taste and breeding," von Herzog said. "Although I would needle you a bit in this matter, Goselein. Knowing of your great skill, as I did, I had commissioned you to make an automaton for war, and you gave me a metal woman. Beautiful she may be, but entirely impractical. She's cold comfort, and too elfin to be an Amazon."

Lily had finished pouring the empty goblet, and brought it close to her chest, mirroring the gestures of the others as she did so, like a solo ballet, motivated by a music only she could hear.

Benjamin smiled and shrugged.

"I'm an artist," he said. "I'm impractical. I thought if I could create a thing of beauty, it would perhaps inspire you to consider other, finer things, than warfare."

Von Herzog thought that was even more hilarious and laughed uproariously.

"My dear boy, there is nothing finer than warfare. We are born to it, every one of us. Soldiers and civilians alike. Even my darling Marina is a warrior, although you would not know it to gaze upon her. Why, the rivalries between her sister courtesans are themselves deadly campaigns, waged with the hearts of men of power and privilege. And, would you yourself not contend that you are in dire competition with other artists of our time?"

Benjamin would not allow the noble horseman draw him out so easily.

"I compete only with myself," Benjamin said. "I am my own worst enemy. I have no adversaries."

"Hah," von Herzog said. "I don't believe it for a second. How can a man—or woman, for that matter—know themselves without taking their measure against another? We are forever in contention. This world was born in struggle and will go down in flames in struggle."

Lily approached von Herzog, extending her goblet to him. The Count clanked his cup against hers and took a drink. Lily mimed his gesture, only to find nothing in her cup once more, in a kind of metallic mummer's farce.

"Your dear Lily agrees with me," von Herzog said. "Even an automaton understands, you silly man. We are ever at war, Goselein. Every one of us. A lucky few of us win, and the rest of you lose."

The sculptor's brow darkened at the aristocratic mockery, and he walked to one of his worktables, where he produced a lengthy item wrapped in white linen.

"Are those the plans?" von Herzog asked.

"In the valise," Benjamin said. "You're right—Lily does understand, for I have given her that understanding. I have seen the shores of Carcosa, My Lord. I have waded along the banks of the Lake of Hali."

Von Herzog laughed in the sculptor's face, while Marina looked on with a courtesan's care, betraying nothing behind her painted visage.

"Where is that, Goselein? Hungary, perhaps?" Count von Herzog asked, gesturing with the goblet, which Marina gamely filled, while Lily looked on, gleaming in the lamplight.

"Beyond the night's sky," Benjamin said. "Beyond imagining."

It was the courtesan who comprehended.

"*The King in Yellow*," she exclaimed as she poured the Count another wine. "Oh, the play. The banned play. The Emperor has banned it."

Plays did not interest the Count, and he took the goblet and drank deep of it.

"Oh?" von Herzog asked, uncaring. "The Emperor has banned so very many things. It's difficult to keep track. But why ban a play?"

"Have you read it?" Benjamin asked Marina, his artist's eyes capturing her again in the yellow glow of the firelight—the trace of a smile, the ardent whisper of sin about her pretty, powdered features, and a feral, conspirator's gaze.

"I have," she said.

The sculptor traded gazes with the courtesan, who cocked an all-too-knowing eyebrow at him, while Benjamin stood awkwardly with the parcel.

"Then you will know of the Yellow Sign," he said.

"I do," Marina said, breathless.

"What are you two babbling about?" von Herzog asked.

"It sits within Lily," Benjamin said. "In the clockwork apparatus where her heart would otherwise be. I daresay it animates her."

"Madness," von Herzog said. "I'm in my cups, Goselein, but you're the one prattling on like a gin-soaked drunkard."

Benjamin unwrapped the parcel he carried, revealing a gilded rapier that was of the same metal hue as Lily.

"An *estoc?*" von Herzog said with delight. "So, you've gilded your precious Lily after all, Goselein?"

At the sight of the blade, Lily moved smoothly past the cavalryman and took the gleaming blade in her slender hand.

Benjamin watched Lily take a few exploratory cuts with her blade, stepping nimbly through the studio.

"I'll wager that Lily can beat you in a duel, My Lord," Benjamin said. "No doubt, you'd not wish to take that wager in front of your Emperor, and risk humiliation."

Von Herzog laughed, spitting wine.

"A duel? With your toy woman? The one *I* have paid *you* to build for me?" Von Herzog wiped his mustache with the back of a hand. "With what could you possibly wager, Goselein?"

The sculptor's dark eyes flashed.

"With my life," Benjamin said. "If you defeat Lily, I'll build your Emperor his Iron Army, My Lord."

"And if she defeats me?" von Herzog asked, setting down the goblet and watching the automaton continue her way through the studio, taking more test cuts with the *estoc.*

"Then she is mine, and mine alone, and your Emperor shall never, ever have my secrets," Benjamin said.

The courtesan slipped a folding fan from the folds of her dress, a grey-hued thing that bore frenzied Barbary script across the ribbing, upon a field of yellow flowers.

"This seems hardly the place for such a thing," Marina said. "A field would be a better place for it."

"Nonsense," von Herzog said, drawing his saber with evident relish. "I worry that I'll damage your lovely Lily, Goselein."

Seeing him draw his blade, Lily turned her mute attentions to the Count, raising her own blade in the Spanish style, pointing her blade at him challengingly, her face as blank as before, her eyes like a doll's. Von Herzog cackled at the image, her golden form motionless, poised and at the ready.

"Don't worry about Lily, My Lord," Goselein said.

"To the first cut?" Von Herzog asked, dropping into a combative crouch, his saber raised. This was the most sport he'd had in some time, and he intended to make the most of it.

"As you say," Benjamin said. "To the first cut, Lily."

And the automaton sprang at the Count, her *estoc* threading the air where von Herzog had been only moments before. He'd sidestepped and had brought his saber around in a sweeping cut that the automaton easily parried, the blades clanging. Lily moved with a terrible speed that caught the firelight in winking sparks that traveled across her perfect body.

Marina watched with interest, with Benjamin moving beside her.

The two combatants took each other's measure, taking a few more exploratory cuts, both of them parrying and dodging.

"How she moves," Marina said. "Like a dancer. So light-footed for one made of metal."

"Light-footed and light-fingered as well, I'm afraid," Benjamin said.

The Count and the automaton clashed in earnest in the studio, separated by an emerald couch that bore a dozen golden stripes, where only earlier Marina had been seated.

"We're better-suited in a field," Marina said. "Truly, that's the proper setting for this."

"I'd not have Lily seen just yet," Benjamin said. "The townsfolk would not understand."

"No, surely not," Marina said.

The clash of *estoc* and saber was a noisy affair, the gilded blade easily able to take the saber's cuts, and the thick saber effectively able to parry the automaton's sword.

"She's just marvelous, Goselein," von Herzog said, breathing heavily as his gilded adversary continued her attack. "Truly, you've outdone yourself. And you've held out on me, for all of your talk of artistry and warfare."

"I'm glad to hear you say so, My Lord," Benjamin said, pouring himself some more wine, while Lily forced the Count back across the studio, toward the glass doors that led to the balcony, which overlooked the courtyard of the villa that housed Goselein at the pleasure of his patron.

Grunting, the cavalryman tried to put his weight to bear against the automaton, but though she was lean of frame, Lily was heavy and would have required the efforts of a couple of strong men or a draft horse to be moved against the will that animated her.

"Life is a struggle," Benjamin said. "Wasn't that what you said?"

Von Herzog found himself shoved against the glass doors, several panes of which crunched against his back while Lily pressed her attack. The splintered shards of glass tinkled on the stones of the balcony, like little chimes drowned out by the Count's soldierly grunts and the metallic clangs of the combatants' blades.

"Yes," Von Herzog said, sidestepping as Lily lunched at him, puncturing the glass with her *estoc*. Seeing her blade momentarily occupied, the Count swung hard at the automaton with his saber, aiming at her neck, only to have Lily bring her free arm up to catch his saber in her upraised, bronzed palm.

Her block had stopped his saber cut with such force that von Herzog's teeth chattered, but he let out a triumphant whoop, all the same.

"First cut!" he said, trying to free his blade from Lily's grip. The automaton wrenched her own weapon from the broken windowpane, while she twisted her other hand in a savage gesture, the saber blade bending, and then corkscrewing before the force she applied with a graceful turn of her wrist. The Count cursed, dropping his blade in order to save his own hand from being broken.

"Hold up your hand, Lily," Benjamin said, and the automaton held up her free hand, revealing not so much as a scratch upon the golden metal.

"No cut? No cut!" Marina exclaimed.

"Nonsense!" von Herzog said, cursing. "She ruined my saber, Goselein."

The sculptor gazed at the aristocrat a moment, and at his creation.

"First cut, Lily," Benjamin said. "Finish this."

Lily then raised her *estoc* and speared von Herzog through the heart with it. So pierced, the Count gazed at Lily and Benjamin in wounded wonder, his legs buckling beneath him as he fell. Lily withdrew the bloody blade, which she'd run through him to the hilt.

As the Count died, the sculptor and the courtesan kissed, while Lily cleaned her *estoc* with the Count's white scarf, which she let drop across his chest.

When Benjamin and Marina parted lips, their eyes were lit with a fervid radiance, and they parted only with greatest reluctance. Benjamin gestured to his valise. Marina folded her fan back into the secret confines of her red dress, grabbing an oil lamp and tossing it in the direction of the fallen cavalryman. The flames engulfed him in a gusty, blazing bloom.

"Come, Lily. Come, Marina," Benjamin said, as they made their getaway. "We're off to Carcosa, as promised."

ONE

Snow only stopped blowing long enough to allow the wind to catch its breath, it seemed to Reeve Finnerton as he worked his way blindly along the demarcated trail. The signal flares had long ago given up the ghost, being mere phosphorescent specters of their former selves, like luminaria strangled by an avalanche—mere points of red-pink light in the blinding dark of everlasting night.

But for the line, held fast by spars hammered hard into the icy ground, Reeve would have long ago been lost. As it was, he pulled himself along, feeling something other than frozen. Enervated, maybe.

The cabin was not in sight, although he knew that it was there. Cal Cassock had given him all the information he'd needed to make the trip to Vancouver and beyond. Even then, on the telephone, he'd been excited.

"It's here, Reeve," Cal said. "I've found it."

"Found what, Cal?" Reeve asked.

"The Wound on the World," Cal replied, as if Reeve should have known that already. And, chiding himself, perhaps his old friend was right about that. There were few things Professor Cal Cassock had been more enthusiastic about than the Wound on the World.

The history of it was apocryphal. The snow never helped, concealing far more than it ever revealed. The native *Kwakwaka'wakw* tribes spoke of the place beneath the Northern Lights, wreathed in green firelight in the skies. It was known as the Place Where No One Goes, at least that was as close as it translated in English decades ago.

Legends spoke of a great monster in the land, like a god-spirit that breathed with the land and gave it both life and death. The god-spirit was named *Alawanak'lak* in one of the lost accounts of the Wound on the World, compiled by Cassock at the University of Washington, where he'd taught Occult Anthropology.

It's where Reeve had met him, during a class on Occult Practices in the Aleutian Islands. Cassock looked every bit the handsome academic explorer, with sandy, wiry hair and a well-trimmed beard. He was hiking-fit and tended to wear corduroy jackets the color of honey.

Reeve was military-strong from a couple of tours with the Army in Iraq and had been looking to replace the hot sands of the Middle East with something altogether colder and more remote. The Pacific Northwest had felt about right to him.

What Cal brought to his classes was enthusiasm, like the kind of professorial teaching that carried with it swoops of his arms and academic exclamations of breathless wonder.

"*Alawanak'lak* was called the Unblinking God," Cassock said over beers in the Krakenpub near campus. "Literally 'He Who Does Not Blink' and was spoken of with great terror by the people in the region."

"Okay," Reeve said. "A legend."

"But not a legend," Cassock said. "*Alawanak'lak* is real."

Reeve laughed, taking a pull of his beer while Cal went on. The Krakenpub patrons were a bunch of literal and figurative punks, but they didn't pay Cal or Reeve any mind, just squeezed themselves some space to drink and dance to overloud music.

"It's not real-real, Cal," Reeve said.

"As real as you and me," Cassock said. "I'm going to prove it."

"How?" Reeve asked.

Cal glanced around them, as if relaying a great secret.

"You know about global warming, right, Reeve?" Cassock asked.

"Who doesn't?" Reeve said, but Cal stopped him with an upraised hand.

"It's melting the north," Cassock said. "I mean, like places that were permafrost, like tundra—they're gone. Or going away. Both. It's unveiling places. Places that long ago would have been under tons of snow. Forgotten places. Hidden."

Cal drank deep from his bottle of beer and ordered them each another. Reeve didn't mind. Cal's enthusiasm was contagious.

"Okay," Reeve said. "So what?"

"So an oil survey team goes up there," Cassock said. "Like north-by-northeast. Many kilometers away from Vancouver. They go up there and nobody ever sees them again. Gone."

"People get lost, Cal," Reeve said. "All the time. British Columbia is huge, man. It's got more land than most countries."

"Right," Cassock said. "So I know what I'm talking about. *Alawanak'lak* is out there."

The server brought them their beers, and Cassock didn't wait to start drinking his. His face was sweaty, even though the Krakenpub wasn't actually that warm.

"All the global warming in the world isn't going to make a myth into reality, Cal," Reeve said.

"Okay, I know how crazy it sounds," Cassock said. "But people disappear out there. They just vanish. Not a trace."

"Serial killers," Reeve said. "Pig farmers. Both, man."

"No, no, no," Cassock said, tipping back his beer. "Not like this. I'm not talking runaways or sex workers, Reeve.

Not strays. It's more like groups. Surveyors. Construction. Rangers. That kind of thing. People disappear."

Reeve smiled at his friend and laughed at him, like really laughed at him.

"Sure, so people disappear," Reeve said. "And you want to, what? Join the ranks of the disappeared? You want to disappear, too?"

"*Alawanak'lak,* Reeve," Cassock said. "The Unblinking God."

He dug out a weathered journal, yellow-jacketed and clearly having been well-used by Cal over who knew how many years. It looked decades old. He opened it and showed Reeve his notes, his tidy script and sketches. Traces of maps and symbols, arrows and crosshatching. Always blue ink. Cal only used blue ink.

"I want to look the Unblinking God in the eye," Cassock said. "To see him for myself."

"Jesus, Cal," Reeve said.

"Okay, okay," Cassock said. "I'm joking. It's a big joke, alright? But there is a place up there, the tribal folks won't go near it. It's a big range, but it's out there. The Place Where No One Goes. I want to go there. I want to observe and take notes. I want to write a book about it."

"You see my problem with it? You want to go to the Place Where No One Goes, Cal," Reeve said. "Don't you think there's, I don't know, a lesson in that?"

"Meh," Cassock said. "I'm not worried. Publish or perish, right?"

It was the last time Reeve saw his friend.

TWO

The yellow notebook arrived in the mail when Reeve was at work on the campus as a curriculum coordinator. He worked in the Chemistry Department, assisting the professors with their classes.

He opened the package and was startled to see Cal's notebook with a hastily jotted note on it, on a Post-It, saying:

Reeve—

THIS IS IT!

Your Pal,
Cal

Reeve felt uncomfortable even having Cal's notebook. He paged through it, like the pages in the back, where Cal had outlined the field trip he was taking with five grad students and a local guide. He included a note in an envelope on that last page, with "Reeve" written in his clear script:

I'm taking a team to the site. They don't know why I'm going. Only you do, and I do. They think we're heading up for an anthropological site evaluation. That's how I pitched it to get the grant money. There's always something somebody's willing to fund. Anyway, I got the permission and I'm heading up there.

The coordinates are in the notebook. I know you don't believe me, and I don't blame you. It SOUNDS crazy. But based on what we talked about, I wanted you to have this notebook, just in case something happened. You'll be the only one who knows about the Unblinking God.

If something does happen, don't come after me. That's the worst thing you can do. And for the love of Christ, please don't bring the notebook, even if you're inclined to do something reckless and come for me. Leave the notebook home, whatever you do. Give it to Rhonda Deerling in Applied Metaphysics or maybe William Rosser in Liminal Anthropology if you absolutely must.

Reeve looked over the date of the letter. It was nearly a month ago. Cal's trip had taken place when Reeve was on vacation in Colorado. He and his girlfriend, Teresa, had gone skiing for a couple weeks, taking advantage of a snowfall there.

He dialed up Cal, but it went to voicemail. He left a message anyway:

"Cal, this is Reeve," he said. "Call me as soon as you get this."

But Cal didn't call him back, and Reeve began to worry. He called Cal's wife, Andrea, but she'd said that Cal had told her he was on sabbatical, had six months off and was going to do research out past Vancouver.

"When did you last hear from Cal?" Reeve asked.

"About three weeks ago," Andrea said.

"And that didn't make you nervous?"

"Should it?" Andrea asked. "Cal said the cell reception is bad out there, and he told me he'd call me as soon as he got back. He said the fieldwork grant was for months."

"Uh, yeah," Reeve said. "Still, you aren't worried?"

"Cal's Cal," Andrea said. "You have no idea how much that Wound on the World stuff was eating away at him. I felt like if he wanted to scratch that itch, he should, if it means he can let it go. Or write a book about it. Maybe both."

"Wow," Reeve said. Andrea had been more than a little of a hippie when she and Cal had started dating. She was incredibly chill, but Reeve couldn't imagine someone so even-tempered to be cool without hearing from her spouse for weeks. Teresa would freak if she didn't hear from him nightly.

Reeve went to the campus copy shop and made copies of Cal's notebook, just in case. The right thing to do was pass the notebook along to the police. That was the simplest, most straightforward thing he could do. But he didn't really want to do that, so he kept it at home, told his girlfriend Teresa about it. She looked at him like he was insane.

"If I disappear, give these papers to the cops," Reeve said, showing her the copies he'd placed in a manila folder. "And give this notebook to Dr. Rhonda Deerling at the University's Applied Metaphysics Department. Tell her it's from Dr. Cal Cassock."

Teresa shook out her black curly hair as she peered into the notebook, which she cultivated into a rock star sort of woolly shag that played nicely with her off-the-shoulder undyed knit sweater and black leggings she wore.

"What is this, Reeve? Like it looks cray," Teresa said.

"Maybe it is," Reeve said. "Just do me that solid, could you, Babe?"

"Of course," Teresa said. "This isn't like some arcane plan to ghost me, is it?"

"Jesus, no," Reeve said. She smiled at him, her soft hazel eyes somehow piercing in their sidelong scrutiny.

"Good, because I wouldn't like that," Teresa said.

"I promise you I'm not ghosting you," Reeve said. She took the notebook and the notes and put them on the kitchen counter, which counted as safekeeping in Teresa's world. "I'm going out there. If you don't hear from me in a month, then send those copies out to the people I mentioned."

He jotted it down on a note and paperclipped it to the folder.

"Reeve, you're kind of freaking me out," Teresa said.

"It's okay, Babe," Reeve said. "I'm just being careful."

"Okay," Teresa said.

It was the last time he ever saw her.

THREE

Following the directions he'd pulled from Cal's notebook, Reeve had rented a four-wheel drive truck which he loaded up with fuel and drove up Highway 99, drinking in the mountain beauty of it, hearing Cal's voice in his head as he traveled.

"The Unblinking God sleeps beneath the everlasting snow," Cassock had said, on that long night at the Kraken-pub. "That's what I've been saying, Reeve. He doesn't sleep anymore. The snow's gone. *Alawanak'lak* is awake, now. He's awake, and he's watching us from the Wound on the World."

"What the hell is that?"

"An asteroid impact," Cassock said. "That's what I think. A crater. Long ago. Before time. Before whenever. The world grew around it. The mountains. All of that. People forgot. Most, I mean. Not all. Some knew. Deep memories. Lost traditions. Lost tribes. I don't know. It's a bad place, Reeve."

"And you're wanting to go there," Reeve said. "Why do I have to be the voice of reason, here, Cal?"

"You only think you are," Cal said, clinking his beer bottle with Reeve's. They were too many beers in to stop now. "You're as crazy as I am where it counts."

When the snow came, it ate up the landscape and left Reeve twisting until he zeroed in on the position Cal had left him, his best guess. Reeve knew how to prepare. He had packed enough supplies, enough to ride out a damned blizzard. He'd brought a lantern, flares, glowsticks, snow-shoes. He'd found the marks Cal had left him on the map, the route to the cabin—just a lonely turn off Highway 99, something nobody would blink twice at amid all the mountains. If the blizzard had come before Reeve had gotten there, he'd never have found it.

But it worked out, and he found the encampment. The other vehicles, a few kilometers off the road. He'd seen the trail marked off by the poles at even distances, connected by the brightly colored yellow-black line. Reeve had latched on and made his way to the cabin, marking his way with flares so he could get back to the truck to unload supplies.

"*Alawanak'lak* came from the heavens, Reeve," Cal said. "From out there. He smashed into the Earth when it was young. Too young. The world was an egg back then—a cracking shell of itself. The Unblinking God sat within the cradle of the crater and he waited."

"Waited for what?" Reeve asked. "I mean, you're telling me that snow keeps him asleep. There wasn't snow back then, Cal."

"I don't make the rules, Reeve," Cassock said. "I'm just telling you what I know. He came from out there, and he's here, now. He's our problem, now."

"Yours and mine?" Reeve asked.

"Mankind's," Cal said. "All of humanity."

Reeve made his way to the cabin, had to shove his way in past the snow-frozen door. Inside, it was dark, and only somewhat less cold than outside. But he felt relief at being out of the pummeling wind.

He took out his lantern and turned it on, grateful for the cold blue-white illumination as he looked around. Six bunks, no trace of anyone. No blood, nothing untoward. It looked abandoned, except for the vehicles parked outside and that Reeve knew they had come here. How had no one reported it?

"People vanish, Reeve," Cal said. "All the time. Nobody can keep up. He takes them."

"Where does he take them?" Reeve asked.

Cal laughed, unwilling to take the bait.

"I have no idea," Cal said. "No idea. Maybe he devours their souls. Maybe he disintegrates them. I don't know."

"Seems to me like you're having it both ways," Reeve said. "You don't know and yet you're sure you know something."

"Yeah," Cal said. "You've got me there. Circumstantially, I'm saying there's a correlation. People in the area. Disappearances. History and legend. It's gotten worse now that he's awakening."

For all of his talk about global warming, Reeve felt like somebody should have told the blizzard. But he knew that weather and climate were not the same thing, that even in a warming world, snow was still possible, at least for awhile. Who knew where it might all end?

Walking through the cabin, Reeve put some logs in the fireplace and lit them up, took solace in the growing warmth of the fire. He saw a map had been thumbtacked on one of the walls of the cabin, showing a trail marked in Cal's writing by dotted lines in blue ink, leading to an X on or near Lake Alicia. Cal had scrawled "CRATER" on that and had put arrows on it with "Wound on the World" on it in big blue block letters.

Reeve laughed to himself, wondered what the grad students had thought about all of that. Maybe they assumed they'd get in good with their prof. But, of course, there was the issue of where the hell everyone had gone. There was no sign of struggle, just as there was no sign of life.

He made trips back and forth from the cabin to his truck, unloading supplies by the waning light of the flares, before he found it necessary to hunker down for the night.

The fire crackled and Reeve huddled by it, while the snow fell outside. He worried that his truck might get buried, and then he'd be in a real fix. Cal had written *"Alawanak'lak"* in block letters on the map as well. Something else had been written on it, near the site of Lake Alicia, near the big blue X:

I am coming for you,
My Dread Lord.
O Unblinking God
of Alawanak'lak,
favor me with
a backward glance
gives me the chance
a backward glance
gives me the chance
to show you
that I mean just what I say
O Alawanak'lak

Upon the Wound on the World
Will I wait for thee
Thee and me, eternally.

Reeve felt real sorrow for his friend. He'd been the one who'd gone to war, but somehow his friend had been the one to go mad. To save his reputation, Reeve had to find him and get him back home. Let him leave all of this behind.

He dialed up Teresa, was pleased to get a call through, even though it wasn't a clear one.

"Hey, Babe," Reeve said. "I'm here."

"Where?"

"The place I told you about," Reeve said. "I just wanted you to know I'm okay."

"Thanks," Teresa said. "Is Cal there?"

"No," Reeve said. "It's snowing here. I'm hoping to head out tomorrow and see where they went."

"Be careful," Teresa said.

"I always am. Remember what I told you," Reeve said, as the call dropped. He tried dialing her again, but was getting a NO SIGNAL message. "Great. Did I piss you off, *Alawanak'lak?*"

He received no answer but the howl of the wind.

FOUR

Reeve slept in the bunk he'd pulled closest to the fire, and despite the circumstances of his presence here, he slept well and deeply. No one disturbed him during the night. The wildlife that was sure to be out there knew better than to brave a blizzard.

He opened the door into the crisp and cold mountain air and saw that they'd gotten at least 25 cm of snow from the storm. Muttering to himself, Reeve strapped on his snowshoes and took his twin red telescoping metal walking sticks and put on some ski goggles to protect his eyes from the sunlight blasting down on him from above. The snow was wet, but the snowshoes let him trudge his way across it, along the path he'd memorized from his mad friend's map.

"What did you do, Cal?" Reeve asked, crunching his way along the trail. The mountains around him were staggeringly beautiful, the fresh-fallen snow lending particular loveliness to everything around him, and the conifers standing majestically in massive splendor.

It would be the easiest thing in the world to lose one's way out here, or to lose one's mind, Reeve thought. But he could see that Cal had marked the trail with stakes and rope like what had led to the cabin. There was, at least, still method to his madness.

From where he was walking, Reeve could see the trail went down to what was frozen Lake Alicia. He didn't relish traveling out onto a frozen lake, so he called out for his friend, in hopes that he'd hear him.

"Cal?" Reeve yelled. "Cal!"

But no one answered. Reeve could see the trail markers went out some distance and stopped where a long red and white pole had been placed, bearing a tattered white flag that bore a red eye upon it, almost a pictogram—like an oval eye that had eyelashes or rays emanating from it, and a great red dot of an iris in the center. The pennant flapped in the wind, and Reeve stared hard at it as he crept closer.

"Cal?" Reeve yelled. "Anybody?"

He walked upon the Wound on the World, Reeve was certain. From here, he could see the rise of the land around it. It was a crater lake. Cal had been right about that. Unlike the land, the walk upon the frozen lake was flat, and the wind blew hard on the snow, whipping it up at him, making him wince as he worked his way to the end of the line, toward the swaying flag on the bobbing pole. The pennant snapped and flapped, almost making it seem like the eye blinked.

Around the end of the line, Reeve could make out smaller mounds in the snow. A half-dozen of them. He poked at them with his walking sticks and chiseled away the crust of the wet snow. He gasped as he saw that he'd uncovered a body bent forward, perched on their knees, their heads bowed low, their arms beside them. As if arranged. It was a young man, frozen solid, and dead, his skin the color of old wax.

As he looked, he saw that the other mounds had been scattered with intention, like a kind of starburst around the focal point of the flag. He cleared the snow off the mounds and saw that they were more bodies arrayed the same way, their frozen, dead faces down against the lake ice, bent forward in a ghastly parody of supplication. Reeve could not tell how they died, for there was no blood, no sign of trauma. He'd seen enough dead in Iraq to know what a corpse looked like, how it died.

None of them were Cal. They had to be the grad students. Reeve took out his phone but had no signal. He took photographs of the scene with a shaking hand.

From his vantage point, he confirmed that the bodies emanated around that central point, where the flag had been placed.

"Jesus," Reeve said, as he walked to the pennant, snapping a shot. At the pennant, upon the ground, the snow had been blown away, leaving only the darkness of the lake ice. He had no sense of how thick the ice might be, but it was apparent that Cal and the others had moved the snow out of the way to expose this part of the lake.

Had Cal somehow jumped into the frigid water? Maybe after sacrificing the grad students? What had happened here? And why had no one discovered this? He didn't know how often people patrolled these remote areas.

All he knew was that he had to get the hell out of here and get to Vancouver. He had to report this, whatever this was.

"It's the Wound on the World, Reeve," Cal said, in his head. "Look closer."

Reeve dragged his eyes down into the darkness of the black lake ice, gazing into the abyss beneath his feet. He had no idea how deep Lake Alicia went, but it looked deep.

As he gazed into it, he could see his reflection in the ice against the everlasting sky. Then he became aware that something was looking up at him from below, rising up, pressing against the ice, cracking it beneath his feet. Reeve's courage fled with his sanity, but his snowshoed feet would not listen to his mind's cries as he gazed into the thing below him.

It was something so massive that it didn't even register as an eye to him at all, but was, rather, a massive red disc within the icy water, like a monstrous sun from a distant alien world, focusing on him, unblinking.

Enshrined

~~~~~~

[FRAGMENT which was found in the Ambrose Grotto in Happy Valley, wrapped in yellow parchment and twine, sitting under a yellow chess piece, with four yellow candle stubs around it.]

Part I: Polishers of the Dream Ether

ONE

In the fog-shrouded valley, the City of Rust slept in the dreary, developing dark, deep and dreamless. Four shadows stirred on the forgotten hillside, slipping past barbed wire barricades and into the golden grove. From there, they could see everything that needed to be seen.

And in that place, they rounded a stone. And then another. And yet another. They danced in a whirling, counterclockwise gyration. An atavistic spasm. Beneath the night's sky.

Unseen. Unheard. Unknown.

The stones sang for them, smooth rock richly veined, all but untouched by the acid rain. The stones throbbed and grew under the attention of the four. And the three became one, and the one became more than prime.

It became everything.

In the becoming, a bolt of lightning arced down from the sky and struck the stone, and the four shadows who had laid their hands upon it. And the four died, consumed utterly by the purple-white light that broke the night.

When the thunder rolled through the valley, jolting the townspeople awake in their homes, the damage had already been done. It had only been one stroke of light-
~~~~~~

ning, on that foggy night, and nobody had seen where it had landed.

Nobody but one.

TWO

Gavin Cleeves had seen the splash of light and the thunderous roar that shook the valley. He'd seen it, despite the foggy downpour, and he had told his friends about it in the morning. At school.

School was the Ironheart Academy, in the heart of the City of Rust, in Happy Valley. There were four hundred children at the school, in uniforms of white and grey. Boys and girls. They wore blue sweaters with the Ironheart shield over their hearts, in red and grey—red heart, grey shield, under which *veritatis et iustitiae* was written in an unforgiving script.

He was a small boy for his age, and his age was 15. Small-mouthed and large-eyed, he wore glasses and had dark hair. He was perennially pale, sharp-tongued, and quick-witted, with an ungovernable sense of style.

His friends were Annabelle Clifton, who had peroxide-yellowed hair and brown eyes and kept her hair close-cropped to better frame her angular face and particularly pointy nose. She did not believe a thing that she saw, and she saw absolutely everything.

There was Connor Shaughnessy, who had black hair that he kept as long as Ironheart would allow, which was something of a knightly pageboy that reached nearly to his shoulders, the almost being the only thing that kept him out of the office of the Headmaster. Connor had a devil's grin and laughed at Gavin far more than he listened.

And Carlton Reed, who was the oldest of them at a newly minted 16, the tallest, and bespectacled. He played chess with himself in the cafeteria, spoke to no one who would listen, saw the world as his chessboard, and himself as the King. His long nose and blue eyes were perpetually in everyone's business.

"Did you see the lightning?" Gavin asked.

"I was asleep," Connor said. "Why were you awake?"

"It woke me up," Gavin said. "The flash."

"Sensitive," Annabelle said. "Light sleeper."

"It was a dream," Carlton said. "You dreamed it."

Gavin's cheeks flushed, while the four of them huddled around a table. The other students ignored them, huddled around their own tables, under the watchful eye of the Cafeteria Minder, Mr. Hegewich, the fat man, who breathed through his mouth as he walked.

"I didn't dream it," Gavin said. "I saw it."

"So, where'd it strike?" Annabelle asked.

"North Side," Gavin said.

"Ewww," Connor said. "Yucko."

Gavin looked at his friends, his only friends, and sighed. He wanted to go see where the lightning struck but didn't want to go alone.

"Don't you want to see it?" Gavin asked.

"Lightning strikes the Earth about 100 times every second," Carlton said, from down the end of his nose, contemplating a Rook he was going to take from himself. "It's only the most common thing you can possibly imagine."

"I don't care," Gavin said. "I want to check it out. Maybe it blew apart a tree."

"Maybe it didn't," Connor said. "North Side? River trash, man. Happy Valley castaways. For real."

"Aren't you the least bit curious?" Gavin asked.

"I'll go with you," Annabelle said. "I totally want to see it."

Connor glanced at Annabelle over the turn of a curly-fry—a long glance—and reconsidered.

"Okay, I'll go," he said. "If only to provide protection."

"Right," Gavin said. "What about you, Carlton?"

Carlton took the Rook and sighed. "You go on ahead. Report on what you see. I'm predicting that it'll be nothing."

He jotted his move down in his worn yellow ledger.

"When?" Connor asked.

"After school, of course," Gavin said. "Meet us by the bikes."

THREE

The three of them met on the north side of Ironheart, past lines of electric cars and huffing SUVs of the waiting parents ushered through one by one, like cattle in a slaughterhouse. The unsmiling policeman hired by Ironheart to navigate the afterschool traffic waved them on like a conductor of an orchestra.

The sky was cloudy and grey but held no apparent promise of rain this time.

Gavin watched the other students leaving, wondering if his friends would stand him up, but then Annabelle appeared, with Connor on her heels, and he felt a measure of relief.

"We only have two bikes," Connor said. "Annabelle can ride with me."

"That's fine," she said. "I called my mom, said I'd be in study group. Would catch a ride home later."

"And she bought that?" Connor asked.

"She buys everything," Annabelle said. "She's my mom."

The boys unlocked their bikes—Gavin had a vintage five-speed that had been his older brother's, a blue bike with a glittery banana seat, high handlebars and a knobby gear shifter. Connor had a white mountain bike, a 21-speed with thick tires.

"I changed my mind," Annabelle said. "I'm riding with Gavin."

Gavin handed her his helmet, which she laughingly clipped on. The helmet had an eightball motif—the black helm with the white circle around a black eight at the crown.

Connor pouted, but accepted it, since it only made sense, given their bikes. Annabelle slipped behind Gavin, who took off speeding. Connor easily caught up, pulling alongside. He stole glances at Annabelle, who smirked at him from her perch behind Gavin, who peddled gamely, like a gundog chasing game.

"Don't wreck, Gavin," Annabelle said. "I don't want to skin my knees."

"I won't," Gavin said, mindful of his passenger, who lightly held her arms around his ribcage as they rode. She smelled of fruit and flowers.

Gavin couldn't understand why a girl like Annabelle hung around them. But where she wasn't very pretty, she was definitely smart. That didn't make her very popular at all. Not with the girls who thought they mattered most at Ironheart. She listened to weird music from a bygone age and wore studded bracelets on either wrist.

The three of them rode through the strangled streets of Happy Valley. The area around Ironheart was like much of the city—there were inklings of past affluence from more prosperous times, but they were larded over with a persistent poverty that had settled like smog on the City of Rust and colored everything with the same shades of despair. Even the pretty things in the City of Rust were tragic and near-forgotten things, in a state of decay.

"This place is a toilet," Connor said as they rode. "It's an armpit of a town. Why Ironheart picked this place to be is beyond me."

"Ironheart was settled over 150 years ago," Gavin said. "When Happy Valley was up and coming."

Annabelle scoffed. "Do you think Isaac Sutter was punking everybody when he named it 'Happy Valley?' I mean, what was happy about it?"

"It's like Iceland and Greenland," Connor said. "Eric the Red was playing tricks on people when he named those places."

"Sutter was playing tricks?" Annabelle asked. "Why didn't he name it Sutter's Valley, though? Why Happy Valley?"

Gavin laughed, pedaling hard with the extra weight, but in no way flagging at his task, lest Annabelle think he was a wimp.

"Only Isaac Sutter knows for sure," Gavin said. "And he's long dead."

FOUR

Their trek took them to Ambrose Park, which was an anaconda of untended green that wound its way through the City of Rust. It paralleled the Dun River, which itself flowed through town. It was said that if Ambrose Park could be put into one continuous space, it would have been nearly as large as Central Park. But because it was a ribbon stretched through Happy Valley, its true size was camouflaged.

Ambrose Park made for good biking, however, depending on which way you rode. Going downhill dragged you into the dilapidated downtown, while going uphill took you to the emerald enclaves of some of the more prosperous and planned communities where the people with money lived. This was from where the denizens of Ironheart Academy overwhelmingly came.

Gavin hunted with his nose as much as with his eyes, since the fog was still hanging heavy around them.

Annabelle caught him sniffing and laughed that plucky chuckle of hers, like a mirthful machine gun, fired in short and careful bursts, always on-target.

"Are you seriously sniffing your way to the lightning strike?" Annabelle asked.

"Maybe," Gavin said. "I might be. Ozone and all. Ionization."

"We are so dead," Connor said. "The Rustics are gonna kill us."

The Rustics were the name somebody at Ironheart had given to the locals, the kids who weren't privileged enough to pass the thick stone curtain wall that separated Ironheart from its surroundings. Those kids went to city and parochial schools, and hated the Ironheart Academy kids, who they saw as invaders.

"They won't. They're on the other side of the River," Gavin said. "The park is ours, man."

"They still sneak in," Connor said. "They're around."

He looked around them uncertainly, eyeing the tangled trees that flanked the road. Ambrose Park was left to its own devices, tended by a few stern Park Rangers, but otherwise trackless, beyond a single paved lane that made its way through it.

"Don't worry about it," Gavin said. "Sheesh."

"They kill people in the park," Connor said. "You could kill somebody here and absolutely nobody would notice. The Mafia dumps bodies in Ambrose Lake all the time. Everybody knows this."

Gavin shushed Connor with an upraised hand, then pointed.

"You know, this isn't actually so far from where we live, Connor," he said. "Oak Shadows is right over there."

And he was right. Gavin had a great sense of direction, and, sure enough, the island of affluence that was Oak Shadows was on the right side of the river, easily overlooked by those Rustics who would have to trek upriver for at least an hour or more before being able to follow the bend to reach it.

But for Gavin and Connor, it was an easy jaunt from there to Ironheart, if you knew the way, which they did.

For Annabelle, who lived in Troy, this was all unforgivably unfamiliar. Her mom would pick her up at the Academy and they'd go up Sutter Boulevard to the well-tended yards of Troy, the neighborhood for accountants and lawyers, versus the old money of Oak Shadows.

"You don't know where the lightning hit, Gavin," Connor said. "Admit it."

"It's right that way," Gavin said, pointing, using the promontory of Oak Shadows as his guide. "It's uphill from here."

They took their bikes off the road and locked them together by a clearing, near an old timber barricade that kept cars from driving over the side. There was a path marker, pointing in two different directions:

CAUSTIC SPRING TRAIL <1 mile
VINE VALLEY TRAIL >1 mile

"Which way, dude?" Connor asked.

"Vine Valley," Gavin said. "Uphill."

The others moaned.

"What's Caustic Spring?" Annabelle asked.

"It's where the stoners go to smoke weed," Connor said.

"Why's Vine Valley Trail uphill?" Annabelle asked.

"Let's find out," Gavin said.

FIVE

They reached Vine Valley Trail after half-marching through the fog, the trees and bushes, where dewy spider-webs blocked the path, fat black spiders huddled in their spiral centers.

"What are you even hoping to find?" Connor asked.

"Sometimes," Gavin said. "When lightning strikes the ground, it fuses the ground and creates a hunk of glass."

"Lightning glass," Annabelle said. "That's *almost* cool."

Connor had taken a stick and was whacking at spider-webs as they went, until soon the stick was a web-wrapped scepter topped with dangling spiders struggling to escape Connor's adolescent boy-whims.

"Gross," Annabelle said, watching Connor take swings as they made their way up the path.

Gavin was mindful of the cloying canopy of trees, themselves black shadows wrapped in thickening fog, and was thinking about turning around when Connor cried out, his stick striking a barbed wire fence.

"Whoa," Connor said, looking around. "You can see everything from here. I mean, if not for the fog."

The barbed wire barricade screened a grotto. A rusted sign with peeling paint warned to KEEP OUT by order of the City of Rust. Someone had painted a strange symbol on it, something none of them recognized, like a coiling, crazy thing.

To their right, over the lip of the trail, swarms of vines were tangled like monstrous grey-brown snakes, having strangled everything in reach.

"Christ," Connor said.

"Dead end," Gavin said.

"Bullshit," Annabelle said, stepping over the barbed wire. She snagged a dirty pink sneaker on the barbed wire as she went over. The boys, seeing her get ahead of them, scrambled after her.

The grotto was itself naturally occurring, with a dripping overhang above them, some thirty feet up. The stones above were dark grey, packed tightly, themselves held fast by tenebrous vines.

Gavin dug out his phone and snapped a picture of the sign and the grotto, of the dangling vines. He sent it to Carlton, with a note: CHECK THIS OUT.

Then they made their way to the grotto, which was a baker's dozen of slippery steps from the trailhead.

"Where'd the lightning strike, Gavin?" Connor asked, while Gavin sniffed the air yet again.

"Not here," Gavin said. "But we're close."

The grotto dripped with water and graffiti, arcane signs in red, orange, olive, and purple. The obligatory pentagram and odes to the devil, band names, and scrawled assertions about the carnal proclivities of any number of people. The waxy stubs of candles of various colors were present in nooks and crannies of the grotto as well. Someone had spraypainted "CARCOSA" on the far wall with an exaggerated arrow pointing deeper into the grotto.

"Carcosa," Annabelle said, while Gavin snapped a shot and sent to Carlton.

In the heart of the grotto was something else, something that was devoid of graffiti, something that stood with dozens of spent candles at its base in mingled cold waxy pools.

"What is that?" Connor asked, the three of them circling the object.

At first glance, it looked like it was a stalagmite, being of a yellowish hue, a sulfurous apparition rendered in stone that looked almost like a man. However, it was a faceless man, with only a blank visage amid the smooth turns of stone that looked as if it could be garments of silk. Someone had taken a jester's hat of yellow and crowned the stalagmite with it, where it hung partly askew, with little tarnished brass bells dangling from it.

They gazed at it gapemouthed, words fleeing them.

Gavin took another a photograph to send to Carlton, managing more of a finger twitch than something that ordinarily would have required a degree of volition. He typed with quick pushes of his enervated fingers:

SOMETHING'S HERE

The three of them fell to their knees before the stone figure as one.

SIX

Carlton gazed at the image Gavin had sent, his eyes poring over the shape and Gavin's last text message.

SOMETHING'S HERE

Gavin hadn't answered Carlton's follow-up texts, and none of them would answer their phones.

"Carlton," his sister Hannah called to him from downstairs. "Mom wants you to set the table."

The youngest of four, with three older sisters, Carlton was used to this household ritual. It was only because of the weirdness of the afterschool exodus of his friends that had caused Carlton to get behind his usual routine. His oldest sisters were twins, Hannah and Hailey, who were 18, and considered themselves the proxies of their parents. And his sister, Emma, was the family spy.

"Coming," Carlton said, firing off another text to his friends, whom he'd grouped together:

SOMEBODY TELL ME WHAT'S GOING ON.

Then he pocketed his phone and made his way downstairs, where the twins were looking at him with the feral triumph of sibling righteousness. Hannah and Hailey were both beautifully blond and were the twofold teen terrors of Ironheart Academy. Emma hunted in their shadows, being more bookish and prone to challenging Carlton at chess when the mood struck her.

"Set the table, Twerpo," Hailey said. "Mom said Dad's going to be home tonight."

"Fine," Carlton said, fetching the stacks of plates, dealing them out like they were cards, matching them to silverware. Family of six, with Carlton at the rock bottom of the hierarchy. His father was a commercial pilot, was gone more than he was there, and their mother worked in City Hall, which was an unusual occupation in Happy Valley, almost guaranteed that she worked steady yet pointless hours attempting to breathe life back into the nearly lifeless City of Rust.

"What were you doing up there, anyway, Carlton?" Hannah asked. "You'll go blind, you know."

"I know," Carlton said. He was used to everything his sisters threw at him, counted on his experience with them as a crucible that readied him to face absolutely anything the world could throw at him.

"Okay, just checking," Hannah said. "Emma? Mom and dad are coming home any minute now."

Their mother had put something in the crockpot in the morning, and the scent of beef stew filled the room. Hailey was making a tossed salad, while Hannah was putting out some bread and butter.

Emma emerged from the den like a wraith, dark-haired and wearing glasses like her baby brother.

"The Ghost has emerged," Hailey said. "Em, you have dishes tonight."

"I know I do," Emma said. "Everybody knows, Hail."

The twins looked up at once, their pretty faces momentarily cold and blank at the prospect of a challenge, but finding none they could detect, they went back to their business.

Carlton snuck a glance at his phone, saw that there was no response from any of his friends. He studied the image of the sculpture/figure they'd photographed, and the shot of the CARCOSA graffiti and the arrow. There was something uncanny about it, sinister. He could feel it, an almost throbbing menace in the thing, and the ridiculous jester's cap it wore.

"What are you looking at?" Emma asked, from over his shoulder.

"Carly's got a girlfriend," Hannah said. "Or a boyfriend, maybe?"

Emma had snuck a peek before Carlton could slip it way. He may have been taller than his sisters, but they were relentless.

"It's a rock formation," Carlton said. "Something one of my friends discovered."

"But you don't have any friends, Carly," Hailey said.

"Good one, Hail," Carlton said, mock-laughing.

Emma's face was showing that she wasn't yet done chewing her way into Carlton's business.

"It looks like a person," Emma said. "Is that in the park?"

"Where else?" Carlton said.

Hailey walked over, her athletically broad-hipped stride already something that would be a liability for her in a decade, but as a young woman, made her very popular at Ironheart. It wasn't Carlton's fault that he could see so many moves ahead—he knew his sisters' fates before they did.

"Let me see," she said, taking a look at the image. "What is, that, a pile of yellow wax wearing a hat?"

"I think it's a stalagmite," Carlton said. "My friends were investigating."

"Weirdo," Hailey said, rolling her blue eyes at him. They all had blue eyes. She set the salad bowl on the table, while Hannah was turning off the crockpot and putting the stew in the center of the table.

As if on cue, Mom and Dad had pulled up, and in they came. Captain Christopher arrived with Mother Amy, the two of them exchanging glances at seeing the kids all in the dining room, waiting for them.

"Daddy!" the twins said in unison, flanking their father and giving him a hug, while Amy hung up her coat and looked on with bemusement.

Emma and Carlton formed the second wave of greeters, after the twins had their turn. Their father received all of their greetings with a white-toothed smile that played off his tanned skin as he put his hat on the hat rack near the door.

"Something smells good," Christopher said.

Amy smiled at how everybody had come together to get dinner ready, and set down her work bag, while Christopher washed his hands in the powder room sink.

"Did you bring us anything, Daddy?" Hannah asked.

"Oh, we'll see," he said. It was kind of a joke they had because he hadn't brought them anything for several years. His gifts were usually topical trinkets that were acquired in the course of his travels. Carlton's favorite had been some jade figurines that he'd gotten for each of them.

He glanced at his phone again, still saw no reply.

WHERE ARE YOU GUYS?

And then, from Gavin:

werehere

SEVEN

Carlton couldn't get through dinner fast enough, volunteering to do the dishes to just give himself an excuse to leave the table. He scrubbed and piled dishes, putting the remainder in the dishwasher, tried to keep a low profile as he did so.

Then he shot upstairs, ostensibly to work on homework, but in truth to text Gavin and see what happened.

CARLTON: WHAT HAPPENED TO YOU GUYS?

GAVIN: werehere

C: WHAT WAS THAT THING?

G: somethingwonderful

C: WONDERFUL HOW?

G: ishardtoexplain

C: TRY.

G: wesawsomething

C: WHAT DID YOU SEE?

G: inthestonewesawit

C: WHAT DID YOU SEE?

G: youwontbelieveituntilyouseeit

C: WHAT. DID. YOU. SEE?

G: gottago

Gavin didn't reply to subsequent texts, so Carlton reached out to Annabelle.

CARLTON: WHAT DID YOU GUYS SEE?

ANNABELLE: sobeautiful

C: WHAT WAS IT?

A: seecarltonyoullloveit

C: WHY?

A: youjustwilltrustmeseeyousoon

C: WHAT DID YOU SEE?

A: illshowyouthen

Then Annabelle went quiet. Carlton reached out to Connor, too, just to see what he might say, but he wasn't much better, giving him only one reply.

CARLTON: WHAT DID I MISS?

CONNOR: everything

Connor didn't say anything else, despite Carlton's repeated texts. Irritated, he looked at the photos that Gavin had shared, and tried to figure out where it might otherwise be within Ambrose Park.

He did some Internet searches for the park, and for statues. He looked at the KEEP OUT sign Gavin had sent, and the photo of the grotto, and did some more searches.

There was an article in the *Rustville Ranger,* the local paper, dated ten years prior:

AREA MAN IMPLICATED IN
RITUAL TRIPLE MURDER

By Elliott Burke

Rustville (AP)—In a surprising twist to the spate of ritual murders carried out over the past three months, police have apprehended Lazarus Coulter, 38, of Troy, who was found hiding from authorities in a disused area of Ambrose Park on Wednesday. Police had received a tip from some hikers who had been chased by Coulter, who had confronted them with a hunting knife along one of the hiking trails.

Authorities said that he'd chased the hikers, who wished to remain unidentified, along the Vine Valley Trail, turning back when they had managed to elude him and call the police.

When the police arrived, they found Coulter in a cave along the trail, wrapped in a yellow robe he'd apparently been wearing. Coulter surrendered to the authorities and confessed to being the perpetrator of three bizarre ritual murders that had occurred over the past few months.

Coulter, who worked as an accountant for Brookhaven Pharmaceuticals, had lived alone in Troy. Police went to his home but did not reveal what they had seen at the Coulter residence, pending further investigation.

Carlton searched for VINE VALLEY TRAIL and was able to locate it. He then searched along it, did some additional searches for Ambrose Cave, Ambrose Grotto, Vine Valley Trail.

He found a website called THE YELLOW FELLOW, which contained a photograph of the stone figure in the grotto, the same one that Gavin had photographed. The website had an eye-rending yellow background, with black type.

Beautiful figure in the Vine Valley Grotto, the writer wrote. Carlton looked at the name of the writer. Her name was Madison "Maddy" Cathcart.

She had dozens of photographs of the figure, taken from various angles, and wrote at length about it on her website.

Not like stone, but something else. Like sculpted flesh, that seamless flow of rock hewn by steady hands. It flows like wax or butter, straight from the ground. I had thought it a stalagmite, but the grotto does not lend itself to such things. It cannot be naturally occurring, and yet it appears unnaturally naturalistic in its location.

Of all places, why here? Why here? I don't have an answer. Only the same question, asked over and over again. Like an echo in the mind within the cavern of reason, shadows on the wall, writhing.

I put a candle at His feet and watched it until the thing had burned out. And then I'd placed another. He rules the grotto as surely as any monarch. Even the vandals don't dare touch Him, beyond whoever put the jester's hat atop it. I've seen plenty of their cryptic marks on the grotto walls, the fearful movements, palsied proclamations.

Fearful, they mark the walls like dogs claiming territory, but He remains untouched. He neither fears them nor cares, standing sentinel, waiting, watching, seeing, knowing.

I know Him.
I have known Him.
All who see Him know Him.
In my heart, I know Him.
I have known Him.
And He has known me.
Beautiful Stranger.
Master of Masks.
Forgotten shadow.
Keeper of the vainglorious vanguard.
Lord of Whispers. I have known Him.

I have known Him.

Most of her website was devoted to poems and sections like that. There were pages upon pages, deep scrolls, long odes to the figure in the grotto. Carlton bookmarked the website for future research.

He texted Gavin yet again.

WHAT DID YOU SEE?

But he got no answer.

EIGHT

Carlton went to Annabelle's Instasnap account (Punk-rawkgrrl789) to see if she'd done anything there. She was always taking Instasnaps of everything. And, sure enough, there was a shot of the same stony figure that Gavin had photographed.

But there were other things there, too. There was a shot of Annabelle looking in the mirror, roughly an hour after the cave photograph. And a video clip of her shaving her head bald, while she whispered something. The hashtag was #thekingdemands #thekingcompels

He replayed the video several times, and thought it was Annabelle saying "The King demands, the King compels, the King demands, the King compels…" over and over while shaving her head with a straight razor.

Carlton dialed up Annabelle, who picked up on the third ring.

"What is it, Carlton?" Annabelle asked.

"You shaved your head," Carlton said.

"You're stalking my Instasnap?" Annabelle asked.

"Why'd you do that?"

"I wanted to," Annabelle said.

"The King demands?"

"The King compels," Annabelle said.

"Who's the King?"

"The King in Yellow," Annabelle said. "The Yellow King."

"Who's that?" Carlton asked. "What are you even talking about?"

Annabelle sighed. "Go to the grotto, Carlton. See for yourself. It'll be clear to you. Look for the Yellow Sign. You can't miss it. And it can't miss you."

Carlton felt a chill run through him.

"What happened to you guys?" he asked.

"Just go to the grotto, Carl," Annabelle said. She only called him that when she was teasing him. "Go there this weekend, and you'll understand. I've got to go. See you soon."

She hung up, and there it was.

Carlton contemplated what she'd said, looked up The King in Yellow, and saw references to a macabre play, to Carcosa.

NINE

"I can't know what's happened to my friends," Carlton said in his vlog. "I'm trying to find out, but I just don't know what's going on. I plan to go to the grotto and see for myself. If you don't hear from me again, I'm leaving this here, just in case. I'm fairly certain that—"

[END OF FRAGMENT. Carlton Reed (16) disappeared the week of September 25, 2017, as did his friends: Gavin Cleeves (15), Annabelle Clifton (15), and Connor Shaughnessy (14). Anyone with information on the whereabouts of these four and/or whoever wrote "Polishers of the Dream Ether" is strongly advised to contact the Redvale Police Department at 555.546.4366.]

The Starving Artist

13 APRIL, 1986, CHICAGO

Permit me a digression, if you will, Selene.

The Yellow Fever seems to have originated in Africa, from mosquitos to humans, by way of some of our primate cousins. The indignity of that, I suppose. And, at least in Africa, when Yellow Fever appeared, it would mostly kill the Europeans, as the local Africans had acquired a degree of immunity to the virus.

One can only imagine the withering umbrage of those haughty Europeans to be laid low by a mosquito bearing something other than malaria. It came to the New World by way of slave ships, they say. Irony abounds. The first catalogued outbreak of it in the New World was in Barbados, in 1647, and the Spanish recorded one in the Yucatan the year after—the Maya called it *xekik,* which translates as "blood vomit" evocatively enough.

It was first officially called "Yellow Fever" in 1744 by a Dr. John Mitchell, accounting for an outbreak in Virginia at the time. Isn't that a wonderful name, Selene? Yellow Fever. The irony is that poor Dr. Mitchell appears to have misdiagnosed the disease, but names stick, don't they?

European soldiers stationed in the Caribbean in that time dreaded appointments there, for the Yellow Fever would take their lives. The casualties were considerable. They even started calling it "Yellow Jack" as a way of putting a name to it, the personal animus they felt by being targeted by the relentless pestilence.

Yellow Jack stalked the soldiers protecting the colonial imperialists and took their lives. The fear was palpable, the terror. There was an epidemic in Philadelphia in 1793, when it was the young nation's capital, killing almost ten percent of the city's population, making it one of the worst epidemics in our country's history. Yellow Jack pranced about on clouds of mosquitos and claimed the lives of the European conquerors.

I don't know why these morbid thoughts keep coming to me. Hungry thoughts, fever dreams from a diseased mind. I don't bleed for my art; I starve for it. Don't worry, I know what I'm doing.

You're still worried, I know. But Leopold has assured me that the audiences are—pardon the pun—eating up the work. It is happening for me, I can see it with my own eyes. They are piling up at Cabaret Vortex every night to see me starve, Selene. I have arrived.

I have Yellow Fever, but not the same as the pestilence of the past. No, it's another fever that lays claim to my spirit. You warned me off of it, I know. I just didn't listen.

14 APRIL, 1986

Cabaret Vortex is the most enchanting of venues, I must admit. Leopold Castaigne is a saint, Selene. He has taken me under his black wing and given me the guidance I was always lacking when we were children. How am I to describe him to you? He is older, of course, like all mentors should be, don't you think? He radiates a handsome madness, I daresay. There is just something magnetic about him in his decadently confident bearing. It was his idea, I'll be the first to confess, but genius is genius, never to be denied.

But I digress, Selene!

I was talking about Cabaret Vortex, and here I was going on about Leopold. I imagine that the two are inseparable, for he poured his blood and soul into the Cabaret, to the point that the two of them can be said to be related, after a fashion. You know the pull of blood relations better than anyone.

The Cabaret is Baroque to the bone, a feast of cupolas and colonnades, and I cannot for the life of me imagine how Leopold was able to afford it, the sea of golden colors that drip from every corner of the place. The effect is one of abject transcendence. I tell you, Selene, Leopold has crafted a temple in the heart of Northalsted. It is a temple, and we who attend to it are but acolytes to the grand designs of Leopold Castaigne.

Sorry, I'm drifting again. I am eating so little, now, I feel myself lighter than a feather, and prone to visions. It's fascinating how one can lift oneself beyond the terrestrial confines of one's existence when you put your mind to it. Leopold has guided me in this. I confess to you that he is my muse.

Never having had a muse before, how can one truly know? It's a bit like true love, I imagine, never having felt that magical emotion. How well you know how thoroughly I have sampled my share of the world's delights. Is that how it might proceed, I wonder?

Mentor → Friend → Confidante →
Companion → Muse → Lover → Mate

I can't truly know, but I hang on every utterance of Leopold. Gods, but that man can command a room. I'm mad for him and his rampant grandiosity. You would swoon. I know that I do.

My head is swimming. I was talking about the Cabaret. The frescoes, Selene! I don't know how Leopold managed to draw forth such painters for the Cabaret, but they are exquisite in their depictions.

I've already mentioned *The King in Yellow,* so you fully understand me, or you should, if you've read it. Leopold read it to me. We acted it out, we two, playing all the parts. He, of course, was the Stranger, the titular character, while I played hapless Cassilda and Camilla both, but I tell you the truth when I say that the paintings upon the frescoed cupolas depict the vistas of Carcosa to unfathomable detail.

Gazing heavenward in the Cabaret is to lose oneself to ecstatic oblivion. And he will not tell me how he did it, or even who painted it, this nameless artisan, maker of masterpieces. But the frescoes are staggering in concept and execution. No one can set foot in Vortex and fail to feel it.

HE is there with us in the Cabaret, looking over us all. Leopold has a gold-leafed idol to HIM in one of the many labyrinthine turns of the place, the Corridor in Yellow, Leopold calls it, where admirers and supplicants can pay their respects. Is it a shrine? Is it, Selene?

Permit me to further paint a picture of Baroque opulence: a golden, gilded corridor, with paintings upon the walls, and columns encrusted with ornamentation, with chandeliers overhead, and the most magnificent carpeting in gold with a pattern of black stars upon it, hypnotic in such elegant simplicity. It's hard not to stare at those lovely stars as you pass, moving inexorably to the idol—"statue" seems too meager a word to describe it. The hooded, robed figure of HIM, seated upon a golden throne. Leopold has candles arrayed in front of it, an altogether decadent profusion of them, tended by some of his employees.

That's not what I am, by the way—I'm *not* one of Leopold's employees. We are partners, he and I. I am the performance artist-in-residence in his glorious Cabaret. People would kill for this honor. I'd vouchsafe that some probably have before, Selene. Oh, wicked, sinful Leopold, how you hold me fast in your entropic embrace!

I'll write more tomorrow, as I'm terribly hungry.

15 APRIL, 1986

I'm back! What a night it's been. Capacity crowds, Leopold was so happy. I could see it in his eyes, in his smile. He has the most magnificent of mustaches—he looks like Nietzsche's godfather, I swear to you. And his artful application of mustache wax, this careful beeswax concoction he acquires, to turn the ends of his mustache into the most diabolical of points. I tell him he looks like Mephistopheles incarnate and he just laughs with that gusty, operatic baritone he possesses.

"Mephistopheles, Michael? T'would be a demotion for the likes of me to be placed in the company of such peerage. I serve both higher and lower causes, you should know by now."

It might have qualified as a faux pas if it were possible for the dictates of the mundane to hold sway at the Cabaret.

But people turned up in droves, beneath the frescoes of the twin suns and the shimmery waters of Lake of Hali. The very best sort of people, dancing as if their lives depended on it while Pallid Mask played from the stage—a stage that I shared with them, I should add—yes, Selene! I shared the stage with that feral foursome and their white masks. The Stranger in his yellow velvet suit and white gloves, while Cassilda played her black bass and Camilla played lead on a custom lemonburst Les Paul and Hildred drummed as if her life depended on it. One man, three women. All masked. All masked!

I shared the stage with them, rapt in my fever dreams as I wasted away. In those moments upon the stage, I forget how hungry I've become. Or, perhaps, I'm hungrier for the applause and adulation of the crowd, the hungry eyes upon me, feasting on me as the band plays their dirgelike neogothic ballads.

Those nights, those infernal nights, they sustain me in my performance. It's a quiet thing, starvation. It's like a fog descending, although not nearly as visually arresting. Slower, subtler, Selene. It creeps up quieter than the proverbial cat's feet if you can even imagine that.

And I'm ashamed to say again that it was Leopold's idea, not mine. I'd been complaining about the plight of the artist, and the sinister implications of the Great Plague, hunting from the venereal shadows like some monstrous, hulking predator. Who can be safe from it, I ask you? It stalks our every step.

"You should make a statement," Leopold said, while we drank the most delectable of spirits he'd acquired from one of the many vendors indebted to him.

"A statement?" I asked, the incarnation of inebriated innocence. Leopold leaned into me, on his bespoke elbows, his amber eyes upon me, a golden grin on his face, his buff-colored Homburg at a puckish angle. He wore a yellow suit not unlike the one worn by the Stranger onstage, and I could see he had a stickpin brooch at his lapel that bore the Pallid Mask upon it in what I could only imagine was porcelain or marble, or possibly even finer things.

"An artist's statement, Michael," he said, as if he needed to explain it to me. "You can give life to the plight of the Blight with your life. And to the plight of the artist, of course. Which is always a struggle for affirmation in the face of what? Apathy? Ignorance? Infamy? Irrelevance? Obsolescence?"

The idea took hold of me, held me fast in its teeth, Selene. It laid claim to me.

"'The Starving Artist,'" I said, and I could see from the way he sat back, his ever-present walking stick in hand, that he was satisfied with that idea. I felt a swell of pride that I had pleased him.

"We'll make a big thing of it, Michael," Leopold said. "Why, we can stage a Last Supper for you—a sensational feast before you begin your fast, or part of the process of your performance. I leave it to you, naturally, to decide. You are the Artist, and I defer to your approach and your vision as your benefactor."

He was gracious that way, so giving. We were there with a dozen or more of his acolytes, the others who followed in his wake. I won't name them because they are but bit players in my own play. Just understand that they were there, and I could see it in their eyes, the covetousness for what I had managed to accomplish in the company of Yellow King Leopold Castaigne.

16 APRIL, 1986

It's not an easy thing to starve. Not for a man, at any rate. I sympathize with you, Selene, with women everywhere, who abstain when they would rather partake of the bountiful harvest brought from Nature. The world is sensation, and the sensation of hunger gnaws away at the glory of life itself, the very building blocks of pleasure.

There are no words for it, the dismal emptiness of it, the void—yes, the void—as one's cells cry out in a chorus for sustenance, only for the tyranny of Mind to hold back the needs of Body. That need is dire and all-consuming: the need to feed.

I imagine I dwell upon The Last Supper out of a remembrance of that precious food, the opulence of it, the bacchanalian table Leopold set for me, all of his hangers-on in attendance, fellow rivals and courtiers eager for Leopold's fleeting favor. Some of them, the more adroit among them, actually praised me for my courage, for taking the stance I did, for daring to take Leopold up on his suggestion.

At that moment, I didn't care. I was the Guest of Honor of the Founder of the Feast. I was being feted, wined and dined by the very best people, and Leopold lavished his lordly attention on me.

"True artists are truly rare," Leopold said, raising his gilded cup of stars to me. "Michael Archer is just such a true artist. All of you would do well to honor him tonight."

And I saw the cups, glasses, chalices, drinking horns, and goblets raised to me, Selene. To me! From friends, rivals, and foes alike, all of them rhetorically riding on Leopold's generous coattails as he praised me that fateful night.

The table set at the Cabaret's Gilded Lounge was exquisite. I don't how Leopold could have possibly afforded it. The man is simply made of money. The tablecloth was a resplendent yellow, upon which he'd had blackened candelabras of tarnished silver set, bearing white candles that burned brightly, there were so many of them. The Gilded Lounge was set with recessed mirrors along the length of it, in golden frames that bore the mocking faces of cherubs and had the dizzying effect of creating the iterated images of infinite selves to any onlooker who dared to look over their shoulder and look into the abyss. And believe me, Selene: I looked myself right in all of my infinite eyes.

Overhead, brass chandeliers hung and added further luminosity to the tabletop conflagration caused by the candles. At the far side, a string quartet of musicians played Handel (Leopold told me this later; I'm impossible with names of those old, dead composers)—two violins, a viola, a cello—all wearing white masks upon their faces as they played, wearing matching cloth-of-gold suits and dresses. I joked that maybe it was Pallid Mask slumming it for my sake, but Leopold only rolled his eyes, told me they were simply classical musicians picking up a bit of extra money.

"They're always hungry for work, musicians are, Michael," Leopold said, refilling my glass. Gods, but the food. Thinking of it now actually brings me pain.

The Gilded Lounge was where Leopold served his most important guests at the Cabaret, and it was ordinarily off-limits to anyone but the most incandescent of VIPs.

"The luminaries who need no illumination, and yet, I provide it for them, anyway," Leopold said with a glittery grin.

I cannot forget the food, which was served, Leopold proudly announced, *à la française,* which, to my artist's eye, meant everything arriving all at once in a carefully choreographed fashion, creating a kind of gustatory tableau that left me breathless.

There were cavalcades of ivory tureens that bore onion soups, creamy mushroom soups, and beef broths, amicably served up by the hovering staffers who wore uniforms of white ruffled shirts and golden knickers and white hose with golden buckle shoes.

There was a phallic avalanche of baguettes in hand-woven baskets upon the table, and diners gleefully tore at them and drowned them in the soups, and when the *pot-au-feu* appeared in grand style, first manifesting as a delectable beef-duck-pork-veal-chicken broth that came forth in the arms of the servers within the most extraordinary of golden cauldrons, inset with tangled visions of twining angels and devils and stars and bulls and nymphs in a staggering ensemble, while the servers dipped deeply of the golden ladles to serve the beguiling broth. When the savory *pot-au-feu* entrée returned to us later, it arrived upon golden platters, piled high with the broth-moistened meat and vegetables.

There were overstuffed yellow peppers filled with sausage and golden rice, a plethora of ornately topped meat pies—I saw eel and lamprey, mince, and pork, as well as platters of steaming lobster attended by congregations of boiled crab, with finger-fat prawns languorously lounging with legions of prostrate oysters on copious mounds of shaved ice.

We were next invaded by a column of *filet de boeuf en croûte* (basically, Beef Wellington, Selene). Forgive me if you can for any details I have missed—I was deep in my cups at that point, and my vision was blurring even as my head was spinning, which remains as much a memory for me as the food. To be at the eye of a storm is a heady thing.

The desserts were opulence incarnate, as to be expected whenever Lord Castaigne is involved—candied dates, plump figs, golden raspberries, blackberries, poached pears and baked apples drowned in calvados and cloves, blood oranges, sliced mangos, and cheeses of every consistency and color—was able to make out Gouda, Emmentaler, mascarpone, fontina, goat cheese, brie, and fresh ricotta, always on the most artful of plates that spoke to Leopold's apparently inexhaustible flair for ostentation, and accompanied by the most delectable of pastries turned into all sorts of convoluted and even erotic shapes made for people's opened mouths, which were absolutely everywhere.

Leopold had also summoned a painter to the party, who was tasked with reproducing the event, who was walking about with a camera, capturing the scene as he went. I hate to say that I don't know the man's name, but he was everywhere taking pictures, for Leopold had commissioned the man to make a painting of the event, one that would adorn an as-yet unannounced wall in the Cabaret, to commemorate the evening.

All for me, Selene! It was all for me, and it was glorious. The memory of it is both precious and painful, as I mourn the irrevocable path of glory that I have taken, to give all for my art.

17 APRIL, 1986

I fear the remembrance of that Last Supper drained me in ways I had not foreseen, leaving me almost crestfallen. The Michael that I was that night is not the Michael I have become—to pass from ingenue to artiste to artist is a painful passage that I would not wish upon you or anyone.

How long has it been since I've undertaken this performance as *The Starving Artist* who Leopold trots out at the Cabaret? Oh, I know, he indulges me. He lets me speak, encourages it, even. The things that I saw, delirious with hunger, caught up in the sorcerous spell of the Yellow King, I am captive to it.

Would that I could stop, Selene.

Can you stop me?

Can anyone?

Can I stop myself, I wonder?

20 APRIL, 1986

I whirl upon the stage before the strength has left me, when the hunger fuels my mad visions, the things I see, I walk through the starry skies and sing ballads of lost Carcosa before the gleeful audience. Each night, Leopold introduces me, like some stage-managed shaman, and each night, I deliver a ravenous rhapsody, the words coming to me as my brain lashes out, borne of cellular desperation as it yearns for food.

Selene, I'm ashamed to say that I don't know what I have said when I was deep in it. At the start of it, I had coherence, things I wanted to share, but now? As *The Starving Artist*, I am something else, someone else, and I am hidebound to the whims of the King. I go where HE wills me to go, like some swaybacked nag. HE could ride me to the Sun, or to HIS double suns, and I would gladly face immolation.

I'm dying onstage, Selene.

23 APRIL, 1986

The painting has arrived, and Leopold is so proud of it, and the artist who made it. He made a show of showing it, unveiling it before the crowds of the Cabaret. He announced it, and me, as I slumped in my golden chair, a fragment of who I had been, wasting away.

"Look upon this lustrous depiction of a most holy night, my lovelies," Leopold said, directing the spotlights on the painting.

And I must admit that it was exquisite. The nameless painter (bad with names, I told you) had signed it in yellow, a hopeless scribble I could not make out, but his Last Supper—which was, in truth, *my* Last Supper—was a stunning monstrosity, perfectly rendered in a fashion that could only be said to mock and honor all that was holy, for there I was, and Leopold, and the other specters in attendance, in the Gilded Lounge, surrounded by the splendor of the meal, which the painter had somehow consolidated into a literally everything at once in an extraordinary scene that carried with it every emotion of that wonderful night, which felt a lifetime away.

The Cabaret crowd cheered and applauded, raising their glasses not in my honor, but in the honor of Leopold and his nameless painter, in the work of art, while I watched onstage, but no longer the center of attention. Leopold could see my pain, and his smile bore something that felt like compassion, although in my state of famine, I could not be entirely certain.

"Behold our beloved St. Michael," Leopold said, pointing to me with his night-black walking stick. "Our current performance artist-in-residence at the Cabaret. See how he suffers for his art, and how far he has fallen from that night when he set out to become *The Starving Artist*. I put it to you, my dear audience—should we feed him? Michael, what would you have us do?"

The painting was beautiful. I was beautiful in the painting. I mean, I was preserved in the work. There was something in that. There was, of course, another sour note, one that stuck with me, for the nameless painter had entitled the piece, *The Lost Supper,* which felt to me like another slice of mockery, the twist of the palette knife, from one artist to another.

I tried to get to my feet, and, to my satisfaction, managed to do so.

"I have made my statement," I said, my voice almost a whisper. Leopold approached me, all but looming over me. I felt so small beside him, although before I had fallen under his spell, I was taller than he was, and heavier. Stronger, I had thought, too.

"What is that statement, Michael?" Leopold asked.

"Feed me," I said. "I beg of you, feed me."

"But your performance is not yet ended, Michael," Leopold said. "What say you, dear audience? Has Michael suffered enough? Should he end his fast at last? How long has it been? You've seen him here every night, in his golden chair. You've listened to him speak of unseeable things, of faraway places. What say you?"

"No!" came the chorus of cries from the crowd, their feverish eyes upon me, glittering.

"No," I said, shaking my head, waving my rail-thin arms in front of me.

"Michael is hungry," Leopold said. "He is so hungry. But is he an artist or an animal, I ask you?"

One of his attendants came forth in golden livery, an insane costume of a powdered wig, golden clothes, and a white ruffled cravat and the knickers and hose and gilded buckle shoes. The attendant wore a white mask and bore something on a golden tray, covered with a lid that threw back the light in flashes as he moved.

The attendant, one of Leopold's youthful disciples, clacked over to me, holding out the covered tray, theatrically removing the lid with a flourish.

Upon the tray, steaming in the bright light, was a cheeseburger.

"Which is it, Michael?" Leopold asked. "Artist or animal?"

I snarled and threw myself at the cheeseburger, snatching at it, dropping it to the stage to the delighted laughter of the audience. Uncaring, I picked it up and took a bite from it, Selene. I know what they say when one restricts one's diet, how one should be careful about reintroducing food, but I swear to you, that burger, wherever it came from, was paradise made flesh.

"Ladies and Gentlemen, Lady Gentlemen, and Gentlemen Ladies, I give you *The Starving Artist*," Leopold said, slow clapping. "Artist and animal both, it would seem."

And the audience all began to slow-clap as I chewed, heedless, uncaring, desiring only the cheeseburger I ate beneath the unblinking spotlight, all eyes upon me again, condiments smeared across my face, to thunderous applause I could hardly hear over the sound of my own chewing.

I MAY, 1986

I am recovered, Selene, if I am not entirely myself, after a few weeks. I have been cast out of the inner circle of the Cabaret Vortex by Leopold, who seemed beyond disappointed in me for reasons I could not fully comprehend. He came at me like a hammer after the conclusion of the performance. And the cruelty of it is that I'm not entirely sure he was even unhappy with me.

"There it is, Michael," Leopold said, from his office. He had a taxidermied polar bear in that office with him, some stuffed monstrosity in a corner that he'd acquired in one of his many adventures. Someone had placed a golden crown upon its head and had festooned it with golden beads that hung from its outstretched arms. I could feel it watching me and could feel Leopold's eyes upon me as well. I am unsure which was the harsher judge.

The Lost Supper was on his wood-paneled wall behind him, the beautiful painting dominating the room in a way that even the stuffed polar bear could not. It commanded the space, and framed Leopold beautifully.

"There is what, Leopold?" I asked.

"You gave up, Michael," Leopold said. "Now you're just another person, another mouth to feed, from my perspective."

"You can afford it, I should think," I said, and he smiled.

"Mmm," Leopold said. "Did you see HIM? When you were at your hungriest, Michael? When you were well and truly starving? When you were raving? Oh, the things that you said upon my stage, Michael. I have them all, you know. Every performance, every utterance. Captured on video, on film. Those are all mine."

"I saw something," I said, and Leopold tasted that on his lips a bit before replying.

"Not enough," Leopold said. "Did you see the stars? The fact is, I don't think you'll ever do anything as good as *The Starving Artist* again, Michael. In fact, I'm quite sure of it. How can you even hope to top that? You gave a month of your life for your art in a way that few ever have. The dedication, the madness of it. Intoxicating. Had you gone all the way, you'd have been immortal. I'd have seen to it. Now, you're just like anybody else. Another useless mouth."

"I'm a survivor," I said. "I'm a living artist. There's that."

Leopold leaned forward on his desk, a beautiful artifact of mahogany, upon which sat papers and a lovely green lamp, and a stunning copy of *The King in Yellow*, richly bound in yellow leather. He caressed that tome with one of his well-ornamented hands, his gold rings bearing precious stones that could cover my cost of living for a year, I was sure.

"Everyone who goes to a bullfight secretly goes in hopes of seeing the matador gored, you know," Leopold said. "To see true courage in the face of almost-certain oblivion, to face it and accept the consequences. The flinching matador? No, he is nothing but a coward. A clown and a pretender."

Leopold loved to speak in that way, those images that spoke of his experience and knowledge.

"You're calling me a coward?" I asked.

"I am," Leopold said. "You were supposed to die for your art, Michael. The painting, the everything. The entire thing. But you flinched. How can you hope to reach Carcosa when you flinch, Michael?"

Selene, the pain of his disapproval wounded me deeply. Worse than the hunger pangs I'd felt in the course of my performance.

"Even hapless Icarus flew until his wings melted," Leopold said. "What would he be if he turned away from the sun? Nothing. That's what you are. Nothing."

Anger welled up in me, that this man, this impresario, this Svengali, this cabaret owner would judge me so harshly for failing to, what? Kill myself that he might have another bauble added to his already overcrowded crown?

"Get out, Michael," Leopold said. "And never come back."

There was so much more I wanted to say, but I didn't say it. I simply left, without a backward glance.

I suppose I flinched.

I won't flinch again.

5 MAY, 1986

The Cabaret Vortex continues, as ever. Implacable. Like the Sphinx.

Leopold has found another star, that nameless painter, the one who captured my likeness in *The Lost Supper*. He had been in the audience on that fateful night, you know. I'm certain Leopold had placed him there, a performance within a performance. Another of his games.

He had captured it, rendered it into another glorious painting—*The Consumer*. It's a Goyasque grotesquerie of me gorging myself onstage, rendered in oil. It's fantastic, a delicious chiaroscuro of light and dark: damnable Leopold onstage, the attendant nearby, white-masked and malicious, while I loom in the foreground, this pathetic specimen, feasting on that cheeseburger, my face that of a rapacious revenant, fully transported by the food, my face festooned with ketchup and mustard, oblivious to anything but my own satiety. It's an amazing work, a true statement. He's perfectly captured me, my humiliation. I could not look more abject than in that moment.

No wonder Leopold has put the man on as his new artist-in-residence. How the man works, stalking about with his camera, capturing things, and then painting them part from memory, part from his photography. He and Leopold were made for each other, a perfect synergy, a parasitic symbiosis between patron and artist. I was a fool to even think there was ever a place for me at the Cabaret, Selene.

10 MAY, 1986

I know I should call you. But the pain of my rejection is still too raw. It's weird, though—every meal I take, I think of my time of fasting, my masterpiece. I cannot look at food the same way again, and even Carcosa dims in my vision, without the Yellow Fever I spoke of before. There is something lost in me, Selene. Or I lost something of myself. I don't know.

They look at me when I attend the Cabaret, now simply part of the audience. Leopold and his performers, the people he plucks and fluffs, the stage-strutters, the damnable Pallid Mask, practically the house band of the Cabaret now, those masked charlatans, playing their dark, throbbing music, captivating the throngs with their songs. But I know them for what they are, and who they are.

Even in the audience, I see them.

And they know me. Not the band, not the band. They float higher than me, now, but everyday members of the audience, the ones who'd been there at my happening, at my moments. They recognize me, they make the smallest of small talk, the curiosity that I have become. I can't hope to get close to Leopold, now; his security won't let me near him. They watch me, too. Not a curiosity, but perhaps a threat.

Is that what I am, now? A threat?

15 MAY, 1986

I hate the nameless painter. What madness could drive a man, an artist, no less, to anonymity? Truly? It's his shtick, isn't it? That's his thing. I had thought it was just my own inebriation, but the man paints with no name, just his signature scribble in yellow. It's the only continuity in his work, that ridiculous, obscene scribble.

Not to deride his work—it's brilliant. He's well-trained and masterful, but good god, no name, Selene! He trades in it, simply calls himself The Painter. That's all he goes by or answers to. It's insanity. I want to see where he goes but since he's fallen into Leopold's orbit, but he's never out of the Cabaret, or when he does venture forth, it's with a bloody entourage.

I never had an entourage. Am I jealous, or merely envious?

20 MAY, 1986

I got kicked out of the Cabaret for good tonight, Selene. I suppose I was causing a scene. Maybe it was another performance, haha, wouldn't that be something? I might have said as much when I'd drunk too much, roaring on the dancefloor.

It was packed, as it always is, and I just couldn't abide it, wondered where the Painter was, which one he was. I know him by sight when I'm clear-headed. I can see him, his pretty face, the high cheekbones, the blond hair, the bright eyes, and always his camera, what he carries with him like a kind of talisman in his long-fingered hands. How I hate him. I really, really hate him.

And I saw him, just a glimpse, because Leopold's security got their meaty mitts on me and they walked me out in front of everyone, howling and making a scene. I was making a scene, Selene. Yes, your baby brother humiliated himself yet again, beneath the gaze of the King on the dancefloor of the Cabaret, in front of everybody. How I howled and wailed.

What I saw, my last glimpse from within the Cabaret, was the Painter, smirking as he took my picture, captured me.

Those images would require release papers I'd die before signing, I can tell you that. If I could afford a lawyer, I'd send one after him.

25 MAY, 1986

I'm going to mail my journal to you, Selene. I want you to understand what's happened to me, what I've done. You're the only one who understands me. The only one who ever has.

I have one more performance piece in mind, one I hope makes an impact. I will not flinch. I must not flinch.

Just know that whatever becomes of me, that I love you eternally, and I fervently pray that you always love me in return.

[Unreceived letter addressed to Michael Archer, delivered to his address in Hyde Park. Opened by investigators after being contacted by Selene Archer.]

30 MAY, 1986, NEW YORK

Oh, Michael, why do you put me through this? You're scaring me. I understand you're trying to raise awareness, but at what cost? Your life? I fear that you're taking things too far, as ever. If I weren't so busy here, I would come see you.

I received the play you kept talking about, the one you mailed to me with your journal, but I haven't gotten around to reading it, yet, I'm so terribly sorry.

Life just intrudes, but I swear I'll get to it. I apologize for the brevity of my note, but I've got a recital to attend.

I'll call you, I promise, if only you'll answer.

[Authorities are investigating the apparent suicide of Michael Archer, found hanging in his Hyde Park apartment on May 27. When questioned by the police, Leopold Castaigne, local businessman and noted philanthropist, expressed great sorrow at the passing of Michael Archer, and had mentioned that his artist-in-residence, known only as The Painter, is doing a retrospective portrait of Archer commissioned by Castaigne in honor of the late performance artist, which will be unveiled in an invitation-only showing at the Cabaret Vortex.]

The Eye in the Sky

ONE

Aldebaran is an orange giant. It has expanded to 44.2 times the diameter of the Sun. It would be as if Aldebaran was a basketball, and the Sun—our Sun—was a pea beside it. On that kind of celestial scale, the enormity of it, it is impossible to imagine. That's because our own Sun is massive to our eyes, and it's nothing compared to Aldebaran.

Nothing.

Aldebaran means "the Follower" in Arabic.

It's 20 parsecs way.

That's over 65 light-years from Earth.

That means that it would take 65 years for light to travel between Aldebaran and Earth. It means that the light we see from it is over 65 years old. Old light, interstellar ghostly afterimages, sights unseen.

The brightness and proximity of Aldebaran makes it one of the easiest stars in the sky to spot. The asterism—the pattern of stars that it appears to reside with—makes it easy to locate. It doesn't ride with the Hyades cluster; it only appears to be, because it's in the same line of sight. It's closer to us than the Hyades. The Hyades are over 150 light-years away.

This is lost on the celestial tourists, the ones who don't actually know.

They don't pay attention to the details, not the way I do.

Aldebaran is a type K5 III star and has a stable habitable zone. That means that it's at least possible that there *could* be life out there. Some measurements of radial velocity have showed a long-period radical oscillation. This could mean that Aldebaran has a substellar companion out there with it. That basically means a planet of some sort, roughly 11.4 times the mass of Jupiter.

Then again, there could be nothing there.

Is it Carcosa?

Is it circling Aldebaran?

Is that where the King in Yellow lives?

Camilla, my wife, told me about it, about the *King in Yellow,* and about the mentions of the Hyades and Aldebaran. She mentioned it to me in passing, in bed, while we were watching television. I could tell it excited her to be able to talk about something astronomical to me.

"Will," she asked, curled beside me. "You know about the Hyades, right?"

And I laughed.

I mean, I was an astronomer. It was my job.

She knew I'd know, but Camilla was like that, asking questions of me that she already had answered in her mind.

"Yeah, of course I do," I said. "Where'd you hear about them?"

And she told me, about the story, the play, and what it meant. What it meant to her. It clearly meant something to her, something profound.

Camilla was not like me. We came together in the middle, like a compromise. She was fire, I was ice. She was sugar, I was spice—or maybe I was the sugar, and she was the spice. It just was one of those things that happened. My job required me to do math and gaze into the skies, not muck around in meetings. It was a good job. I was well-suited for it.

Camilla told people's fortunes. She was a fortune teller, like walked people through their mundane miseries with stories of prophecy and destiny, of opportunities to be gained over the horizon. People actually paid her for this, these clients of hers.

I focused on what was out there; Camilla saw things down here that couldn't be seen. Somehow, we made that work between us. One of the many ironies between Camilla and me was that she was a professional astrologer, and I was a professional astronomer. We made it work.

She wore her brown hair shoulder length, wore glasses. She had big brown eyes and a smattering of freckles like stars across her face. I had blue eyes and glare-resistant eyeglasses I wore almost constantly, except when I went to bed. My blond hair was thinning, but I wasn't bald, yet. I was taller than Camilla. She liked that about me, I think. She'd comment on it from time to time, how she liked that I was tall.

"No idea why they'd mention those places," I said. "They probably thought they were cool names to use."

"It's in Taurus," Camilla said, something I already knew. But her knowing it as the constellation of Taurus meant something else to her. "It's in Taurus, with Aldebaran. With Aldebaran, Will."

She had an upturned nose and a toothy sort of smile, a bit of an overbite that I thought was cute. She was a Taurus. I was a Capricorn. She'd done our charts and had declared that we were a perfect match of Earth Signs. She said we'd build our own castle one day, our own citadel. That's just the word she used: citadel.

"The Hyades are estimated to be about 625 million years old," I said.

Camilla whistled. "That's really old, Will."

"Yes, it is," I said. "Although, in truth, it's a celestial wink."

"I'll give you a celestial wink," Camilla said, squirming against me, winking. I liked the arch of her eyebrows.

It gave her a faintly diabolical bearing that she wielded to great effect. I couldn't ever deny her when she asked for something.

"What got you thinking about the Hyades?" I asked, mildly curious, because normally she didn't care.

She reached over to the nightstand, held up the yellow book, upon which was the spectral figure I assumed the story was named after, while I turned off the television.

"Why would they mention the Hyades and Aldebaran?" Camilla asked. "It has to mean something, Will."

"Probably because they sound sinister," I said. "Maybe a little threatening. Not Aldebaran—Aldebaran is *always* mentioned in science fiction. Everybody just loves Aldebaran. It's fun to say, even. Aldebaran. But the Hyades? Feels more menacing, maybe. But it's really just a cluster of stars, nothing more. There are stellar clusters all over the place. It's a big universe."

"Yes," Camilla said. "TOO big, if you ask me."

That made me laugh and prompted Camilla to treat me to a little poke, as she set down the book and turned off the light. We were together in the dark, gazing at the ceiling.

"You know what I mean," she said. "Can you look at the Hyades? Can you look at Aldebaran for me?"

"I'd have to book time at the observatory," I said. "That takes a while. And, frankly, the Hyades are some of the most-studied stars in the sky. It'd take something special for me to justify telescope time on that particular cluster."

"I understand," Camilla said, sighing. "I was just curious."

Lying in bed, staring at the ceiling, where I imagined there to be stars, the wheels turned in my head a moment or two, maybe even longer.

"What's supposed to be in the Hyades and Aldebaran?" I asked, at last.

"Something," Camilla said. "The King in Yellow. Hastur."

"Hastur?" I asked.

"Yes," she said, in the dark. I could see her profile as she spoke.

"Who's Hastur?" I asked.

"We're not really supposed to speak about him," Camilla said. "I shouldn't have brought it up."

The caution, even fear, in her voice gave me pause. Camilla and I had been married a decade, had a daughter, Nicole, and an otherwise utterly normal and happy suburban family life in Oak Park. Part of why we'd moved to Oak Park was because it was a place where we didn't have to be scared. What's more, it was marginally less light-polluted than proper city living, although I had secretly longed for an appointment in Mauna Kea, it was something we were considering once Nicole was off to college. Right now, Nicole was away at band camp, marching, playing her flute, piccolo, whatever woodwind it was.

Of course, now that Camilla had brought it up, it got me wondering, and so I started doing my own research. I skimmed the stuff she talked about, reviewed the lines in question, which were really throwaway mentions, like so much stardust.

On a whim, I went to my own amateur observatory—amateur only because it was in my home, versus an official observatory. Here I had my own telescope, and turned it skyward, chased down Aldebaran and the Hyades and gazed up at them, nestled in the bull's head of Taurus.

Taurus was one of the very oldest constellations, having been featured in the mythologies of the Sumerians, Assyrians, Babylonians, Egyptians, Greeks, and Romans.

Aldebaran was the glaring red eye of the Bull, glowering at Orion across the sky. It was the angry Eye in the Sky. I imagined the Bronze and Iron Age civilizations, bathed in fearful darkness at night, looking up at the stars and painting their constellations to bring them the comfort of mythology.

Taurus was said to be painted on a cave from 15,000 years ago, in a place known as the Hall of the Bulls. I imagined those ancient cavemen, for whom even the Bronze Age civilizations would have seemed hopelessly advanced, gazing skyward into the red eye of Aldebaran and the Hyades, and seeing something there. Something that would move that ancient soul to paint it on the walls of a cave in Lascaux. That's in France.

I hopped the stars with my telescope to find Taurus, and turned my expensive telescope to bear upon it, gazing into the crimson glare of Aldebaran.

For the Babylonians, Taurus was Gugalanna, the Bull of Heaven, sent to punish Gilgamesh for spurning the advances of the goddess, Ishtar. He was the first spouse of Ereshkigal, who ruled the Babylonian Underworld, a forlorn place of shadow, devoid of light.

I could see Aldebaran and the Hyades glittering at me through the telescope, could feel the piercing gaze.

What had they seen?

TWO

I got to Bierce Observatory early, having been able to request time from Mr. Masters, who grudgingly cleared me for the time, and I was able to book an hour of telescope time, gazing up at the Hyades, hoping to find something worth seeing, something that everyone else had somehow missed.

I didn't know what I was looking for, exactly. Certainly nothing anybody else wouldn't have found before me.

That was the thing: I didn't really know what I was even looking for; I had only taken a peek for the sake of Camilla. I was being a supportive spouse.

The Hyades rewarded me, opening themselves up to my celestial scrutiny while Aldebaran glowered. Star clusters almost never endured; they inevitably scattered off into space, and I assumed the Hyades would themselves spin off in millions of years, for parts unknown. It was the nature of gravity, the fickle, moody mistress of space-time.

Looking at the V-shape of the Hyades in the head of Taurus, I could only wonder how the ancients had seen a bull, and what could have made them draw those images in the heavens. While the first direct evidence for people noting constellations showed up in clay Mesopotamian tablets from around 3000 BC, most of their constellations, which would form many of the classical Greek constellations, were formed in the period from 1300 to 1000 BC.

Again, what drove them up into the stars in that era? Religion, more than likely. Speaking of that, in mythology, the Hyades were tied to Dionysus, their name meaning "rain-makers" because of ostensibly endless tears they cried, where they were eventually rewarded by the gods and turned into stars in the head of Taurus, for whatever reason. I suppose there were worse rewards than being turned into stars, especially by the shambolic standards of the ancient myths.

Nothing jumped out at me before my hour of observatory time was used up, and Masters was giving me looks while I lingered.

"The Hyades seem beneath your scrutiny, Will," he said.

"Seemingly, seemingly," I said. "There's method to my madness."

"Is there?" Masters asked, watching me go, stroking his grey-bearded chin, like he was some sort of sage, or even a wizard, maybe.

THREE

"What did you see?" Camilla asked, while making dinner. It smelled like barbecued meatloaf and roast potatoes, maybe green beans, too. She was trying to seem kitchen-casual, but I could feel her intensity, the way she leaned into my words.

"Nothing out of the ordinary," I replied. She didn't like that answer, I could tell, but an answer was an answer, whether you liked it or not.

"There must be *something*, Will," she said. "Something you missed."

I'd seen that she'd done a Tarot spread before I'd gotten home, so she was clearly thinking about things. She'd scribbled something on a notepad, a kind of sigil I didn't recognize.

"Did you see this?" she asked, pointing to it.

"What's that?" I asked.

"It's the Yellow Sign, Will," Camilla said, in a tone that made me think she thought maybe I was an idiot. "I thought maybe it matched the Hyades, that maybe you'd see that."

"Uh, no," I said. "They don't mesh up."

I drew out the Hyades Cluster for her on the notepad, for reference. A little reality to offset whatever it was she was expecting.

"You have basically the five brightest stars of the Hyades becoming giants—Gamma, Delta 1, Epsilon, Theta Tauri A, and Theta Tauri B. They're located here," I said, pointing with the pen I was using. Epsilon Tauri, known as 'the Bull's Eye' has a possible gas giant exoplanet orbiting it."

"That's it," Camilla said, her eyes lighting up altogether too brightly. "*That's* Carcosa, Will."

"Or not," I said. "Just another exoplanet, Cami. The cosmos is full of them."

But I could tell she wasn't hearing me. Her mind was light-years away. I knew, somehow, that I was in for it.

FOUR

With Nicole away at band camp, Camilla and I made the most of having the place to ourselves. It was kind of like parent camp, just a bit. When you're a parent, you have to be on your best behavior. You have to set some kind of an example.

In that regard, I feel like Camilla and I were exemplary parents, at least before Camilla had gotten that *King in Yellow* crap in her head. It was one of those things, like a mind virus, what people used to call memes before the other, the Internet memes became the thing everybody thinks about whenever memes are brought up.

The mind virus meme, the original meme, was this idea that would take life in your head on its own and be easily transmitted. Those memes, the real memes, work like genes, in that they evolve, self-replicate, adapt to selective pressure, mutate. I mean, I'm not a biologist, sociologist, or an anthropologist, but that's what memes do.

What I'm thinking is the Yellow King is a meme, and it takes hold of a person's brain, somehow. They start thinking about it, maybe obsessing about it, sure as hell talking about it a lot. Camilla was talking about it a lot.

Like Camilla pointed out that there's a character named "Camilla" in *The King in Yellow*—the play, I mean. This hit her big-time, like she couldn't stop thinking about that.

"It means something, Will," Camilla said. "She's my namesake. That's not an accident; it's fate. It's talking about me."

"Fate, Cami?" I said. "It's a coincidence."

She scoffed, raising her eyebrows. "Pretty heavy coincidence, if you ask me."

I researched memes on my own. There's an entire school of learning on it—mimetics—the study of memes. Once you start seeing them, it's hard to not think about them. Like according to some professors, religions are very tenacious sorts of memes, with some built-in evolutionary advantages over rational thought. Like preaching the value of faith over experience-driven evidence, for example. And tethering social altruism with a religious affiliation, there's the capacity to accelerate a religious meme's capacity to proliferate because people believe they can gain personal and societal rewards from embracing the religion.

Things like holy texts and proselytizing helps pass it along from generation to generation, and the demonizing of infidels, heretics, blasphemers, and apostates helps punish those who aren't followers of a religious meme. Religious memes reward adherents and punish disbelievers.

Anyway, that's what this Yellow King thing is, as I see it. It's a meme, and Camilla's captive to it. Not me, though; I see it for what it is. It's become a bit of a thing with us, honestly. Camilla wants me to believe in it—the King in Yellow, Carcosa, the Yellow Sign, the Pallid Mask, all of that junk.

"It's out there, Will," Camilla said. "He's out there."

"It's not real, Cami," I said. "It's all pretend, Babe. Unreal. Made up."

She gritted her pretty teeth in a way that made me feel like she wanted to bite my head off. She leaned forward and grimaced at me.

"You don't understand," Camilla said. "Did you even read the play?"

I hate plays. I mean, since high school, I hated them. And I was in Theater Club. Maybe that's what did it for me, not sure. I mostly helped build the sets. I didn't act in the plays.

"Sure, I read it," I said.

"Liar," Camilla said. "If you'd read it, I mean, honestly, deeply read it, you'd understand. You're only *pretending* to understand, Will. Stop humoring me."

It was late, and I was tired. Arguments with Camilla made me tired. I decided to take a shower. I told her as much.

Showers are sacred to me. They're just perfect for reflection. Even the sound of a shower is soothing to me, reassuring, even. Whatever problems I might have in the world, they went away when I was in the shower.

I was thinking about Camilla's obsession as I was shampooing, scrubbing the day off of me, and pretty soon, I wasn't bothered about it. Not even when she came into the bathroom and just stood there, blurred by the shower curtain and the fact that my glasses were on the sink.

"What's up, Babe?" I asked. "Could you close the door, you're letting in a draft."

She didn't answer, but went back out, closed the door. I didn't think anything else of it until I got out of the shower, toweled off, and even without my glasses, I could see that Camilla had drawn that bizarro Yellow Sign on the bathroom mirror. The steam from my shower had mostly covered it, but I could see it there, the occult tracery of it.

I wrapped my towel around my waist and slipped on my glasses, which were steamed up. I went out and called to her, putting my glasses on the nightstand so they could defog.

"Camilla, are you alright?" I asked. "Babe, you're taking this all much too seriously."

"I'm in the bedroom," she said from somewhere. I couldn't be sure from the way her voice carried.

Now, for me, that was a sexual call to arms, so I went strolling in there, thinking something was about to happen. But when I went in there, Camilla wasn't in bed. It looked like maybe she'd been in bed but had gotten out.

"Where are you, Babe?" I asked, but she didn't answer. I thought maybe this was some foreplay sort of hide-and-seek, so I playfully went to our closet and opened it, clicking on the light, but she wasn't in there.

Then the bedroom lights went out, so I was standing there by the light of the closet, looking out into the darkness of our bedroom, trying to see her by squinting.

"Get in bed," she said, and I could see her, backlit by the hallway light. She looked naked, and I was fine with that. I took off my towel and flicked it to the foldout towel rack we kept by the closet, because Camilla hated whenever I'd just lob a damp towel on the floor.

I got to our bed and slipped into the cool covers, that great feeling when you were clean and the sheets were clean and life was good, and you wife was putting the moves on you. She watched me from the doorway.

"Care to join me?" I asked, patting the empty space beside me. I went to put on my glasses, but she stopped me.

"Don't," she said, and she walked up to me, putting a cool hand over my eyes. She climbed atop me, straddling me. This happened, and we surfed the sexual stratosphere awhile, and I could hear that her breath was muffled, somehow, even as I got where I was going after a few well-timed hip thrusts. But she stayed atop me even after it was over, hand over my eyes.

"Um, Cam?" I asked. "Do you mind?"

And she sang something in verse, something I might have understood had I read the play:

"Song of my soul, my voice is dead,
Die, thou, unsung, as tears unshed
Shall dry and die in
　　　　　　　　　　Lost Carcosa."

"That's great, Cami," I said, trying to pry her hand off, but then I felt something cold and metallic pressed across my throat, and I stopped. "What the hell?"

"That's Cassilda's song, Act 1, Scene 2, Will," Camilla said, her voice still muffled and strange to my ears. "You'd know that if you'd read it."

My head was reeling, I wasn't sure what to think, or what the hell was going on. Was it a knife against my throat? Was that it? I didn't even know what that would feel like, since when in life do you find yourself with a knife against your throat, right? When do you find yourself locked between your wife's thighs, knife at your throat, while she's singing some obtuse verse to you about some mumbo-jumbo that's somehow gotten locked in her brain? I mean, when does that ever happen? It doesn't. It never happens, and I was starting to get pissed, I mean, like actually mad, but when I moved against her, to try to pry her off, she'd flex her thighs and I'd feel that knife—I was sure it was a knife, now—press harder against my throat.

"Don't, Will," Camilla said. "Just don't."

I thought maybe negotiation was the way to go, at least until I could get myself free of whatever was going on.

"Cami, please, I'll read the play, I swear," I said, but she just laughed, and it was a desolate kind of laugh, made strange through the muffling.

"No, you won't," Camilla said. "You could have joined me in the dream ethereal, Will. We could have gone to Carcosa together, you and me. And Nicole. The three of us by the shores of Lake Hali, beneath the waning light of twin suns, Will. We could have gone there together. I asked you to help me, I asked you to believe me, to believe in me."

"Enough, Cami," I said. "Get off me right now."

"You don't believe, you can't believe, you won't believe, Will," Camilla said. "In me, in us, in them, in it, in *him*."

And her cool hand, the one over my eyes, came off, and I saw her looming over me, the bluish-white planes of her pallid-masked face looking down upon me through black, sightless eyes, bright in the light of the night, before she slit my throat and I could see the black stars of Carcosa clearly at last.

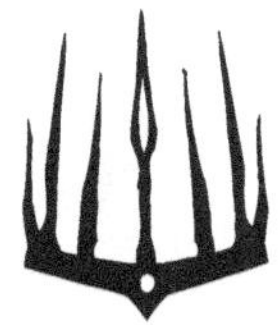

The Thing in Yellow

Thatch put it on his livestreaming feed, so what was I supposed to do, ignore it? I mean, he was there, brandishing his secondhand copy of *The King in Yellow* like he hadn't just learned about it the other week, when we'd been talking about stuff we could talk about. Just same as ever, pale-faced and google-eyed, his brown curly hair like some stupid high hat, and he's holding it up to his cam and he's raving, like actually raving. Lunatic biz.

"It's all right here," Thatch said. "Act Two, for me and you. Storytime, all. Feel me?"

And then he's reading from the play, like he's literally reading from the Second Act, playing all the parts. Narrating it, like it was some crazy bedtime story.

Now, I'm thinking maybe it's a stunt, or, like, a ploy to boost engagement. His podcast and mine compete, although neither of us would admit to that, cuz we're friends. His is *The Thatch Weave*, while mine is *Delta Skelta*, but we both do occult stuff. It's our bread-n-butter, and we split the country between us—I have everything east of the Mississippi, and he has everything west. It's not fair, really, cuz I did both our logos, mostly because Thatch is graphically hopeless, whereas I have an eye.

We've been on each other's shows, okay? We're not enemies. We tag team that way, because we're members of the occult Community. It's what we do; we're there for each other. We support one another, we're always there for each other, working the tout, crosslinking and namedropping each other when we have the chance.

Then Thatch just comes out with his nutty livestream, reads the play, video broadcasts it, and then sets himself on fire while the cam's still running.

Yes! Totes not making that up, which you'd know if you'd seen it, but, like, if you'd seen it, then it's already too late for you. I mean, he read it, then he burned himself up right after he finished. He was laughing while he burned, until the fire took his breath and he couldn't even scream. Thatch died on-cam, and people were going crazy, like his audience.

Only I don't know if they're legit cray from the play, or just from seeing Thatch burn himself alive. This isn't something anybody can really know, for true. You don't walk away from something like that unscathed, is what I'm saying.

But it's worse than that, because the broadcast was used as evidence, and I swear to you that everyone who watched it—whether cops, federal agents, psychologists— they all went crazy, too. Bonkers.

How does that manifest, you're probably wondering? Who can judge sane from insane, especially nowadays, am I right? You know I'm right. We're all on thin ice, that much I know. Walking, skating, running—it hardly matters because the ice is thin. It doesn't care, except maybe for physics. Like if you were really skinny or light, maybe you'd make it. But most everybody else? Dead in the water.

The point is, nobody's really in a place to judge what's crazy, not anymore. I just know because I know about it, like what that play can do to a person. I know because I know the history of it, and because I didn't watch Thatch's stream; I only know because he introduced it, and I just tuned out because I didn't want to go crazy. It was only later when I heard about what happened that I realized just how bad it got.

I was, like, the onlooker, the objective observer, or at least as objective as I could be where Thatch was concerned. I bounced past his reading, went to him burning himself alive. That got me wondering, too—like did he prepare all of that? He got himself a copy of the play and read it, and it boiled his brain, and he then planned his livestream death. I talked to him between the point where he got it and the livestream, too. Zero indication, if you ask me. We were on the phone.

"Hey, I picked up *The King in Yellow*," Thatch said. "Got it off eBay."

"Yeah?" I said.

"For sure," Thatch said. "I don't see what the big deal is."

"The second act's what gets you," I replied.

"For real?" Thatch asked. "I only just started."

"Yeah," I said. "That's part of the trick, I think. Like Act One is normcore, but Act Two is, I don't know, yellowcore."

"Yellowcore," Thatch said, laughing. "I'm totally stealing that, Delta."

"Steal away," I said. We were friends like that—we stole from each other all the time.

My own fans were all up in arms, leaving me comments and messages, wanting me to talk about it on *Delta Skelta.* They were all up in my biz, and I didn't want to ride on Thatch's death like that, but people wanted to talk about it.

"Hey, all," I said. "I just wanted to say how sad I am that Thatch killed himself the other day. That's not cool, and if you're ever feeling suicidal, call this hotline and talk to someone, please?"

And I mentioned the number a couple of times, trying to be the responsible one. It's what you do. But then people were messaging me and leaving comments, asking about

The King in Yellow and then I was like having to talk about that, too. It's like a fire you can't put out, once it's started.

Yellowcore's one of those things where if you start talking about it, you can't stop. I think that's part of its curse, maybe. Put yourself in my Doc Martens for a minute—if I don't talk about it, it's like I have something to hide, maybe. Thatch's video was already going viral, like people were making copies of copies and watching it. It went straight to the dark web, I mean, quick as hell, it was there, being passed around and there were like watch parties, called Thatchburns. People would dare each other to watch or would even tie people up and make them watch it. Sick shit.

Then I start paying attention, like noticing when weird stuff starts happening, like people doing crazy things. People do crazy stuff all the time, you know? How do you spot Yellow King-crazy from everyday crazy? Yellowcore jumps out at you, once you get tuned to it. And this goes back to even knowing what counts as crazy anymore.

For example, someone named Kissilda posts the Yellow Sign on the comment board, I mean, what the hell? And people start commenting on the comment, like they're talking about it, and Kissilda's talking about the Yellow Sign and what it means.

It's on my feed, and I'm deleting comments, because I administer my own feed on my page, and I want it to be a safe space for people, and here people are being creepy on it, and weird.

Kissilda reposts, and it's back, and people start doing more, and pretty soon, my board is awash with Yellow Signs from a bunch of users, and they're slagging me, like I'm somehow the villain, here. Yellowcore whackos start swarming my page and clogging up my feed. They're all over me, swarming like bees.

"Hey, all," I said. "Not cool. This Yellow King stuff is brain pollution, y'all. You need to just avoid the hell out of it, alright? Don't be picking up copies, don't be watching Thatch's last broadcast, and avoid the Yellow Sign."

My portal gets hacked, and somebody slaps the Yellow Sign all over my site, and they screw with my profile picture—it's me, but they color it yellow and bleach my face white. The whole site goes yellow, basically, with the text turned to black. It's eyeball-burning.

I am calling my provider, and they're telling me they can't do anything about it, and I'm super-skeptical, wondering if maybe they're in on it. Because now I'm thinking maybe everybody is in on it, or at least a lot of people are. More than before.

Going out, like in the city, I'm feeling weird. I'm seeing yellow EVERYWHERE. It's just jumping out at me at every turn, and I'm thinking maybe I've become infected, too. Is that a thing? Get me the brain bleach, STAT!

This whole thing, like from Thatch onward, starts triggering my anxiety big-time. I mean, four-alarm brainfire going. I don't know what's coming or going. Not on drugs, by the way—not including my anti-anxiety meds, which are just my baseline. I'm saying nothing else.

And it's still freaking me out. I feel like maybe people are following me, although why would they be following me? I'm not involved, beyond knowing Thatch, and being his friend. It's just a feeling, like when you're out and you see somebody glance at you, or when a dog watches you walk by and just sort of stares at you. What the hell? It's weird.

They can't get me access back to my site, or maybe they won't, because I feel like the company might be in on it or something. That could happen, right?

Now, I have to stress to you: I didn't read the play; I didn't watch Thatch's reading of it. I'm sane, I'm sane, I'm sane. Sure, I saw the Yellow Sign when that damned Kissilda slapped it on my portal, but are you expecting me to believe that even *seeing* the Sign is enough to make someone go insane? Is that what I'm supposed to believe? Nothing has that kind of power. It's just not possible.

It can't be, can it? THAT would be insane. Nothing could possibly be that toxic, could it? I understand the power of symbols and all of that, how symbols affect people. I told you how I designed our logos, so, like, I put that to work in my analysis of the Yellow Sign. Because that's really what it is, you know? It's a logo for the King in Yellow. Not the book, but the entity. The whatever-it-is that's behind it all.

While I'm processing all of this, I now see that somebody's come up with an app, can you believe that? I saw the Yellow Sign in the app store, and I loaded it on my phone, I don't know why I did, except that I wanted to see what the app would even do. Yellow Signpost. That's what they call it.

Don't chide me for being stupid. I was in a place, emotionally. Thatch killing himself, and me wanting to get to the bottom of it. An app is just an app. Am I supposed to believe that some cosmic juju will come down on me for loading an app on my phone? Identity theft, maybe, but celestial retribution? I don't see it.

Keep in mind that I'm refusing to concede that the Yellow Sign has any sort of power over me. The app's created by some shop called Hello Yellow, like they're the ones doing it. And I load the damned thing on my phone because I want to see. Now I have Yellow Signpost on my phone, and I click on it to open the app, because I want to see what it does. That's how we learn—we learn by doing.

It shows me where I am, and where other followers of the Yellow King are relative to me. They're like little yellow blips on the map. That's what it does. It gives push notifications of upcoming Yellow King-related events and activities, too. That's all I can see it doing. Harmless geofencing type stuff.

Some maniacs at Hello Yellow created this app, and I'm wondering how it even identifies these people. Are they fellow Yellow Signers? Is that what it is? Am I one of them, now? Is that what it's saying? Or it thinks I am because I loaded the app?

So many questions.

I tell you this, though—whether it was legit or not, the Yellow Signpost was definitely helping me track the others, because I was seeing more and more on the interactive map, like the little pinpoints where people were. There were chatrooms, too, like people talking to each other. Back and forth, meeting up, hooking up, whatever. A lot of crazy chitchat, back-and-forth broadsides about the King, Carcosa, all of that rot.

It was almost too much information. However, I did notice when some of them took their own lives, like I'd cross-reference them with Yellow Signpost. There's a correlation, like fatalities and users of Yellow Signpost. I'm going to talk to a reporter about it—Elliott Burke, an investigative journalist. He believes me, tells me that it's legit and that I need to get the brain bleach for real, but the way he says it, I don't even know what he means. What are we talking about, here? I can't unsee what I have seen. It's like it's tattooed on my brain or something. Is that what trauma is?

Anyway, I am trying to set up the meeting with the reporter, and he turns up dead. He fell to his death down the stairway of his building. You know, he lived in one of those old buildings that has the stairs, and he just went over the side, fell a bunch of floors. Dead on arrival. They think it was an accidental death, or maybe a suicide. Not sure.

Literally the guy I was going to meet about Yellow Signpost, about Thatch, about everything related to the King in Yellow. This is one of those things I feel like would be great for *Delta Skelta*, but I'm afraid to podcast it. I'm afraid to talk about it, because maybe that'll draw more people to it. Or maybe it'll draw bad people to me.

It puts me in a bad place. Then I get a push notification that says we should all go to Northerly Island. There's a pavilion out there that can seat 7500, so I'm thinking this is a lot of crazies to be in one spot, but the Yellow Signpost is pinging about some Thing in Yellow, this special event, like it's taking over my phone, just flashing the Yellow Sign, and if I don't respond, it just gets more insistent, like an alarm I can't turn off.

Or maybe I'm just seeing and hearing things. That is entirely possible. However, when I went out to Northerly Island, there were people there, like this big procession of people with their phones out, their faces lit yellow. They looked like a bunch of ghouls to my eyes.

I mean, they were all just walking and talking animatedly with each other, their eyes all big, like google-eyed the way Thatch's were. All sorts of people—lots of young people, some old, even, and lots of people in between the poles of youth and dotage. Just people walking and talking, talking and walking. There's only natural light out there, so I'm only seeing them by the light of their phones, their faces all lit ghostly like mine. Plenty of them are wearing yellow, and it makes me feel self-conscious that I'm not. I'm wearing my Suck Junkies concert tee from '96 and I'm feeling *very* out of place and out of sorts. I'm not feeling like myself.

We pass this banner somebody made, this big yellow banner that says THE THING IN YELLOW and it's a big banner, like somebody got that printed somewhere, big black letters on yellow. The poles are being held by these white-masked weirdos in yellow uniforms, and they're just standing there, ushering people along.

"Check out the creeps in the masks," I say to no one, snapping some shots of them, wishing my phone could give me better resolution in the dark. They just look like dead-faced blurs.

I see some people with ROAD TRIP TO CARCOSA signs and pointing arrows and the Yellow Sign scrawled on them. I'm almost reassured by the sight of the Yellow Sign, because I feel like I can understand it, I know what it is, and that makes a bit of sense in this crazy thing I'm observing real-time. I wanted to capture it from my phone, just going live, so I did, like I just started filming and babbling while going along. Pretty bad, right?

"Hey, this is Delta, and I'm at Northerly Island, attending this flash mob Thing in Yellow event. Stay tuned, I'm hoping it'll be worth the walk."

Get this: there's vendors along the way, like people selling Yellow King t-shirts and lemon ices and stuff like that, and it's like a massive flash mob, a yellowcore party scene, except I'm not sure what is going on or even why I'm there. I see a boat along Northerly, like a yacht, maybe. A big boat, and it's moving along the island, and I see people jumping into the lake, swimming after it. More and more are jumping into the water, and the yacht is zigzagging slowly away, people swimming after it, all crazy-like, churning the water as they try to reach the boat.

"I'm not seeing police," I said, panning around, just seeing more yellow-faced walkers, tracking on their phones, eyes wide.

Somebody says some bands are playing the pavilion, it's what they're saying, and I'm thinking maybe that's for real, maybe bullshit—it's just weird to think a band might set up on the fly like that. That's just crazy. Maybe they're in the yacht, because it's playing music, some creepy-ass songs I don't know.

I reiterate: I didn't read the damned play. I'm safe.

They say there's safety in numbers, but there's another side to that. There's danger in numbers, too. Any good mob can tell you that.

Is this a mob?

Am I part of a mob?

No way.

I'm immune to mob logic.

I'm sane.

I'm sane.

I'm sane.

I'm sane.

I'm sane.

I'm sane.

I'm sane.

Pallid Masquerade

ONE

Constance checked her phone for the dozenth time, rolling more than a little from the Molly she'd taken before she'd hooked up with her friendoids, who were nowhere to be seen near The Yellow Sign, the neon electric banana-yellow swirl looping hypnotically on the overhead, around, and around, and around, and around. The Yellow Sign was spraypainted big on the side of the building, captivating Constance as the Molly kicked in, pacing back and forth, stretching, twitching, yawning, fidgeting.

She looked good tonight, in a silver jacket and matching tight pants, vintage Pallid Mask tee she'd picked up on eBay for a steal, one of the super-rare pink ones that had come out in 1987. It was so broken-in it felt so soft, like super-soft and snuggly, and Constance loved it.

Maskers had been piling on as soon as the band had announced their 25th anniversary reunion show, as they hadn't toured in at least a decade, had been holed up in a studio for years. Nobody had seen them play live since Cabaret Vortex shut down for good in '92.

She double-thumbed them on her phone, seeing them blur before her eyes:

OMG WHRU?

Desmond DuSable was first to respond, of course, given his propensity for yellowjackets amping him up to the veritable redline of cognition. Dez was Black and beautiful: tall, lean, wiry, abundantly enthusiastic about absolutely everything, and unattainably accessible. He was a hardcore punk revivalist, a huge Bad Brains fan, and viewed Pallid Mask as a sort of benign indulgence, even a kind of guilty pleasure, to show that he was broad-minded in his musical interests, and not some strident hardcore edgelord.

ONDAWAY, STANZA!

Constance smiled, glanced at herself in the club window—her black pageboy was perfectly presenting in the chill night air, her immaculate bangs and black lipstick and silvery eyeshadow making her look like the quintessential Masker, not that anyone would notice. The invite for the Pallid Masquerade New Years' Ball had a mandatory mask notification—no one would be admitted without a mask. She loved that about PM, the way they were about stuff like that.

She'd prepared like any good Masker would, getting an official PM mask from their band merch site, one of the stick masks they sold, with a Yellow Sign emblazoned upon the forehead, where it mattered most, marking her as part of the congregation. Some would use ribboned masks or (God forbid) elastic to affix their masks to their faces, but Constance knew that anyone who was anyone would bring a stick mask. There was a degree of artful affectation in the stick mask that required a level of physical and emotional investment on the part of the wielder, and there was also the opportunity for the mask to flirtatiously flip aside if one wanted, which was always a nice thing to be able to do if someone struck your fancy.

She flipped through her friends and found Vera Hunt, pinged her, too. Vera had been her roommate in college, and it bugged her that she was running late, too. Vera wore her blond hair Valkyrie-long, and there were rumors she might color it for the show, but Constance thought she'd probably chicken out, because that's what Vera did. She was more shy than Constance, prone to tagging along. And, in Constance's current condition, that was just fine by her. She loved Vera for her shyness, which was cute and charming. She'd tell her in person when she saw her. Vera was an absolute vanilla bean dream.

VERA YO-YO?

Vera was slower to respond, but as Constance started rolling a bit, Vera's response seemed somehow more transcendent to her, her phone feeling like it was a mile away, and her black-lace fingerless gloved hands were connected to her on balloon strings. Constance stroked the lace netting of her gloves between texts, savoring the softness of them, the intricate mesh, which felt heavenly to her.

ALMOST THERE, CON! SWEAR!

Constance smiled, watching Maskers lined up and going into the Yellow Sign, two-by-two, two-by-four, ten-by-ten. They were mobbing the entrance, and Constance was having to fight the urge to just go in and ditch her BFFs. She wanted to get *moving*.

Punctuality was one of her strong suits, which she felt added a nice counterpoint to her otherwise capricious nature. She'd been doing abundant freelance graphic design work to pay the bills, and was flirting with a half-dozen agencies that seemed at least somewhat inclined to take her on. She texted both Vera and Dez in a new thread:

HOPE U BROT MASKS!!

Dez again, quick as a wink:

DUH! OMG! 4-GOT! SIKE!

Vera, slower, again:

YUP. LOL.

Constance could see the Pallid Mask tour bus on the side street, this masterful abomination in yellow and black, like crazy-looking, with the Yellow Sign on the side of it. She wondered how that went, like state-to-state, people seeing it, maybe not knowing what it was, what it meant. It struck her as funny, somehow, but that might've been the Molly.

As she stared at it, she wondered if maybe the band was in there. They could have been in there, gearing up for the show. No one had ever seen who the band members were. Not really. They wore their white masks, nobody knew who the hell they even were—the blond-haired Stranger, lead singer, was a riddle and an enigma. They all were.

He was perfect rock star slim, always impeccably attired in yellow, like in some Venn space between David Bowie, Bryan Ferry, and Brett Anderson—right at the nexus of those three. The Stranger brought a kind of fey sexuality to his performances, with a strong tenor that oozed seduction and charisma, the kind of frontman intimacy that could carry forth even in bigger venues, larger than club settings. Mask never played arenas, always favored clubs or opera houses, theaters, those more casually intimate kinds of venues, but even in places like that, the Stranger would take the audience in his velvety embrace and hold on tightly.

There was Camilla on the bass, prone to black lace and tats, plonking away, with blue hair all long, always kind of wild, like she was an alien lioness. Camilla kept a steady beat, but would dance while she played, the kind of head bobs and shimmies that conjured up a limbic kind of propulsion to her part to play onstage. A transhuman metronome as part of the rhythm section, Camilla was stoically sexy, if such a thing was even possible. She brought it to every show she played, and Constance admired her for it, thought her fingers had to be incredibly strong to punch out those bass lines with such steadiness.

And Cassilda on the lead guitar, prone to a yellow leather jacket and black miniskirt and boots—could be booties, could be knee boots, could be thigh boots. Always, always boots. Her hair was invariably varied, depended on her whim, Constance ventured. Often spikey, often black, but not always. Cassilda was a staggeringly good guitar player, in that postpunk sort of dirgelike way she had, with waves of sound and cascading, droning arpeggios that carried with them a portentous sense of futility and doom-saturated madness propelled by rampant, interconnected pedals. And Cassilda would often scream when she played, which Constance kind of loved.

Hildred, the drummer, most often wore her hair in braids and had the most fanlike of looks, like always in a yellow tee with the Yellow Sign on it in black. She favored bondage pants and worked a heavy double-bass drum kit with the kind of pneumatic intensity of a piledriver with the ON switch duct-taped into place. Constance always thought it was maybe a statement on the part of the band that they held onto Hildred, didn't opt for a drum machine the way some Industrial and Noise bands had done. Constance was kind of touched by that commitment to their drummer.

The more she thought about them, the more Constance wanted to get on that bus and give everyone in the band a great big hug. She wanted to tell them how much she loved them. She'd taken a step toward the bus when Dez and Vera popped up, calling to her.

"Stanza!" Dez said. "Oh, my Angel of Darkness, just look at you, Grrl!"

Vera grinned, too, having double-braided her hair in two thick plaits that framed her round face. She had given her eyes that cool linear black treatment that made her look like Pris from that BLADE RUNNER movie that had been part of a film studies class she'd taken. She'd whited up her face, too, and had black lipstick. The whiteface was a nice touch, and she'd worn some sort of shimmery silver dress with a black leather jacket and some wicked black chonky boots that made Constance somehow feel underdressed.

"Veer, you look fantastic!" Constance said, hugging both Vera and Dez with a fervor that was bracing. They hugged her back. "You both look totes adorbs!"

Dez had arrived in black slim jeans and a gorgeous black velvet blazer and a stunning yellow overcoat that only he could possibly pull off. He had opted for a ruffled black tuxedo shirt and was wearing some pointy-toed black monkstrap leather shoes.

"Okay, so, I was totes ogling the bus," Constance said. "But we need to get inside like NOW, you guys!"

TWO

The Yellow Sign was packed to capacity, and Constance thought maybe the place was overbooked as a venue, that maybe PM should have opted for the Vic or Metro, maybe the Riv or even the Aragon. Had they underestimated the turnout, or was it all part of the plan? The place was stuffed with people, and everybody was brandishing or wearing their masks, which looked just unbelievably wonderful.

Dez had one of those Venetian Bauta stick masks in bone-white, which played very well with what he was wearing, while Vera had opted for a yellow-ribboned tie-on white she-mask, some lacquered number she'd picked up somewhere with red lips and black eyebrows.

Constance was scanning the venue, the sea of white-masked faces, the other attendees, loving everyone there, loving her friends, loving the moment. So much velvet and leather, so much glitter and gloss, and the place was just humming with excitement. Even the basement brickwork was calling to her to caress it, which she did in passing, just sliding her open fingers across it until Dez pulled her away with a laugh.

"Such a great idea," Vera said, after they'd picked up some glowing yellow drinks that were being served up by the Black Star Distillery, where masked women in sleeveless sequined outfits served up drinks that came from cans.

"Are these energy drinks?" Dez asked, taking a sip. "Tastes like, I dunno, Lifesavers mixed with lighter fluid."

Constance took some satisfaction that she and Dez had prepared with their masking for easy drinking, while Vera just nursed hers, since she'd have to slip off her mask to drink.

Not to be catty, but come on, Vera, Constance thought. *Think it through, Grrl.*

It did taste like an energy drink, Constance decided, but in her present state, she loved that about it. And who didn't like more energy? Some corner of her brain warned her that maybe not the best dance partner with the Molly, but she waved that off.

The Yellow Sign had two levels, like the main floor being where the main bar and restaurant was, with the basement being the performance space, so people who wanted to just hover could hunker down in the main floor, but Constance knew that anybody worth their stripes would take the basement, which was spacious and had satellite bar stations on the wings. Only tourists stayed on the main floor, although with the crowds tonight, even upstairs was packed.

"Mask has to be, like, pushing their 40s, now, right?" Dez asked. "I mean, like OLD."

"Ancient," Constance said, swilling her Black Star, liking how much it jazzed her up, thinking it might play nicely with the Molly, after all. "I mean, yeah. But they're really kind of forever, you know what I mean? A band like that, they endure, they transcend, they fly above the rest of us. And with their masks, I mean, maybe they're not even them, you think of that? I don't think of that, but I mean, it could totally be true. They're a concept, as much as they are a band, when you really get down to it. They're a thing, and we're in with that thing that they represent, and are just feeling it, right? And so long as they are who they are, and we are who we are, and everybody's who they are, it all works seamlessly, whether it's five years on or five times five years on, yeah?"

Dez laughed at her, "Oh, you are rolling, Stanza."

"Who's opening for them?" Vera asked.

"Lethal Ingestion," Constance said.

"I don't know them," Vera said, fiddling with her drink. Constance could see she was on the fence about what to do.

"They're okay," Dez said. "They try too hard by half, you know? Volume over substance. You'll see what I mean. I don't envy them, though—this crowd is like all Maskers."

"'Poison Pill' wasn't a bad album, Dez," Constance said, but Dez shrugged, his face unreadable behind his Bauta. "They tapped into a sort of bumper car demolition derby fast-track gas pedal rally sport crash collision with infinity in their jagged sound and uncompromising lyrical trouncing of boozy-boujee audience expectations that take a jet set swagger and fuse it with the anxiety of auditory annihilation delivered in the flangerified form of Doppler-shifting decibels, Dude."

Dez laughed even harder, his shoulders shaking. "Yeah, okay, Stanza. You go get it, Grrlfriend! I'm just saying, Lethal's just the sacrificial lamb at this gig. Everybody's here for the Mask."

Constance was deep in it, now, and everything was just glowing to her. Even the load-bearing poles that kept the floor from crashing down on their heads were beautiful to her, festooned as they were with silver tinsel and Xmas lights. Constance wanted to rest her head against them, feel the tinsel on her cheek.

"I just love you both so much," Constance said, hugging them again. "I'm so glad you came out here with me tonight. You're what everything's about to me, and I mean that from the very bottom of my heart, to like the tippy-top."

She hugged them so fiercely-but-tenderly, and they hugged her back, her friends.

"Great way to ring in the new year," Dez said. He worked in advertising as an account executive, while Vera was a schoolteacher, teaching math to middle schoolers at a private school. "I mean, like, hello, 2011, right?"

"Yes!" Constance said, almost too vigorously. Vera handed Constance her energy drink with an apologetic shoulder shrug. "This is the year that something's going to happen, I can feel it. Can you feel it? I mean, I feel it. I'm feeling it right this instant."

"You take mine, Con," Vera said. "I can't, you know, with my mask and all."

"Aww, poor Veer," Constance said, taking a hefty drink. She was already feeling the effects of the first one, the way her heart was rat-a-tatting from whatever speed they put in there, on top of what she'd already taken. She could tell Dez was feeling it, too, because he was talking faster, his words coming out in a blur to her.

"I'mgonnagofindajohn," Dez said, saluting them, while Vera and Constance held their space in the capacity-crowded basement.

"God, if there was a fire in here, we'd all be dead, wouldn't we, Con?" Vera said.

"Oh, yeah, way dead," Constance said, snapping a picture with her camera. "Although there are several exits and I'm not even anxious about it, I'm feeling way good, like way, way good."

She pointed to them for Vera's sake, knowing that Vera was a worrier. That was part of their dance, like Constance saw herself as the fearless trailblazer, and Dez was the jaded sensualist, while Vera was the winsome worrier. They formed a stable kind of triad when they were all together, and it always seemed to work out.

"Everybody looks so young," Constance said. "I feel, like, I don't know, out of place at an anniversary show, but whatever. I mean, were some of these fans even born 25 years ago?"

Vera laughed, shaking her head. "We're not much older than they are, Con."

"Yeah, but you know what I mean," Constance said. "So much youth, so little time. Can't imagine any of these kids even liking Mask, honestly. Not even Lethal, really."

The crowd got to cheering when Lethal Ingestion came out. The front man, Boy Howdy, wearing a green-and-black gas mask and a black tank tee with a white star on it, black jeans, and combat boots, with a butcher's or chef's apron across his front with the chemical name for lithium printed on it in black, in a square, like:

3   6.94
Li
Lethal Ingestion

"Funny," Vera said. "Very on-brand, I guess."

"What?" Constance asked. She was getting distracted from all of the sensory input, like so much going on at once, drawing her eye.

It looked like Boy Howdy had a microphone hooked up to his mask, like he was eating the mic. His guitar, a Gibson Flying V, was glossy black, hanging limply at his hip.

"Howdy, Chicagooooons, we are Lethal Ingestion," Boy Howdy said, flapping his arms like he was some tattooed flightless bird. The other band members appeared, as Lethal Ingestion was a power trio, with Johnny Fulsome on the bass, and Ranger Rex on the drums. Fulsome was a hulking, black pompadoured man in a sleeveless black Lethal Ingestion tee with grey slacks and yellow Chuck Taylors, while Ranger Rex came out wearing this leather daddy ensemble that had him basically shirtless up-top except for a couple of ringed strips and in leather pants and flip-flops on the bottom. He had a black-and-grey forest of dreadlocks for hair, held back by a lone hairband. He waved before jumping behind his kit and counting off 1-2-3-4 and propelling the band into a deafening set that got the Yellow Sign bouncing.

Vera dug out her earplugs, these yellow numbers she had, stuffing them in her ears, while Constance rode it out, drinking away, feeling the raw power of the band, if not their songwriting ability. She figured Mask put Lethal out there as a study in contrasts, the way bands sometimes did, to make them stand out all the more. Lethal was definitely going for it, trying to make that killer impression, with Boy Howdy technofuzz-bellowing lyrics about oblivion and ecstasy while crashing through solos with his Flying V.

"Oh, I just hate these guys," Vera yelled. Constance was more willing to roll with it, especially in her own buoyed mental state, and just bounced around with the crowd, who were throbbing almost in spite of the band. The noise was ungodly, but Lethal Ingestion was bringing it in their trainwreck-spectacular sort of way.

Constance could see more Maskers turning up, clusters of Shadows who were just knifing through the crowd in this slow, a strange procession pushing their way to the front, sort of gliding. All of them were garbed in shadow, and it was making her uneasy, despite her high. She thought they were wearing robes, maybe, the way they moved, but the robes flowed around them like liquid, in a tumbling cascade, and she thought she was possibly seeing things. She pointed them out to Vera, waving her free hand at them, stabbing the air in front of them with an outstretched finger.

"Yeah?" Vera asked. "So?"

"Shadows, see?" Constance said. Vera turned her own head to scan them, her face unreadable behind her mask. "Do you see the Shadows, Vera?"

But with the stage lights flashing green and white and red and blue, it was hard to make them out from the other audience members who were thrashing about in the pit. There was a ton of motion, now.

There was a subset of Mask fans who liked to turn PM shows into pit brawls. They would just throw themselves at each other and clomp and stomp. The Shadows didn't look like they were doing that. They were just standing there, a dozen of them, staring at the band onstage.

Constance snapped a shot and sent it to Dez.

THREE

Dez had turned up after Lethal waltzed offstage, with some more energy drinks in hand, which he gave to Vera and Constance.

"Where were you, Dez?" Vera asked. "You missed Lethal Ingestion."

"Did I?" Dez asked, laughing.

The crowd was definitely fired up, now, and itching for Mask to come out. Constance didn't think the audience qualified as ugly. She'd been to plenty of rough shows over the years, but the plethora of energy drinks and other pharmaceuticals, plus, of course, abundant alcohol, was likely swirling together to create a rising tide of hormones and libidos that would drown everybody in the room if they weren't ready for it.

Constance's own hallucinatory vibe was in full swing, and the Shadows weren't moving.

"Dez, you see the Shadows, right?" Constance asked. "I mean, you see 'em?"

Dez looked around, confused, while the house music played.

"There's shadows all over the place, Stanza," Dez said. "We're in the Yellow Sign. There's shadows in literally every corner."

He pointed to the painted walls, the black-painted brick set with yellow stars, like endless bunches of them that looked like the night's sky through the eyes of a half-mad manga artist.

"Okay, I gotta go see'em," Constance said, pushing into the crowd, heading for the pit, leaving Dez and Vera behind. In her brain-state, the crowd was a blizzard of blurs, of flashing light and color amid the darkness as people looked on their phones or played with glowsticks they'd picked up at the concessions area on the main floor, cracking them and glowing yellow. The yellow glow was dazzling to her eyes, each time someone gave one a tambourine shake, mixing the cocktail of chemicals to produce the glow, which would seem to flare to her eyes.

Her heart was pounding as she went, just galloping in her chest as she remembered that she was still carrying her can of Black Star, which she downed, tossing it in a trash bin near the Dark Star Distillery kiosk, where a masked model stood, wearing a black-sequined jumpsuit. A fishbowl was at her station, full of glowsticks.

"Take one," the woman said, when Constance approached. "You look like you need it."

Constance grabbed one, then two, then three, and cracked one, hanging it around her neck, grateful for the glow.

"These are for my friends back there," Constance said, gesturing.

"Sure, sure," the woman said.

"Do you see the Shadows?" Constance asked, pointing toward the front of the stage, where she'd last seen them. They were harder to see, now.

"Sure, I see them," the woman said. "Absolutely."

"Where'd they come from?" Constance asked.

"Carcosa, for sure," the woman said. "And where they're heading. You know that, right?"

"Yeah, I mean, like, yeah, yeah," Constance said. "I'm an old-school Masker."

"Hah," the woman said. "You mean, like, what, the Caberet days? You don't look that old to me."

"No," Constance said, distracted, trying to make out the Shadows, who were blending in because the stage lights were muted while the roadies were setting up for Mask. "No, I mean, like, after that."

"Like new old-school, is that what you mean?" the woman said.

"Like in '98," Constance said. "I saw them play in '98."

"Ah, yeah, okay," the woman said. "Yeah, right before they went studio-only. Okay, yeah, so, you're kinda old-school, I mean, like, kinda. There are some real old-school fans here, too, like first-wavers from the '80s. Maybe those are the Shadows you're talking about. They're the ones that look like cops and grannies, like there, and there, and there."

The Dark Star marketing maven pointed them out with her fingers, like she was shooting them with a finger-pistol—Constance could see an older couple in black leather jackets, the man with silvery hair fully pomped up, while the woman had purple hair in an elaborate coif and was wearing a purple flare dress with combat boots. They looked to be in their 40s or 50s and were wearing Yellow Sign medallions and pendants. The woman had a golden tiara on her head and was mask-whispering to her guy.

"Yeah, I guess," Constance said. "How can you tell who's old when everybody's wearing masks?"

"You can always tell," the woman said. "The weight of the years, man. Life weighs you down. Gravity, entropy, all of that. It just pulls you to the ground, until, you know, you end up IN the ground. I mean, unless you transcend, of course."

Constance swayed on her feet, wanting to give a hug to the drink-marketer.

"You are a philosopher," she said. "I'm Constance."

"I'm Amnesty," the woman said.

"You are not," Constance said.

"Totally," Amnesty said. "This job makes you philosophical. I've seen things."

"Like what? Have you seen the Shadows?" Constance asked.

Amnesty served up more cans to partygoers, and Constance could see that she was giving them away for free. Promotional stuff often came to shows, and it looked like Black Star Distillery was no exception to the practice.

"Oh, I've seen Shadows," Amnesty said. "Every show, the Shadows show. Sure thing. And I've seen other things. But, like, you know, Constance Old School. You know."

Constance's phone buzzed against her thigh, and she fumbled with it to check. It was Dez:

STANZA, STOP FLIRTING WITH THE DRINK GRRL AND GET BACK HERE.

"Okay, so, I gotta go chase Shadows, now," Constance said.

"Good luck with that," Amnesty said, watching her go.

FOUR

Pallid Mask came out right as Constance had pushed her way to where she'd last seen the Shadows, when the room erupted into applause and the lights went out, with only the yellow glowsticks offering illumination. PM just came out, smooth as glass, with the Stranger looking god-like in his yellow suit and white gloves, his white mask, grabbing the mic.

"Hello, Chicago," the Stranger said. "It's been a while, hasn't it?"

And everybody started screaming.

"You know who we are, and you know why we're here," the Stranger said.

This close, it was really loud, as they blasted into "Infinity's Kiss"—one of their classic openers, with Camilla and Cassilda twining bass lines and guitar licks back and forth, while Hildred struck out the beat, while the Stranger leaned out over the audience, underlit, a small sea of hands reaching out for him as he sang of loneliness and fear, of broken hearts and broken dreams, and the kiss of infinity.

From where she stood, pummeled by the thrashers, she could see a sea of white faces, the masks, and not a sign of the Shadows, who seemed to have retreated to the fringes of the crowd, now, and she was not entirely sure if she had ever seen them.

Camilla strutted near her in some sort of bustier-harness with a flared ballerina-type dress of black, dancing with her bass as she carved out the rhythm, each note a hammerblow that threatened to knock Constance off her feet by the time "Blissful Vista" folded into the melody, a sort of seamless segue carried off by the caramel-creamy utterances of the Stranger, who was owning every moment.

Constance was getting plowed into by the pit crew, who were jumping all over themselves and each other to the music. Not that she didn't mind the pit, but at 28, she was okay with stepping it back a little. Plus, she wanted to link back up with Dez and Vera, who were definitely backhangers.

But to be so close to the Stranger, to see him just almost in arm's reach, it was intoxicating, especially when he'd reach out and run his hands cross the outstretched audience appendages, straining for a touch.

All she had to do was reach out, so she did. Not being as tall as some of the others, it was a harder thing, but she did it, all the same, and his hand passed over hers, clasping her hand for a moment, and she gripped him tightly, and their eyes met, or so she thought, mask-to-mask, and she let her mask slip a bit, so he could see her pretty face, her eyes upon him, but he had already moved on, head turned, free hand outstretched.

His hand had been warm to the touch, his grip both sure and steady, and Constance felt herself get weak as she shoveled her way back to her friends, feeling a sense of triumph.

"Look who's rejoined us, Veer!" Dez said. "Did you find the Shadows, Stanza?"

"Better," Constance said. "I touched his hand. The Stranger's hand."

"Nice," Vera said. "What was that like?"

Constance gave them glowsticks while she formed the words, because the words were tumbling through her again as the band had pushed through to "Stranger Danger"—which had the Stranger actually wading out into the crowd, followed by yellow spotlights that illuminated his every step and interaction.

"It was like the baleful blessing of a sunlit beam interwoven with a dream," Constance said. "The last kiss of the dying, as they pass from day to night, beneath the blinking black stars and the distorted chug-chug-chug of electric guitars."

"Oh, I wish I was recording this," Dez said, laughing at Constance, snapping her picture.

The Shadows were still apparent to Constance, on the fringe, on the edge of vision, lurking, looming, waiting, waiting for their cue. Something was happening, something was going on. She could feel it, could sure as hell see it.

"We walk wildly into the night air, without a hope, without a care," Constance said. "Heedless of the Stranger Danger that we face, knowing that in that moment, our lives erase."

Her words were matching the Stranger's as he sang them, while she rendered them as spoken word, feeling poignant and pointed, while he had left the crowd and was back onstage, looming over the audience.

"I long to see the you and me," Constance said. "Whispering our way through eternity."

Vera and Dez laughingly cracked their glowsticks, underlit in yellow, while the stage lights switched to a netherworldly indigo, bathing the room in a surreal glow that made everyone's masks shine brightly.

"I'd face disgrace, for just one taste," Constance said. "Of Stranger Danger."

Try as she might, she couldn't pry her mind free of the lyrical onslaught of Pallid Mask, as they went through song after song, and Constance writhed and sang along, while Dez and Vera danced and laughed with her, her heart pounding, and, to her eyes, the Shadows were on the move again, coming together, one by one, until they grew and formed something behind the band, behind flailing Hildred and the grand banner of the Yellow Sign, where Constance could swear she saw something beyond the Shadows, like a black-wrapped tunnel that showed a distant city on an alien shore, reflected on itself by a lake, beneath the cross-eyed light of a pair of stars, which doubled the shadows of everything in Dim Carcosa, and she could see the band was playing and the Stranger gestured to the shimmering gap, the "Mortal Portal" he was singing about.

"This mortal coil, our fleeting fling, as you must dance, and I will sing," Constance said, her voice rising. She thought Dez and Vera could see it, just maybe, because they were taking pictures and yelling to each other, while Constance could see some of the audience running onstage and dashing through the portal, to the faraway place, while the band played on as if nothing was happening. The oldsters were racing for it, she could see them running, pushing, huffing, puffing, diving for it. The light was night-bright, only deepening the shadows in the Yellow Sign.

Was it happening?

Was she even seeing this?

Constance couldn't be sure, and knew that there was only one way to know, as she opted to "Glow with the Flow" as the Stranger sang and hurled herself through a fleeting break in the crowd, the null space made by the passage of the others, while Dez and Vera called after her, their voices drowned out by the searing sound of Cassilda and Camilla blazing away, running past the Stranger, who noted her passing with the barest turn of his head and, she fancied, a sidelong glance, past Hildred, whose sweat was flying free as rain as she struck the drums and in the barest nick of time, Constance had crossed the threshold from here to there as the song had ended, the portal passed, old and broken bones crunching beneath her booted feet, and all at once, the sound had ceased, and she gazed upon the sights unseen, lost amid the in-between, enraptured by the doubled dancing Shadows and the ecstatic wails of the Yellow King's most rabid fans.

Yellowjacket

The work in her studio didn't stop until Isabella was finished with it, when she knew that it was done. And what a majestic thing it was, her Yellowjacket.

It sat on the mannequin, and she admired it from a distance. The line was exquisite, and her weeks of pattern drafting and ceaseless draping of the finest lambskin leather had produced something she was confident that Emma would love.

The notched lapel collar and asymmetrical zip closure, the dual front waist pockets, and lone chest pocket, with full-length zipper sleeves and shoulder epaulets created a powerfully chic statement. And if that wasn't enough, putting the Yellow Sign on the back of it, with Carcosa Kings upon it stitched in black leather, surrounded by a spray of black stars, like it was an artifact from some otherworldly biker gang, it was just too perfect, a crowning touch.

Only Isabella didn't want to give it to Emma anymore. The young pop starlet was always stealing the spotlight, and while Isabella was supposed to make it for her, that had been the commission, now that it was nearly done, she didn't want to part with it.

Isabella looked at her fantastic Yellowjacket and in her full-length mirror, wanting very badly to put it on. Her long, dark curls and darker eyes would play perfectly with the canary-colored biker jacket. She and Emma were the same size, and that had made the design efforts easier than they otherwise would be.

Emma's manager, Thane, turned up, of course, with his infallible instinct for bad timing, even though she'd been expecting him. He came sauntering into her studio like he owned it, giving Isabella's Yellowjacket a long-faced frown beneath his spray of red hair, lacquered to within an inch of its life, while he wore a white ribbed mock turtleneck with a royal blue blazer and grey stovepipe pants and black pointy-toed leather shoes that made him look like a time-traveling ambassador from Swinging London, although she knew he came from New Jersey.

"Is that it?" Thane asked, pointing with a flip of his chin.

"It is," Isabella said, while he stalked around it, shark-like, pursing his lips. He passed by her worktable, with all of her sketches, her inspirational copy of *The King in Yellow,* all the legwork that went into the crafting of the fabulous Yellowjacket.

"Who the hell are the 'Carcosa Kings', Izzy?" Thane asked, folding one arm under the other and tapping his cleft chin with a finger.

Isabella smiled, knowing this particular dance with clients. She never worked with anyone who was simply happy with the work; they always had to deconstruct it, even criticize it as a way of putting up rhetorical buttresses to shore up their own achingly apparent lack of design talent.

"They're nothing," Isabella said. "A fictitious gang I made up."

"Right," Thane said. "I had hoped there'd be an actual yellowjacket on your yellow jacket. But I'm just seeing stars and a splashy logo and whatever-the-hell that is. Is that a glyph? A sigil? A symbol?"

"It's the Yellow Sign," Isabella said.

"I don't even know what that is, Izzy," Thane said, waving a hand dismissively in the air.

Isabella thought she'd explain it to Thane, but knew that the more she talked, the worse it would go for her. Conversely, if they were dissatisfied with it, then perhaps she'd be able to keep her Yellowjacket for herself, provided she could deliver what Emma actually wanted.

"She wanted to stand out at the Glitz," Isabella said. "This'll make her stand out."

"She wanted yellow," Thane said. "On this we are agreed. But a biker jacket?"

"Yes," Isabella said. "Tailored, beautifully crafted. I mean, look at it."

She walked to it, caressing it, savoring the feel of the soft leather, showing him the lining, which was black cotton printed with still more stars, the Hyades cluster in a dazzling spray of yellow.

"She was really thinking more of a leather trench coat," Thane said. "Not a biker jacket, Izzy."

"She's better-suited for the biker jacket, I promise you," Isabella said. "It'll highlight her figure, versus looking, I don't know, blocky and monolithic."

Thane's eyebrows raised at that, and he paused in his pacing around the mannequin.

"Are you saying the Divine Miss Emma Dash is 'blocky and monolithic', Izzy? Please tell me that's *not* what you're saying," Thane said.

Isabella cleared her throat, forced a smile on her lips, leaned in a bit. This was part of their dance; not a duel, so much as a joust, as the two of them made punitive passes at one another, with intent to harm.

"Of course not," Isabella said. "But trenchcoats can be so bulky. Whereas the tailoring of this contrasts the masculinity of the biker jacket with the sharp lines of a feminine cut. Emma will look fantastic in it."

Thane sighed, and Isabella maintained her composure, for much hinged on the favor of Thane, where Emma was concerned.

"You're saying Emma's fat," Thane said.

"Petite," Isabella said. "She's got the same build as I do."

"Ha," Thane said. "Please, Izzy. Don't. Just don't. Think of this from my perspective. Glamjam's at the Glitz this year. Emma wants to own everybody there, and all signs are pointing to yellow as THE go-to color this year, so she wants to make an impression. This feels, I don't know, almost burlesque to me."

"There's nothing burlesque about a biker jacket, Thane," Isabella said. Thane pawed at the Yellowjacket, his hands flicking against the soft leather. He was one of those people who saw with his hands.

"Beg to differ, Izz," Thane said. "A yellow biker jacket most definitely IS burlesque. Honestly, I feel like you're trying to upstage Emma. Maybe even mock her a bit."

Isabella held out hope that maybe he'd pass on the Yellowjacket. Thane stroked the zippers and buttons of it, tugging and unceremoniously probing it, as if he were any kind of judge of quality.

"People see this, and they're going to talk about the jacket," Thane said. "And not about Emma. That won't do. She'll come down on me about it. That's the sad reality, Izzy. I'll be the one who catches the javelins on this one, should you fail to deliver. You're the designer, people just leave you alone in your studio to work your magic, but I'm her manager. I have to think about an entire playing field, a battlefield filled with rivals, contenders, pretenders, usurpers, adversaries, enemies, critics. I have to think about how Emma will look relative to her peers. What you made here, yes, it's a statement. Undeniably a statement. But is this the statement that Emma wants to make? That's my question for you."

"You don't like it?" Isabella asked.

"Not what I said," Thane said. "I'm asking you to tell me what statement Emma hopes to make with this jacket."

Isabella took a sip of coffee from her worktable and walked up to Thane, who was a head taller than she was, was used to his height intimidating. There was the matter of why Isabella had made the Yellowjacket to begin with.

From her perspective, it was to honor the Yellow King, and had nothing to do with Emma. Emma was only the delivery system for the Yellowjacket. It would get her seen, and, more importantly, it would get Isabella's work seen, and most importantly of all, it would get the Yellow Sign seen. The more eyes upon it, the better. That's how she saw it. But that wasn't exactly something she could relate to Thane, whose mind worked in autobahn-like linearity.

"I think Emma says with this jacket that she's chic, outgoing, and fun," Isabella said. "She's utterly unafraid to get out there a bit and make a definitive fashion statement, and to be brazen."

"And we already know that about her," Thane said. "That's what I'm trying to wrap my head around with this. Is there more?"

He stopped poking the Yellowjacket, whipped out his phone and began snapping pictures of it—front, back, side—while Isabella thought more about what she might say, without being entirely certain of what she should say. Isabella found that bouncing clients' own words back at them sometimes proved persuasive, so she did that, while he beamed shots to Emma.

"Okay, I confess," Isabella said. "It's got a bit of the burlesque in it. But Glamjam *demands* the burlesque. And it being at the Glitz this year, I think it just cries out for it. Emma needs to stand out on her terms. Everybody else is going to be swimming in sequins, Thane. Emma's going to look like a fashionable badass."

Thane smiled distractedly as he finished sending, treating her to a half-smile.

"Oh, I like that," Thane said. "Emma Dash, the fashionable badass. You're a sorceress with scissors, Izzy, but you're not bad at wordsmithing, too, if you're looking for a second career."

"One's enough for me, especially with clients like Emma," Isabella said. She sipped the rest of her coffee, while Thane casually perused her worktable, her reams of sketches for the Yellowjacket design, the vistas of Carcosa, the twin suns, the sea of black stars, the moons, the Lake of Hali, the alien architecture, splayed out on the worktable like confetti of the cosmos.

"Crazy stuff, Izzy," Thane said. "So *louche*. You're just always so louche. Probably what we love about you."

"Better to be louche than a douche, I guess," Isabella said, and Thane chuckled at that, until Emma pinged him back, his phone chirping. He glanced at it, his half-smile setting into a neutral frown.

"She hates it," Thane said.

"What?" Isabella asked, secretly relieved. Maybe this meant Yellowjacket could be hers.

"Yellow patent leather trenchcoat, ASAFP," Thane said, holding his phone out for her to see the text from Emma. "And that's a quote, as you can see."

"Okay," Isabella said. "I can do that. I'll make her look like a gilded goddess."

Thane liked the sound of that, judging from the way his half-frown went back to a half-smile.

"You do that, Izzy," Thane said. "Keep it simple—the client is always right."

"Always," Isabella said. "Now, if you'll excuse me, I need to get to work."

Thane nodded, glancing at Yellowjacket.

"What's going to happen to that?" Thane asked. This was a very dangerous part of the joust, because Isabella knew that Thane could actually appreciate how fantastic Yellowjacket was, and it would not be beneath him to want it for himself, even if only as something he might be able to sell off somewhere. Isabella would die before letting someone else wear Yellowjacket. She might even kill before letting that happen, if necessary.

"Oh, I'm going to take it down," Isabella said. "I don't let anything go to waste around here. Reduce, reuse, recycle. That sort of thing."

"A pity," Thane said. "What if I bought it from you?"

"This? Oh, no need," Isabella said.

"But maybe I want it," Thane said.

"It's a lady's biker jacket, Thane," Isabella said. "It's not made for a tall fellow like you."

Thane reached out and touched Yellowjacket again, and Isabella wanted to rescue it from his covetous attentions. One bad word from him and she'd be on Emma's blacklist, so she had to tread carefully.

"Can you redesign it for me?" Thane asked. "Made to measure?"

"It's not your style, Thane," Isabella said. "Let me ideate on it awhile and get back with you. In the meantime, leave me to get Emma her yellow patent leather trenchcoat, pretty please?"

Thane accepted that as a flag of surrender, and backed off, which was good enough for her. He released Yellowjacket, turned his back on the mannequin.

"Okay," Thane said. "But I'm holding you to it. I want something of my own from you once you've got Miss Emma all ironed out."

Isabella beamed at him, nodding as if in agreement, which at least appeared to persuade him. She shooed him out of her studio, her pinking shears in one hand, snipping at him like they were hungry for his blood.

"Okay, okay! Keep that pinking piranha the hell away from me," Thane said, laughing. "I'll leave the sartorial sorceress to her incantations. I'll be back in a week, and we'll do this all over again. Just promise me you'll deliver for Miss Emma so we can put all this behind us. I cannot wait until Glamjam's in my rearview mirror, Izzy."

"I promise you won't be disappointed," Isabella said, escorting him out the door, which she locked behind him, using the bar lock she used when she well and truly didn't want to be disturbed. She watched him go, then went back into her studio, where Yellowjacket was waiting for her. She slipped it from the mannequin form and put it on, savoring the feel of it, the heavenly creak of the leather, the savory scent of it.

"I promise that I'll never let him have you, Yellowjacket," Isabella said, feeling the tingling-yet-pleasant burn of the Yellow Sign into her back as she whirled before the full-length mirror, the inimitable sense of collusion with the cosmic. "Nobody but me. Nobody but us."

She looked herself over in the mirror, and knew perfection when she saw it, feverishly grounded in her own grand designs.

The Yielding Pillar

THE SKIP INTO OBLIVION

"**C**arcosalt Corporation still mines here in Lake-shore Springs," said Annabelle, the young woman in her sharp yellow uniform with the company logo on her breast, along with her nametag identifying her as the tour guide, and her smart yellow and black cap that bore the Yellow Sign upon it. "But tourism has taken precedence over mining these days. The Shrines in the Mine have a wide variety of sights to see for tourists."

Boris Zajac sized up the young woman, who gazed with big brown eyes at the thirty-odd tour group at the Carcosalt Mine Gift Shop, the next group slated to take the trek underground. The facility wasn't particularly lovely up top, he thought, showing some salt domes and conveyor belts and yellow trucks, all bearing the Yellow Sign. Every-thing did, to his jaundiced eyes.

They had to watch a 20-minute safety video on how to conduct themselves in the mines and would be given a portable lifepack to carry with them, which carried an hour's worth of oxygen, as well as a yellow and black tag system that ensured they could track everyone who went down into the mine. Annabelle also informed them that there were additional oxygen waystations available in the mines, as well as two emergency areas equipped with food and water to last them for three days.

"But it's perfectly safe, I can assure you," Annabelle said. "Most of these precautions are a legacy of the miners and the hard work they did in the mines."

"So, why are we carrying oxygen packs?" Boris asked.

Annabelle was unfazed by his question, merely smiled at him.

"We're going to be over 1800 feet underground," she said. "And while our ventilation systems are in good working order, we try to ensure that every contingency is covered in the event of a breakdown in the equipment. In a salt mine this deep—one of the very deepest and largest in the world—we're talking about an alien environment. We'll be beneath Lake Erie in some of it, and the Carcosalt Mines cover over a hundred miles of tunnels."

He was young, strong, and fit, as was to be expected for a former soldier. He could see his reflection in the gift shop glass—short hair, blond, strong features, blue eyes, a sharp chin. Boris had been carefully chosen for this mission, brought here from Chicago.

Annabelle pointed to the map of the mines with a white-gloved hand. The mines were themselves crafted in the obscene shape of the Yellow Sign, which was an additional affront to his sensibilities, looking like a spreading cancer, or some infernal blossom.

The Gift Shop was small, carrying yellow t-shirts and black sweatshirts bearing the Yellow Sign, and it offended him even more. There were jars of yellow-hued ritual salt, as well as assorted bath salts and Yellow King Cream Ale, brewed with pride by the Black Star Distillery since 1895. There were pendants bearing the Yellow Sign in gold and silver, and other assorted items for purchase, as well as copies of *The King in Yellow* in nicely bound little volumes, the Yellow Sign stamped on the covers in black.

"Okay, the skip's ready," Annabelle said. "This'll be a long elevator ride—a full five minutes, believe it or not, so if anyone needs to use the restroom, please do so before we make our descent."

The other tourists were entirely ordinary to Zajac's eyes—they were mixes of overweight older couples, some art students, some clueless families.

Annabelle was watching Boris, while the others were milling around.

"You look so serious, Mr. Zajac," Annabelle said. "A man with a mission, perhaps?"

"Do I?" Boris asked, managing a smirk. As a member of *Synowie Srebra,* he understood the need to front at times. The Sons of Silver, an underground Polish paranormal paramilitary organization worked nonstop for centuries in its investigation and interdiction of the many unsavory aspects of the supernatural. But somehow, dealing with these Carcosa cultists was worse than hunting down vampires or werewolves, to his mind. There was just something so off about them.

"You can't trust anything you might see, hear, or even feel," his handler, Patrik, said. "Once exposed to the insidious toxicity of the Yellow Sign, you may find your perceptions eroded. The King in Yellow is like a kind of spiritual radioactivity. You must be vigilant, Boris."

"I am vigilant," Boris said, gripping the symbol of the *Synowie,* which all agents wore—the silver pendant that was its own powerful symbol—a cross with a ring at the nexus of the intersection of the crosses with two diagonals arcing to either side. It had been said to have been designed by early monks of the order, a kind of ward and warning for all who might cross them.

"Right now, yes," Patrik said. "But in the field, who can say for certain?"

Boris shook off his daydream, seeing Annabelle looking him up and down.

"Yes," Annabelle said. "You seem driven by a furious purpose."

"I'm, ehh, claustrophobic," Boris said, figuring it was as good a lie as any. "This is part of my therapy—immersion therapy, basically. Facing my fears."

"Ah," Annabelle said. "There's nothing like the mines, to be honest. They're the most beautiful things I've ever seen. And you won't believe how peaceful they are. We have five shrines down there, in fact. You're Polish, aren't you? Have you heard of the Wieliczska Salt Mine?"

"I have," Boris said. "That's partly why I'm here."

"I'd love to see them one day," Annabelle said. "Although I think what we have here is lovelier than those old, grey salt mines in Poland. The salt in our mines is purest white. It's otherworldly, unlike anything you've ever seen. Artists and sculptors, poets and writers, musicians—all come to our mines because of the atmosphere. You know, Pallid Mask played here in '93. Before my time, but it was apparently quite a thing. Why else are you here, Mr. Zajac?"

"Conquering my fear, like I said," Boris replied. "It's not every day one travels 1800 feet underground."

"Over 1800 feet, to be honest," Annabelle said. "Nearly 1900 feet, truth be told."

"It said 1895 feet on the brochure," Boris said.

"Yes," Annabelle said. "The year rock salt was first discovered, and, coincidentally, the year *The King in Yellow* came out. Have you read it?"

"No," Boris said, perhaps a little too quickly. He'd been briefed on it but hadn't read the profane and cursed text. The *Synowie* had a number of old copies of it in their archives, but there were strict provisions around not reading it, particularly the second act, where the curse was said to afflict any who read it. Boris didn't entirely believe in the curse but knew that the *Synowie* leadership was gravely concerned about its effect on people.

"I have," Annabelle said. "Many times. It's unlike anything I've ever read, or ever will read."

Her eyes flicked to the rest of the group, who were ready.

"If everyone would follow me to the skip," Annabelle said. "You'll find your tags waiting for you. Simply take one and snap it in half, putting the black half on the numbered hook. Keep the yellow half with you. Oh, and please take a hardhat."

She pointed to the headlamped yellow hardhats that bore the Yellow Sign upon them in black.

"While I'll be keeping you in our tour group, the mines are massive and it's very easy to get lost if you're not careful," Annabelle said. "Outside of the tour areas, it can get very dark. In fact, darker than anything you've ever known. So, the headlamp helmets are mandatory. Just take one and adjust as necessary."

The others quickly donned their helmets, while Boris hesitated. He did not like the idea of wearing anything bearing the Yellow Sign, but could see Annabelle watching him, even as she was tending to the others. He held his breath and slipped it on, adjusting it so that it fit well.

"Okay, everybody onto the skip," Annabelle said. "Prepare yourselves for a very, very long elevator ride."

"One express elevator to Hell, going down," said a man roughly Zajac's age, and he laughed with his friends as Annabelle sealed them into the elevator.

"Or Paradise," Annabelle said, as they began their descent. "The rock salt crystal you'll be seeing is known as halite, appropriately enough. And the salt basin you'll be seeing is over 400 million years old, incredibly enough, from a time when this region was once home to an ancient inland sea. Long, long ago. Long before mankind even walked the world."

Down they went, Boris wondering where he should place the explosive he was carrying in a special belt he was wearing. The key was finding the right spot for it. The skip was a natural conduit that connected the salt mine to the surface world, but what needed to occur was that he had to terminate the mine.

The room-and-pillar mining typical of salt mines meant that there were assorted load-bearing pillars left intact to provide support for the areas that were cleared. The necessity of leaving much of any salt mine intact in this fashion is one of the reasons why salt mines would often go bankrupt, as the cost of leaving so much ore untouched reduced the profitability, particularly depending on the demand for rock salt and the efficacy of surface mines and brine beds that offered easier extractions.

Still, as Annabelle pointed out, the state of Ohio still generated millions of tons of rock salt for the roads in these and other mines.

"But, as I said earlier, the Carcosalt Shrines in the Mine offer us enough tourist traffic to make any extraction secondary to the overall effort. Oh, and I should mention that while our tour route covers two miles in the mine, it's only a small part of the overall mine. You may find a few artists here and there in the mines—they are licensed to carry out their artwork in the mine and are usually accompanied by a Carcosalt employee. You'll see them here and there. I just wanted to let you know, because you won't believe how silent it is down there, and how few people are actually in the mines."

"What happens if the skip breaks down?" an older woman asked, clutching her husband's forearm.

"We have a very long ladder in the event of emergencies," Annabelle said. "With rest stations along the way, as it's a very long ascent. However, our mechanics and engineers have a very good track record regarding the skip, and breakdowns are rare."

The mother of a small family (two towheaded children: boy and girl, and a husband) raised her hand to ask a question, once she was acknowledged by Annabelle.

"What faith are the Shrines in the Mine?" the mother asked.

"It's more of a metaphorical shrine," Annabelle said. "When Carcosalt purchased the abandoned mine, there was a commitment on the part of our CEO—Vance Borland—to turn the space into something new, a unique sort of venue for artists and scholars. A kind of shrine to learning."

"I don't buy that one bit," Boris said. "There are easier places to establish something like that."

Annabelle was unaffected by his interjection, maintained her smile.

"The salt mine is a unique habitat," Annabelle said. "With the money that's been put to it, Mr. Borland has created something unlike anyplace else, Mr. Zajac. We've had all sort of creatives come to the salt mines and make their own mark in the darkness. I think you'll find it an overwhelming experience."

The presence of the children on the tour caused Zajac some concern with what he had in mind. He was prepared to sacrifice his own life if it meant ending this blasphemous place, but not if it meant killing innocents.

What he needed to do was somehow manage to lose himself within the mine, so that he could hopefully be left behind, which would have the other tourists cleared, leaving him to do the work he had to do without fear of collateral consequences. He didn't consider whatever artists might be lurking in the mines in that same way.

"What happens if someone gets lost in the mines?" Boris asked. It couldn't hurt to know how they might respond.

"We'd make a good faith effort to recover them, once we've determined that they're missing through our tag system," Annabelle said. "But the mines are massive, and it's entirely possible for someone to disappear down here. It's happened before. I would urge everyone to simply stay with the tour group when we're down there, to follow the designated route I take you, and everything should be fine. If you do find yourself apart from the group, you'll find some yellow wayfinding markers on various walls, which should help you navigate your way back to the skip, which is kind of the hub of all the spokes. When in doubt, make your way back to the skip, and we'll find you."

"What about photographs?" an older man asked, wearing a short-brimmed tweed fedora, wearing some black-rimmed glasses. He'd unceremoniously mashed his hard-hat atop his fedora, which made him look like a madman.

"Take all the photographs you like," Annabelle said. "Carcosalt has nothing to hide. In fact, pictorials help draw more tourists, which we always favor."

I'll bet, Zajac thought.

"How are the tunnels supported?" Zajac asked.

"Great question, Mr. Zajac," Annabelle said. "This mine, like so many salt mines, uses a room-and-pillar extraction technique, which is kind of like a carefully arranged checkerboard, where rooms are emptied of salt, while load-bearing pillars support the mine's internal structure. Historically, salt mining was very dangerous, but room-and-pillar mining and the advent of the internal combustion engine has made it one of the safest kinds of mining today. Speaking of that, we have a tram waiting for the tour group at the bottom of the elevator, so you won't have to walk the two-mile tour route. The way that we'll go is we will board the tram and drive to each of the shrines, as well as visiting the Salt Garden and Lake Halite. I'll announce these as we arrive at them, so people can get off the tram and take pictures."

That led to some relieved exhalations from some of the tourists, and Boris assumed it would let him slip away unnoticed at some point, although he thought Annabelle had been keeping her eyes on him the entire time. It could also have been his nerves.

"You said gas-powered vehicles?" a middle-aged man in a caramel-colored turtleneck asked. "Won't we suffocate down there? And how could you get vehicles down in the mine?"

"I'll take the last question first," Annabelle said. "Every vehicle you see in the mine has been brought down in pieces and assembled on-site. It's the only efficient way to get them down here. Further, you may see some broken-down vehicles. There's a vehicle graveyard in the mine, as there's no point in taking broken vehicles back to the surface. We'll make a stop at one of them on the tour, so you can see it. And regarding exhaust, yes, of course, in an enclosed space, you would suffocate from a running motor, but we have carbon monoxide scrubbers scattered throughout the mine, as well as in your lifepacks. Further, our ventilation system extracts bad air and pumps in good air, so the diesel engines you encounter will not be a problem."

"Why not use battery-powered vehicles?" the man asked.

"Alas, the highly salinated air in the mine is rough on battery packs," Annabelle said. "Diesel power is far more functional in the mine. Oh, and I should add—while the mine is odorless, you'll definitely taste the salt on your lips. There's a respiratory health benefit for breathing the salt air of the mine, something you'll appreciate if any of you have respiratory conditions such as asthma or bronchitis or any allergies or colds. You'll leave the mine feeling much better than you did when you first arrived."

Within the skip, Boris could see them passing layer after layer of rock, and could see the long darkness overhead, which made him feel uneasy. He wasn't truly claustrophobic, but it still hasn't the most pleasant of sensations.

"We're almost to the bottom. I hope you're all as excited as I am," Annabelle said, as they reached the great metal door at the bottom of the skip. She opened the security cage and pressed a big yellow button to one side, and the massive metal door opened, revealing the mine.

THE FIRST SHRINE & THE SALT GARDEN

It was, indeed, odorless, and there were clusters of lights covering the massive carved corridors of the salt mine. A yellow-hatted driver waited silently on the yellow and white tram, looking them over. He looked to be a young man to Boris.

"This is Gavin," Annabelle said. "He'll be our driver. Won't you, Gavin?"

"Yes, Belle," Gavin said. "Sure will."

Annabelle took a seat near Gavin, guiding the rest of the tour group to the tram. Boris sat in the back, seeing that the tram was made up of three cars, pulled by the cart.

Beyond the chatter of the tourists, the mine was dead silent, and Boris felt unnerved by it. He could see some oil-stained salt near the skip, but in the distance, barely lit, he could see great masses of white rock salt, carved and hewn. People were already taking pictures.

"Everyone aboard?" Annabelle asked. "Okay, away we go. This tour should take about an hour, and if you have any questions, please don't hesitate to ask them of me."

Gavin the Driver revved up the tram, and off they began rolling, the tires crunching on rock salt. Boris sought to appear nondescript, even as he was casing the place. In the back, he had the uncomfortable feeling of seeing things pass into darkness as they moved beyond the halo of light that was around the skip.

"You're welcome to turn on your headlamps if you like," Annabelle said. "There's a switch on one side."

The tourists quickly flipped on their headlamps, and Boris could see their light beams crisscrossing as they looked around, illuminating the ghostly white salt walls as they passed them, with the long, dark corridor ahead, and the pillars of salt flanking them at various points.

The temperature was surprisingly warm, even comfortable, although Boris was anything but comfortable as the tram drove them deeper into the complex.

"We'll be coming to the First Shrine shortly," Annabelle said. "In one of the oldest parts of the mine."

The tram rolled up to a white-columned structure, a cryptlike edifice hewn from the salt, where it stopped, allowing the tourists to get out. Boris hopped off, mindful of the soft crunch of his shoes on the salt, and the taste of the salt, which was everywhere, carried on silent motes of airborne salt specks that hovered around them. Annabelle walked to a switch and turned on a light, which turned out to be a chandelier hanging overhead, a gleaming light that threw off an amber radiance.

"The chandeliers you will see in the shrines are themselves crafted from salt crystal," Annabelle said.

The First Shrine had a statue of a robed figure within it, seated upon a throne, one arm upraised, the other upon the throne.

"Who's that?" one of the tourists asked, pointing to the figure.

"It's the spirit of the mine," Annabelle said. "Symbolized as a salt sculpture."

"It looks scary," the mom said, holding her children close.

Boris watched the tourists snap shots of the statue with their phones, while he walked around, looking at the carvings along the walls, the words someone had carefully carved into the salt, along with depictions of stars and space, of planets and suns:

> *Galatea, my beloved. I cannot hope to find you as you are, but will seek to set you free, I promise you. Entombed in the block, let me find you. I swear you will not be abandoned. I can see you, now. Can you see me?*
>
> *I've worked so hard on you, can you feel me through the stone, I wonder? Keep your secrets if you must. I forgive you for them. I could never be mad at you, Beloved. Do you see me sweating as I*

carve, I wonder? Your white eyes are far from sightless.

Patience, I beg you.

I will see you again.

"Who did all of this carving?" Boris asked, blinking away what he'd just read.

"Miners and sculptors, mostly," Annabelle said. "Who wanted to do honor to the work they were undertaking on behalf of Carcosalt Corporation. For many who worked here, a stop by the First Shrine was a very common practice."

Boris could see that someone had carved benches in front of the throned statue, could only imagine the mindset of the people doing this. Around the base of the statue were the stubs of innumerable burned candles, all of them yellow, and in varying states of use.

"Seems kind of crazy to burn candles down here," Boris said. "What, with air being so precious and all."

"People take what comforts they can," Annabelle said. "Now, if you'll all just get back on the tram, we'll make our way to the Salt Garden."

Everyone reboarded, people casting uneasy looks over their shoulders at the First Shrine as Annabelle shut off the light, bathing them in darkness, except for their headlamps, and the headlights of the tram.

"Let's have some fun a moment before we go," Annabelle said. "Everyone turn off their headlamps, just for a moment. Gavin, turn off the headlights, too. Just for a moment, let's experience the true darkness of the mine."

The tourists did as they were told, and Boris did so in order to blend in, and, in a moment, they were smothered in absolute darkness and silence, except for the nervous laughter of the tourists, trying to comfort each other.

"It's amazing, isn't it?" Annabelle said, her voice crisp and clear in the dark. Boris held his hands in front of his eyes but could not see them. "Take a moment or two to take it all in."

The young children with the mother and father began to whimper, and headlamps started turning on, the beams cutting lines across the darkness,

"Yes, it's something else," Annabelle said, as the tram headlights came back on. "A reminder that we come from darkness, and to darkness we will all invariably go."

"Cheery thought," one of the tourists said, another of the men.

"There's lasting peace in the void," Annabelle said. "Some even call it 'The Solace of Oblivion'."

"Again, creepy," the man said. Boris had decided to hold his tongue if he could, just to lower his profile. He didn't want Annabelle to get used to questions from him and then notice when he went missing.

Annabelle laughed, smiling at them.

"I suppose one could think that," she said. "But it's really all how you look at it. Now, as we near the Salt Garden, I have to ask that you refrain from touching any of the sculptures you see. The oils on your skin could harm the statues. You're free to photograph, but please do not touch."

Boris watched the tram drive through the seemingly endless tunnel, widening into a big room that was filled with statues, and was illuminated by a half-dozen overhead lights. The other tourists ooh'd and ahh'd at the sight of all of the statues.

"Welcome to the Salt Garden," Annabelle said. "We're very proud of this place. Every sculptor who has come to the mines has contributed a statue here, going back generations."

The tram stopped in the middle of the Salt Garden, which was bisected by the route of crushed rock salt. The tourists got out on either side of the tram, marveling at the statues, which depicted all manner of forms—people, animals, monsters, and more. The statues caught the headlamp lights, their white forms made even more ghostly by the illumination.

Boris eyed the ceiling overhead.

"Are we under the lake?" he asked.

"We are, in fact, Mr. Zajac," Annabelle said.

"What keeps it from flooding us?" another man asked.

"There are leaks, of course," Annabelle said. "But it's water-soaked rock that leaks, versus what you're probably imagining, thinking of the mass of Lake Erie above us. There are no direct leaks like that, just subsidence here and there, some leaks."

"Are we in danger?" the mother asked.

"No, you're perfectly safe," Annabelle said. "Carcosalt has subsidence monitors stationed throughout the complex. If any mine levels shift, our engineering team becomes aware of it and remediation efforts are undertaken."

"But a breach would flood this place, wouldn't it?" the mother's husband asked.

"It could, yes," Annabelle said. "It would have to be a significant breach."

"Please, can we stop talking about mine breaches and flooding?" said one of the older women tourists. "Tell us about the Salt Garden."

"First established in 1955, the Salt Garden was created as a kind of artistic sanctuary for sculptors in particular, who were very near and dear to Mr. Borland's heart," Annabelle said. "He's been a big patron of the arts over the years, with fondness for sculpture. The halite in these mines is the perfect sculpting material, as you can see from the works depicted in the garden."

Boris wasn't much of a student of the arts, thought the sculptures just looked like creepy people gaping at them, imploring, waving, begging, gesturing, brandishing—all manner of motions captured in salt. The idea of this being a garden of any sort struck him as profane, and he could only imagine the mangled mindset of a sculptor who might venture into this tomb to contribute a sculpture to this place.

"What happens when it's full?" a man asked.

"We have expanded the Salt Garden as necessary," Annabelle said. "In fact, most of the statues you see here were actually carved out of the rock salt itself, as the garden has grown."

Boris saw a statue that looked like him, which gave him pause as he looked upon it, his headlamp illuminating the white face of it. He sought an inscription, and found one:

> *I am here, across space and time, I am here. I am one with the dream ether. I have waded in the shores of the Lake of Hali, and I have become pure. The tides of time and the Phantom of Truth hold me in this place eternally. Mark my passing in the endless dark.*

Annabelle approached him, smiling, her own LED flashlight shining on him.

"He looks like you," Annabelle said. "Isn't that something, Mr. Zajac?"

"He looks nothing like me," Boris said.

"Like brothers," she said. "Are you ready to rejoin the group?"

And, to his surprise, he saw that the others were all waiting for him, and he alone was standing in the shadowy Salt Garden, surrounded by the statues.

"Yes," Boris said, shaking off the reverie that was afflicting him. He strode out of the Salt Garden, Annabelle on his heels, and took his place at the back of the tram, keenly aware of the headlamp beams of the others and the yawning void to either side of them. He pressed a hand to his chest, against the sliver of silver he wore, the pendant of his order.

"Next stop is the Lake of Halite," Annabelle said. "It is the Second Shrine, in an area we also call 'the Spa'—

indeed, patrons sometimes show up here to soak up the salutary benefits of salinity. So, we will arrive at the Spa shortly."

The tram started up again, and Boris found his head turning of its own accord, gazing back at the Salt Garden, unsure how he had managed to lose time while he was there. He looked upon it until the tram had taken him so far from it that his meager, solitary beam of light was no longer sufficient to illuminate it.

THE SECOND SHRINE & THE SPA

"The Spa is one of the more popular destinations of the mine," Annabelle said, as they reached it. "The entire mine complex is a work in progress, but you can see we have made great strides here at the Second Shrine."

And what a sight it was, being this grand salt cavern carved with colonnades and columns, vaulted arches, and balustrades. Everyone jumped off and explored, with one side facing the illuminated Lake Halite, which was re-markably still and carried with it the most extraordinary color in its luminous depths.

"Everything you see here is carved from salt," Annabelle said. "The railings, the columns, the tables, the benches. All of it."

Boris could see that the walls here were festooned with carvings, much like he'd seen earlier, but in greater profusion in this place. Another great, hooded statue stood at the far end, overlooking the place, and lit from within, giving it a particularly striking impression.

He couldn't see any patrons here, despite Annabelle's assurances that it was a popular place within the mine. Indeed, besides the tour group, nobody was here.

"Wedding parties make use of the Second Shrine, we find," Annabelle said.

"People get married down here?" the mother asked, scoffing. Her children were running around on the carved flooring, which bore a pattern of interlocking circles, almost like bubbles.

"They do," Annabelle said. "It's a one-of-a-kind setting, unforgettable."

The tourist cameras took pictures, while Boris felt himself growing unsteady. It was all too much, this bizarre place.

"Patrons will lay on the slabs you see to one side and bask in the healing radiance of this place."

"Do people swim in that lake?" one of the men asked.

"No," Annabelle said. "The Lake of Halite is a closed environment, and we would not want it being polluted by people swimming in it. People can be messy. Even your breathing affects the salt by introducing humidity, so we are mindful of interactions between patrons and the mine."

"Where are the patrons?" another of the men asked, the man with the hat.

"This is off-season," Annabelle said. "We find people enjoy coming here in high summer, when they need the unequalled peace and tranquility afforded here."

Boris felt uneasy, wondered if donning the Yellow Sign hardhat had somehow compromised him. Was it that simple? Or was the King so powerful that even such slight contact could affect a person? Was he affected at all?

He walked to the carved balusters that separated him from the Lake of Halite and leaned on his elbows, gazing into the illuminated water, which was still as death. He could make out the salt-encrusted rock shapes within the water, but there was nary a ripple upon its flat, mirrorlike surface. Indeed, he could see himself reflected in the water, his headlamp shining a solitary beacon light, like a lighthouse.

Part of him wanted to vault the balusters and dive into the lake. The salinity of it was likely so great that he might float upon it, maybe even walk upon the water. Wouldn't that be a sight?

Glancing over his shoulder, he could see the others were occupied with the main part of the Spa, taking photographs of themselves standing before the great statue of the King, as Boris was certain that it was the King in Yellow being so depicted. He wondered what half-mad sculptor would have worked to create such a looming figure carved out of salt.

It would only take a quick step; one limber lift and he could do it. But he composed himself, remembered who he was.

"I am *Synowie Srebra*," he said quietly to himself. "I am part of God's own army. I am here on a holy mission, to end this place, this abomination in salt."

"The Spa has proven popular with some celebrities, who rent this place out for special events," Annabelle said. "There are individual and group rooms along the far walls where people can really take in the essence of this Shrine."

Gavin the driver came up to Boris, looking him over. Gavin was smaller than Boris, dark-haired, wearing glasses.

"Feeling salty?" he asked, giving Boris a small-mouthed smile.

"It's all too much," Boris said.

"Yeah," Gavin said. "I know the feeling. My friends and I, we knew the King. We saw Him. In a cave, even. Chasing lightning in a cave, can you believe it? Five years ago. A lifetime ago. Time passes strangely here."

"Does it?" Boris asked. Gavin nodded. "Wait until you meet the Yellow Cardinal."

"Who?"

Gavin smiled at him, cocking an eyebrow.

"You know about Yellow Cardinals?" Gavin asked. "One in a million, they are. So's he. One in a million."

Boris looked the shorter man in the face, resisting the urge to grab hold of him and shake the truth out of him, whatever that precisely was.

"Who is he? Does he run this place?" Boris asked. "Is he in charge?"

"Run? In charge? No," Gavin said, smiling. "Nobody's in charge down here but the King. But the King lets the Yellow Cardinal roam, you know what I mean? When in Rome, you roam."

"But we're not in Rome," Boris said. "We're in Ohio."

Gavin nodded, chuckling. "If you say so, man. If you say so."

The tram driver walked away, laughing to himself, shaking his head, while Boris tracked him with his head-lamp.

Annabelle let everyone take their pictures before shepherding them back to the tram. Boris consulted his brochure map, seeing where they were relative to the start. The next stop was the Third Shrine. His encounter with Gavin the driver had shaken him out of his weird thoughts, had given him some clarity and focus. He watched everyone reboard, felt the tram lurch as it got rolling again.

THE THIRD SHRINE & THE VAULT OF SALT

"We're nearing the Third Shrine," said Annabelle, smiling at the tourists. "And what we like to call 'The Vault of Salt'—one of the most architecturally significant portions of the mine, in fact."

They rolled into a dazzlingly colonnaded room, with an astounding number of columns arrayed at tight intervals that seemed to go on forever, or at least quickly into darkness. Annabelle directed everyone off the tram and told Gavin to drive to the far end of the room.

"This was the work of CEO Vance Borland's father, noted architect, Jack Borland, sometimes known as 'Yellow Jack' and 'Yellowjacket' by his peers, for his fondness for amphetamines and the use of yellow motifs in his design. Jack Borland epitomized Neo-Classicism in his style and this work was considered his masterpiece."

"It's a bunch of columns," one of the tourists said.

"Yes," Annabelle said. "A colonnade, we call it."

"It's insane," another tourist said. "Who'd put all of these columns in here like this?"

"It was Jack Borland's vision," Annabelle said. "And quite an undertaking, too—for these columns weren't placed, you see. They were carved out of the salt, one by one. The entablature, the lintel, all of it, carved from one massive block. It took thirty years to make, in fact, and is the largest single room in the mine."

"How many columns?" one of the old men asked.

"There are five hundred columns here," Annabelle said.

Boris gazed at the columns with incredulity that anyone would throw so much time, money, and effort into the creation of such a place.

"The goal was to create the feeling of an ordered forest," Annabelle said. "With the Borland touch to them, of course."

"It's obscene," Boris said, unable to contain himself. "Who would even do this? For what purpose?"

"Art, for one thing, Mr. Zajac," Annabelle said. "Art and architecture. Because he could, because he felt compelled to do so. He sought to make his mark on the world, and in this Vault of Salt, he did so."

The columns were adorned with words as well, winding up the length of them in a hideous profusion of tangled language that Boris could only just make out by the light of his headlamp:

Galatea, I can face you without shame in this place, don't you see? In the bosom of the world, I am cradled, finding solace in sacred geometry, though you would spurn me for my architectural affectations. You wound me beyond measure, but I make my mark here, I make my stand, and in this place of shadow, I am, at last, delivered. You would mock me, Cruel Mistress, for the sake of the King's favor, and who am I but a humble fool, a Jackanape, compared to Him?

This place is my salvation and my sanctuary from your wanton, wicked whims, and though the King would take you for His own, I am yours, entirely. How I have tried, Galatea, and how you have left me in the void, untended and upended. I go to die, without so much as a eulogy from you. This is my eulogy and my salvation, my sanctuary and support.

I am no King. No King am I. And you? Would you be His Queen? Is that how you would seek to steal your fate? The King takes no consort; we are all His subjects, in the end.

Boris dragged his eyes from it, could see the babbling was carved on all of the columns. Not the same words, but the same sentiment, the wounded ruminations of a madman multimillionaire from the past.

The tourists fanned out between the columns, taking delight at their height, and how the light from their headlamps danced between the salted stones. The whiteness of the columns between the darkness that separated them was particularly jarring to Boris, and he felt almost queasy as he moved between them.

His heart thudded in his chest, and, for a moment, Boris thought he might detonate his bomb in this monument to madness, but he stayed his hand, for the sake of the innocents, who did not deserve to become entombed in this rock salt rubble.

"Come along, everyone," Annabelle said, calling out, waving her flashlight. "Let's walk in the Borland Forest toward Gavin and his tram. Use the Buddy System if you must, for we cannot leave anyone behind."

And Boris walked with his mind reeling, his eyes drinking in the light and shadow of the endless-seeming rows of columns, adrift in his own thoughts, seeing glimpses of Borland's words in passing, like snatches of madness:

> *...your winsome kiss makes me feverish...*
> *...I'm lost both with and with you, Galatea...*
> *...I lay claim to what is mine and what is mine in this mine is all mine...*
> *...lost Carcosa's lonely shores bear the burden...*
> *...pugnacity in pantomime, the ardent argent agent...*
> *...in the wake of a wake, this funereal mien is unbecoming...*
> *...there can be no divinity in trinity, only two can make three...*

Until he forced his eyes to the white-carved ground and walked as quickly as he was able, each column looming in his peripheral vision as he passed.

"Who could write such words?" Boris said, crying out. "To create these pointless columns is bad enough, but to carve those mad words around them like that? Insanity! Insanity!"

Annabelle paused the rest of the group a moment, walking up to Boris, taking his arm in hers, guiding him along.

"I know how it must seem to you, Mr. Zajac," she said. "I was like that, too, once, years ago, so many years ago. Uncomprehending. The turns of phrases that leave you dazed and dazzled. I know your pain better than most. The play's the thing! Isn't that what the Bard once said?"

Boris couldn't shake the unease, the winding tight of his mind, or the unwinding, perhaps.

He was *Synowie Srebra*. He had a holy mission. He must destroy this unholy place.

"But what if I haven't got enough with me to do the deed?" Boris asked, blurting it out. Thankfully, Annabelle appeared to misread him, to fail to understand why he was here.

"You have more than enough in you, Mr. Zajac," she said. "You'll find all that you need and more as we make our way to Shrine Number Four."

THE FOURTH SHRINE

The others kept their distance from Boris, so he had the back to himself, sagging in his seat, while the tram made its way to the fourth shrine. He scarcely turned his gaze to the moving white carved walls they passed, the tram tires crunching the ground as they made their way. His headlamp began winking out, until it finally went dark.

"My headlamp went out," Boris said. "Hey, hello?"

"Just stay with the group, Mr. Zajac," Annabelle said. "And you'll be fine."

Boris took off his helmet and gave it a swat or two, trying to jolt the light back on, but it stayed dead.

How long had it been? She'd said the tour would take an hour, but it already felt like a lifetime. The family with the children, they were getting impatient, squirming and fidgeting, while some of the older couples leaned on each other for support, and the man in the tweed hat fanned himself, stealing backward glances at Boris.

"The Fourth Shrine is the last shrine of the tour," Annabelle said. "The Final Shrine—the Fifth Shrine—is far off the tour route loop and is not open to the public."

That prompted some grumbling from some of the tourists, which Annabelle quelled with some soothing words.

"It's magnificent, though," she said. "Beautiful beyond belief."

"I'll be the judge of that," one of the men said, clearing his throat.

They rolled into the Fourth Shrine, which was kind of like a ballroom, with a half-dozen halite chandeliers hanging luminously overhead, the floor polished smooth. At the far end was a kind of U-shaped chapel carved from the salt, with a white altar upon it, with yellow silks upon it, as well as chalices of gold. In the back of the chapel stood a beautiful statue, the very epitome of womanly beauty rendered in the Neo-Classical style.

"If you've consulted your brochures, you'll see that this is the Chapel of Galatea," Annabelle said. "Someone very dear to Jack Borland, being Galatea Penrose, who had been Jack's wife until her untimely death in late January of 1968 in an avalanche in Davos. Jack Borland put a lot of love and attention to this place, which is why we consider it the most beautiful of the shrines—except, of course, for the Final Shrine."

And Boris had to concede that it was lovely, as the flooring had been carefully carved into a checkerboard pattern, although entirely in white. There were carved scenes of revelry upon the walls, as well as mountains and unfamiliar cityscapes on the other side. Everything possessed a lovely shine to it, while Annabelle spoke with the studiously casual fluidity she'd used on the entire tour.

"The mirrored shine you see on the flooring is from the shoes of countless pilgrims as they walk on them, Mr. Zajac," she said. "Each step you take helps make the Fourth Shrine shine all the brighter."

All at once, Boris realized that the other tourists were gone, and there was only Annabelle and Gavin standing there, looking at him. He whipped his head around, trying to find the others, who were nowhere to be seen.

"Where is everybody?" Boris asked.

"They're gone, Mr. Zajac," Annabelle said. "One could even say that they were never here. Or that you made them all up. Or perhaps even that HE made them up for you."

His *Synowie* training kicked in, and Boris dropped to one knee and drew the small pistol he was carrying, a snub-nosed revolver, which he pointed at them.

"What is going on?" Boris said, still confounded by the disappearance of the tour group. He couldn't have hallucinated them. They could not have been illusions. They were here with him. They had been real.

"We know why you came here, Mr. Zajac," Annabelle said. "We always knew. And you're quite right—you don't have enough explosive to destroy the Shrines in the Mine. Not on that little belt you're wearing. That might not even be enough to destroy a single pillar, right, Gavin?"

"For sure, Annabelle," Gavin said.

"How could you know?" Boris asked. The *Synowie* were so secretive, so careful. It didn't seem possible.

"Some of your brotherhood have read *The King in Yellow,*" Annabelle said. "Some of them have slow-danced with the Phantom of Truth. Right here on this ballroom floor, in fact."

Boris raised the pistol, pointing it at Annabelle and Gavin both, alternating between them as he drew forth his explosives belt.

"I'm not afraid to die," Boris said.

"Oh, we know," Annabelle said, while the two of them walked slowly toward him.

"I will blow us all up," Boris said. The detonator had a key he'd have to get from his pocket in order to activate it.

"We know, we know," Gavin said, and then all of the lights went out, just as Boris shot at Gavin, the pistol report deafening thunder in the silence of the mine. He moved from his position in the dark, slinging the belt bomb over his shoulder as he fished for his keys.

"Are you scared of the dark, Mr. Zajac?" Annabelle asked, her voice echoing. Boris ignored her and got out his keyring, felt in the dark for the nubbed key that could activate the detonator. He'd have to shift his grip again to ready it, so he did so, stabbing the key into the detonator in the dark, giving it a quick turn. He saw the little red LED light go to yellow, and he quickly flipped the switch and watched that light go to green.

"I think he's afraid," said Gavin.

"This bomb is armed, now," Boris said, using the tiny light from the bomb to provide a tiny bit of illumination.

Then he heard the tram start up, saw the headlights turn on, and saw Annabelle and Gavin speed out of there, even as he fired another pair of shots after them. He ran after them, watching them recede down the tunnel, moving far faster than he could run.

"Oh, God," Boris said, watching the light of the tram move ever smaller, the sound of it fading, until all he could hear was his breathing in the dark. He went to his lifepack and opened it, remembering the safety video, and quickly cracked it, shaking it, grateful for the cool yellow light, the only illumination around him.

The silence was worse than he could have imagined.

"Okay," he said. "She said it was a loop, so I'll just head the way they fled, and, eventually, I'll reach the skip."

It wasn't a great plan, but it was better than no plan. Boris began walking, mindful of the crunch of his shoes on the crushed rock salt, acutely aware of just how feeble the light of the glowstick was, how all-consuming the darkness was around him.

He remembered her saying the tour was two miles round-trip, which meant he was probably only a mile from the skip at most. He also remembered something about the reflectors and waymarkers that would help someone find their way back. He'd use those. Maybe the belt bomb he carried couldn't destroy the mine, but if he was able to reach the skip, he could disable it, which might make it at least more difficult for the cult to get down here. At least that might buy the *Synowie* some time to take stronger countermeasures. The larger issue that the order had been compromised by members of the Yellow Brotherhood was a far graver concern. He took out his cell phone and attempted to dial out, but, of course, he had no signal. Not this deep underground. Everything hinged on reaching the skip.

THE YELLOW CARDINAL

He'd walked for an hour, trying to follow the exhaust smell of the tram, looking for waymarkers, hoping upon hope that he'd not taken a wrong turn and lost his way. If he had, it would go very badly for him, but he was no less determined to make his escape.

Boris was so determined that he only barely became aware of another sound in the dark, something behind him. A kind of scuffing sound. He only became aware of it when he stopped a moment to get his bearings in the blackness and he heard it. In the silent mine, any sound was magnified.

Scuff. Scuff. Scuff. Scuff.

Someone was following him. Slowly, but following all the same.

"Hello?" Boris said, calling back behind him. His voice echoed, but the steps in the darkness continued.

Scuff. Scuff. Scuff. Scuff. Scuff.

"I've got a gun," Boris said. "And a bomb, for that matter."

Whoever it was, they were some distance behind him, so Boris decided to keep going. There was no point in wasting time down here. He kept moving, holding out the glowstick ahead of him like a lantern, figuring if there was any kind of tunnel break or wall ahead, he'd see it before he ran into it.

He paused again, could hear the scuffing continuing, growing closer, now.

Scuff. Scuff. Scuff. Scuff. Scuff. Scuff.

Cursing, he fired a lone shot behind him, the revolver blinding him a moment with a flash as the pistol deafened him again.

"I hope you're using silver, *Synowie,*" said a voice that made his teeth clench. It was a dreadful voice, a rasping thing. "I'd be disappointed if you weren't."

Boris wasn't, alas. He hadn't assumed he'd be needing it in this place. Further, he didn't know if such a thing would even work.

"Who are you?" Boris asked, listening to the scuffing growing closer. If whoever it was got close enough, he might be able to squeeze off a killing shot.

"Why, I'm the Yellow Cardinal," the voice said. "I believe you've already heard of me."

"The one in a million," Boris said, raising his pistol to eye level, keeping the glowstick in his other hand, and his bomb belt slung almost like a bandolier on his shoulder.

"The one in a million," the Cardinal said, very close, now. "Only two shots left, Mr. Zajac. Or did you bring more bullets with you? Can you load them in the dark, I wonder?"

The Cardinal's voice put him very near to Boris. Then, something shot out of the darkness, catching his gun arm and giving it a twist. The pistol fired again, and again, before clicking on empty cylinders while Boris sought to free himself, but the Cardinal's grip was strong, far stronger than he would have thought, giving him a yank that knocked him off his feet.

And then Boris could see the Yellow Cardinal standing there, looming over him, cutting a commanding figure in his yellow attire of biretta, mozzetta, and cassock, with a white rochet. Around his neck hung the Yellow Sign in gold, the blasphemous symbol dangling from his neck with heft as leaned into him, twisting his wrist painfully, illuminated only by the feeble yellow light of the glowstick.

His face looked ghastly, a kind of withered, desiccated corpse. His yellow eyes were like the yolks of eggs, devoid of irises, his chalk-white teeth bared against the grey-black husk of his salt-cured skin. Behind him, barely visible in the faint light, Boris could see an entire congregation of withered, salted specters, gazing at him with the hungriest of eyes that gleamed like the Hyades on a clear night.

"My Son of Silver, you have finally arrived," the Cardinal said. "We will ride on a skiff across the Lake of Halite, toward the Final Shrine, where you will meet the King and pay homage to Him."

With only the barest hint of a prayer left in him, his mind slivered into the etheric dreams of Galatea, Boris used his free hand to flip the switch of his belt bomb detonator, and he briefly saw such stars shine in the darkness, before there was, in the end, only everlasting darkness yet again.

An Inkling

ONE

When I say she was hot, I mean she was smoking, like hellfire. She came in by herself, wearing a grey trenchcoat and shades, had this long black hair and militantly severe bangs, the palest skin, and bright red lipstick. She wore some high-heeled black boots and had matching black leather gloves, and even wearing that coat, I could tell she was something fierce underneath it all.

She came into Second Thoughts like she was sneaking through the front door, like she didn't want a soul to see her. I knew what she wanted before she'd said a word, because at Second Thoughts, they all came in kind of like that: the usual cocktail of guilt and embarrassment, wanting to get that tattoo removed, the one they got when they went out with their friends one night drunk, or the one with the boyfriend's name etched on their ass—the boyfriend they'd since broken up with.

The stories all came in every shape and size, as varied and as similar as people are everywhere, the same litany of shame and regret. Having worked at Second Thoughts for a decade, I'd seen and heard it all.

But this woman was terrified, and that was something new.

"Hi, I'm Taylor Park," she said, in this sultry purr that was, I have to add, devoid of any kind of come-on; she was scared. She shot out her hand for me to shake, which I did, feeling the cool comfort of the leather as we shook.

"Kyle Rossi," I said. "Owner/operator of Second Thoughts."

She didn't smile, just flicked off her shades, revealing her beautiful face that looked to be perhaps half-Asian, maybe—an imperial bearing with big dark eyes that were in some fetching place between grey and light brown, with a straight nose and devilishly kissable lips.

"They said you could help me," Taylor said. "I went to Ink Incorporated and they said you were the best guy around for this. Half-magical was how they described you."

I was surprised that the chiselers at Ink, Inc. had fanned someone my way. Leif Janssen over there wouldn't send me a client if the world was about to end, so the fact that he had done so with Ms. Taylor, here, was something attention-grabbing.

"We specialize in removals, yeah," I said. "Latest, best Q-switch laser tattoo removal."

Taylor just waved away my pitch like it was a mosquito buzzing around her ear. "Can we just have the consultation?"

"Sure," I said. "Fine."

I gestured to the back, where she could disrobe behind a curtain and show me what the damage was. Judging from her reaction, it had to be something worse than having "JUICY" as a tramp stamp.

"I've been to three other places," Taylor said, from behind the curtain.

"Really?" I asked. "Did they botch it?"

"You might say that," Taylor said.

"Who'd you see?"

"Besides Ink Incorporated, I went to Backpeddlers and before then, to Skinchangers," she said. Her voice actually shook a bit. I knew the guys at those places, was surprised that I was the fourth place she'd gone to.

"You should have come to me first," I said.

"I didn't know," Taylor said. "It's not like it would have made a difference."

The desolation in her voice was jarring.

"Okay, I'm ready," she said, and I put on some latex gloves, just a thing I did at the consult, just to be more professional, more clinical.

I went in and there sat Ms. Taylor in her black bra and thong, on the table, with every inch of flesh below her neck inked in white masks, almost like skulls, only not. Like death masks, only with open eyes, like black orbs.

"Whoa," I said.

And when I say every inch, I mean every inch. Her body was covered in white masked faces, and on every one of them, across the crown of it, was a name in tiny yellow letters. You could make those out clearly. Desmond. Lina. Cabe. Potter. Bliss. Mark. Shannon. Barbara. William. Sarah. Emily. Luke. Marcy. Ann. Patrick. Allison. Tony. Aaron. Brian. Val. Frank. Chrissy. Tad. Randy. Ron. Zeke. Betty. Veronica. On and on and on it went, these piles of masks immaculately inked in radiant white, all over her body, some big, some smaller, but all of them with names on them.

"Wow," I said.

"I know, right?" Taylor said.

The first thing I have to say is that the work was fabulous. It's hard to exactly quantify that, like you think masks are masks, sure, but these were beautifully rendered on the canvas of Taylor's pale flesh, and the way they were placed, there was real attention to the terrain of her body, for lack of a better term—they flowed seamlessly and flawlessly across her flesh, so much so that you almost felt like you were gazing across a landscape.

I'd never seen such amazing inkwork, ever, and so ridiculously thorough. I had to wonder how many years she'd been at this, and who had done the work. That said, however, the proliferation of these masks all over her body was also bizarre and off-putting. It looked insane.

Taylor watched me study her with a caustic gaze, a cynical silence.

"Before you ask me where I had this done and why," Taylor said. "Let me just tell you that I didn't have this done, and I have no idea why it's happening."

Her words stopped me a moment because I was going to ask her those things. I'd seen a lot of regretful bodywork in my days at Second Thoughts, like rampant misspellings or just plain bad tattoo work, or poorly placed tats that just didn't work right. I was like a Father Confessor to these folks, helping them through their pain and shame and erasing the past with a deft hand and a bitchin' laser that just made it all go away.

"What do you mean, you didn't have this done?" I asked.

"I mean that I didn't have it done," Taylor said, leveling her gaze at me. "It's been going on for the past year, and I'm really scared, Kyle."

"Scared?"

"Petrified," Taylor said. "I'm running out of skin. I mean, you can see that, right?"

I looked at her mask-covered body and could only agree. Blurring my eyes, she almost looked like some kind of painted animal, like a cross between a jaguar and a zebra—the eye sockets of black dotting her all over, and the white of the masks (surely titanium dioxide, judging from the intensity of the white—I can tell you right now that this would be a major bitch to remove).

"Yeah," I said. "I'm trying to process all of this."

"All I have left is my face," Taylor said. "From the neck up. That's what I have left. It's saving that for last."

"What is?" I asked.

Taylor turned around, an almost savage turn of her back to me, and pointed to the tattoo at the base of her spine, this maddening yellow scribble, like the calligraphy of a madman, on the forehead of a dead-white smiley face with crosses for eyes.

"That little fucker down there," Taylor said.

I knew what the Yellow Sign was, sadly, because I'd done enough of them over the years, like people who thought it'd be cool to have the Yellow Sign inked on their shoulders or at the napes of their necks, whatever. Or city-scapes of Carcosa or even the King in Yellow, or homages to Pallid Mask. Not like I gave much thought to it, but over the years, people would come in with those same requests, and they became ingrained in my head, somehow. I know, *The King in Yellow* play, whatever. I don't read; I just ink skin for a living.

But there it was, the Yellow Sign, perfectly rendered on her skin, with a couple of masks very close to it, one saying "Shelby" and the other, "Vanessa."

"Shelby and Vanessa," Taylor said, like she was reading my mind. "My best friends."

TWO

"Shel, Vanessa and I were regulars at the boat party out on the lake that happens every summer," Taylor said. "You know that one."

"Yeah," I said, and I did. Everybody knew about the Playpen, where the boat owners would turn that area of the lake into a nautical bacchanal, where yacht owners and speed boaters and cabin cruisers and overtanned boozers-with-bucks would crank up the volume and get their liquor and hard-ons going all summer.

I'd been out there a few times, myself, because the skinfest was just beyond belief—the chicks and the babes and the woo-woo girls and the dolls and hotties were all there in force, drunk as skunks and scantily clad, while the wannabe alpha boys and the codgers who owned the boats or the rich-ass prickbags who weren't old yet would grind in there in their multimillion-dollar yachts and play this ongoing dickwag every year.

"I don't know how it happened," Taylor said. "But that's where Shel saw the tat on me. I was sunning myself on the deck of this guy's yacht, and she's like 'Bitchin' tat, Taylor,' and I had zero recollection of even having gotten a tattoo—I have to add, you know, I'm a Sagittarius, so I had a tattoo of the Archer symbol here."

She lifted her black hair and showed me the nape of her neck, where I could see the bisected arrow that symbolized Sagittarius, all by itself beneath that head of hair she had. Taylor let it fall.

"That's among my only bit of volitional ink," Taylor said. "I'm not like Shel, who had these sleeves, had this blue-black cobra with red eyes circling down one of her arms, the hood of the cobra at the back of her hand, richly-detailed, like scales that looked like they were lit by neon."

"Shelby Cobra," I said.

"Yeah," Taylor said. "Her friend Monique did it. Real creepy, but totes steady hands, an artist. And Shel thought maybe Monique had inked that symbol at my lower back. 'Dude, did Monique do that?' she asked me. 'What are you talking about, Shel?' I asked. And she showed me, and I was like 'Omigawd, did you guys have that done to me, like, last night?' And it was a reasonable ask on my part, because we'd gotten totally drunk on some blue cocktails some guy had been serving up on his boat, and I swear I lost at least 13 hours of my life that night."

Recounting it seemed to make her feel better, so I just let her go at it, while I studied her back.

The inky masquerade was even thicker here, like mountains of them, again, beautifully rendered with that kind of detail you might see on Yakuza guys or something. Just gorgeous work. Taylor watched me a moment before continuing. If I blurred my eyes, I swear I could see a cityscape, too—the skyline of Carcosa, rendered in tattooed white masks across her body. It was one of those things you had to kind of stare at to properly see, or maybe only see out of the corner of your eye.

"We were able to reconstruct it the next day, like on Pictogram and Flutter, like photographs Shel and Vanessa had taken, maybe me, too, or someone with my camera. We looked through it and we were at this bar, *Las Brujas,* and there was this guy there, he's in there with Shel, Vanessa and me, really handsome, nicely dressed. Like dark hair slicked back and the most devilish grin, and these eyes. You can see him in the shots."

She held up her smartphone, showed me her Flutter feed, showing me the apparent scenes of debauchery, gave me a sense of her night.

There's Taylor, laughing in a drunken tangle with her friends. There's the guy in there, photobombing them

"Tio," Taylor said. "His name's Tio Amarillo. Shel told me that later."

There's Taylor being held down by unseen hands, and there's Tio, holding his hand out, like a magician with an upraised palm, and in the palm of his hand, as if it were a playing card, was the Yellow Sign tattoo on that white frowny face, grimacing at me in the Flutter frame. It looked like one of those tattoos you applied with water.

There's Tio theatrically licking the Yellow Sign tattoo in his hand, posing, sidelong glance, with blurry Taylor in the background.

There's Tio leaning over Taylor and applying the tattoo, hand pressed at the base of her back, and then there's Shel and Vanessa in the frame, flanking the tattoo, laughing their asses off, while the Yellow Sign coils between them, almost serpentine, on the frowny dead-face.

"It could have been any of us," Taylor said. "I was just the one who passed out first, so, you know, I got, like, the short straw."

The Pictogram shots showed much the same, although they were less dynamic than the Flutter feed. Las Brujas red neon bar sign, Tex-Mex décor inside, crowded bar, Taylor and her friends, Tio and the tat.

The Inkling—that's what I took to calling it—it was a temporary tattoo. It should have washed off the first time Taylor had showered.

"I didn't even know about it until Shel, who was totally screwing with me, pointed it out. "It was no big deal," Taylor said. "No harm done, except that the thing wouldn't come off. I mean, I tried to scrub the thing off and nothing happened. I tried just normal scrubbing, then a loofah, then this apricot exfoliating scrub, and that didn't work. Nothing worked, and the thing just stayed on me."

It was unreal, the expanse of maskwork across her body, all carefully rendered, all of them with names on them in inked yellow, all of them in piles, covering every inch of her skin.

"Who did all of the masks?"

"It did."

THREE

I could tell from how she said it that she was dead serious. She just looked at me with these desolate, flat eyes of hers, the eyes of terror and hopelessness.

"When did the first mask appear?" I asked, almost incredulous that I'd even asked that question at all.

"I don't exactly know," Taylor said. "I just know that I'd tried to call Shel and Vanessa up to go out the night after they'd played their little prank on me and neither of them were home. So, I left them messages and hung out on my couch a little bit, like in a funk, but I hate just sitting home and doing nothing, but I also didn't want to go out to the Playpen by myself, wanted my wingmen—wingwomen—with me."

"Let me guess: they were dead?"

Taylor nodded. "Yeah. A car accident, apparently. A freak accident. Shel was driving her Shelby Cobra, with

Van riding shotgun, and this truck just smashed into them, and they veered off Lake Shore Drive and went into the lake and drowned. They had to send police divers down to get them, but they say that they were both unconscious at the time of the crash, and they drowned in the dark."

The memory of it clearly still haunted her, as Taylor fought for composure.

"I was really upset about it, losing both of them that way," Taylor said. "I went to their funerals and everything, naturally. Shel and Van were popular, had a great turnout. People were so upset. They were both pretty and happy, and to die like that, it was just awful. Closed casket, obviously, because they were a mess. I saw the photo of Shel's car getting pulled out of the lake and nearly lost it. Bad things shouldn't happen to good people, you know? To beautiful people like that?"

I surveyed the masked landscape across her body and sighed. If I could even do this work, it would take many sessions to remove, and would be terribly uncomfortable for her, to put it mildly. It would be expensive.

Taking out my smartphone, I snapped some photographs of the Inkling, and of the accompanying masks. I wanted there to be some record of this. Taylor didn't notice, or didn't mind, just kept talking.

"I was in a funk for about a week," Taylor said. "I didn't go near the Playpen, just because the thought of going near the lake again just filled me with fear. It's weird, like how you can see something like that, something normal, and then have something bad happen, and then it's just awful. The lake was like that for me, after Shel and Van died. It was like 'you killed my friends.'"

Taylor sighed, and I was unsure whether to talk about the job at hand, or to talk to her more about what had gone on. Given what the job would entail, I thought I'd just ask her more about her story.

"When did you find the masks?"

"Like a week later," Taylor said. "I was out of the shower after doing cardio kickboxing, and while checking myself out in the mirror, I saw that there were two masks on my back, that Yellow Sign right there near them, just like you see. I took my smartphone and I snapped a picture of it, and saw the names on the masks, and I nearly dropped my phone. Because I know that I hadn't gone out anywhere that week, had been sulking since Shel and Van had died, and I knew that I'd not gotten any tattoos in the meantime. What's worse, I knew that thing was mocking me, you know? It was totally making fun of my grief, and I don't know how, exactly, but I had this notion—"

"An inkling?" I asked.

"Huh?"

"You know, an inkling," I said. "Like a notion."

"Um, yeah," Taylor said. "I had this thought that the little shit was behind it, somehow. I know that sounds totally stupid and nuts, but that's what I thought. Maybe it was just an accident, maybe it was just bad luck for Shel and Van, but either way, I went out to get that tattoo removed. That's when I went to Skinchangers and tried to have it removed, but those guys couldn't remove it. They burned the hell out of my back and tried various shit, but I didn't want to get scarred or anything, so I got out of there. And when my skin healed up, there was that little shit, smirking at me, mocking me. I mean, who ever heard of a tattoo you couldn't remove? And its expression had changed—the frown had become a smirk."

"That's crazy," I said. "You came to the right place. We'll get it off you."

Taylor seemed less than convinced. Her demeanor changed a bit as she thought about it. "Everybody says that, but none of you can do it. I'd heard you were the best at this kind of thing, so that's why I'm here."

"What else happened?"

"What else? More masks," Taylor said. "At first, it was people I knew. Like Raj, this DJ I knew at Zephyr—he was stabbed to death coming out of that club. I read about it on my phone, and there it was, Raj, 28, found stabbed outside of Zephyr. It was sad, because he was really kind of darkly sexy and cool, and made good money as a DJ, and to just be stabbed like that, out of the blue, it just really makes you think."

I looked and saw the Raj mask near the Inkling, almost as an afterthought, but it was there.

"I saw it a few weeks after Raj had been killed," Taylor said. "I'd put that thing out of my mind after what had happened at Skinchangers, just how bad that had hurt. But when everything healed back there, and I was out with one of my friends, like we'd gone to a bar, and, you know, like, one thing led to another, and he's like 'Um, who's "Raj?"' and I was like 'Oh, he was a DJ at Zephyr. Really cool guy.' And my friend was like 'No, I mean, like why do you have a mask tattoo with his name on it?' and that completely killed my mood and I almost lost it, and just jumped right out of bed and freaked out, went to the mirror and looked, and there it was, sure enough, like three motherfucking masks, now: Shelby, Vanessa and Raj."

She turned and looked me in the eye, like I was the one who was supposed to explain it to her, to make it alright. She looked like someone used to getting whatever she wanted, so I could see how this would mess with her.

"I went to St. Michael's," Taylor said. "I trotted right over there and went to the priest, Father Ranklin, and I told him about it, and he tried to reassure me, but I was just really scared, like I was thinking I should become a nun or something—fat chance, I know, right? But I was freaked out, and he asked to see the tattoo, and I showed him, because he seemed like an okay guy, I mean, for a priest, and he asked me why I'd gotten that done, and I had told him that I hadn't gotten it done *per se,* but that it had been done to me, kind of as a prank. And he told me that they didn't deal with tattoo removal at St. Michael's, obviously, right? And I just asked him to throw some holy water on it and say a prayer over me or something, and while he was reluctant to at first, I managed to persuade him, and he did splash some holy water on it, and do you know what happened?"

"Did it hiss and smoke and blister?" I asked.

"Nope," Taylor said. "Nothing happened. Not a damned thing happened. Ranklin said a few more prayers, splashed some more holy water on that little shit, and not a thing happened, and Father Ranklin was really upset, like he was really concerned. It was awkward, and so I got out of there, like embarrassed and just sort of freaked out. And I went home, and I was just really upset, and I stripped down and put on some pajamas, and what should I see? A fourth mask, staring right at me. The name on it was Adam. And I don't know any Adam, so it was just bizarre. But there it was, another mask. Then I saw on my phone that Father Adam Ranklin had committed suicide at St. Michael's. He'd hanged himself from the bell tower. No, I can tell you that this absolutely horrified me, because I'd only met with the man a few hours before, and that mask had appeared in the time it took from me to get home from St. Michael's. What the fuck, right?"

I'd seen the suicide of Father Ranklin in the news, the grisly image of him hanging, and had remembered that.

"I hardly knew the guy," Taylor said. "It was that little shit, fucking with me again. Like maybe punishing me, or Father Ranklin, maybe, for fucking with it. There was like a message, there, like it was maybe warning me that anybody who tried to do it harm was dead."

"What about the guys at Skinchangers?" I asked, already knowing what had happened. There had been a bizarre murder plot there, where the employees had been herded by some gunmen and locked into a storeroom in back while they'd robbed the place, and had then set fire to it. The owner-operator and his half-dozen employees had all burned to death in the fire.

Taylor gestured over her right shoulder, to the seven masks clustered like grapes, wreathed in yellow fire: Clyde. Poppy. Jan. Mick. Cynda. Trey. Vin.

"The fire was a new thing," Taylor said. "See, I'd had this phoenix tattoo on my shoulder, and those masks just obliterated it. It was like the thing was mocking me still further. It put those masks over the original tat, and there it was."

"Why'd it wait?" I asked. I knew how they worked at Skinchangers—subtlety was not their strong suit.

"It took me awhile to figure it out," Taylor said. "By then, I was just, like, completely freaked out. But then I knew—it waited until the whole crew was together. Like you know how people's schedules vary. It waited until they could all be in the room at one time, and then it swooped down on them. It had been during a birthday party for the owner, so everybody was there. Then it happened."

"Wow." I said.

"I know, right?" Taylor said. "Just, wow. I'm probably endangering your life just sitting here talking to you about it, Dude."

I was in a weird place, because it was clear to me that Taylor totally believed what she was telling me, but it was just too weird to be believed. I mean, all I had was her word that this was going on—for all I knew, she was just some nutcase who built this story around her tattooing to give it some kind of meaning.

Given what I did for a living, I heard all sorts of stories from people. People loved to tell stories about their tattoos, and the removal of them invariably revolved around the stories of tragedy and personal loss—at whatever level, from actual, profound personal loss to some completely shallow tales of woe from a poorly-planned night out or a bad memory that lingered like a hangover.

Looking at Taylor, I thought she was absolutely sincere in believing what had happened to her had occurred—it was real to her, I would wager, and if something was real to you, then it was real enough, unless you were nuts, in which case, you wouldn't know any better.

But the inkwork was incredible. Even if the motif was pretty straightforward, the degree of detail in the masks, the way they perfectly followed her curves, the way somebody had taken considerable care in the application of them—this amount of bodywork would have cost a fortune.

"Now I'm, like, talking to the little shit," Taylor said. "I'm begging it to leave me alone, to stop killing people."

"But it didn't, uh, listen, right?" I asked.

"No," Taylor said. "Then I started seeing names on there that I didn't even know."

I didn't know what to think, tried to approach it professionally.

"Based on factors like your skin color, the square footage of the tattoos, the colors used, gosh, it's going to be pricey. I'd put it at about $27,000 over about 18 to 20 sessions."

Taylor didn't blink at the cost, which I actually thought was pretty fair. I felt bad for her, offered my lower rate. A job like hers might run to nearly $60,000 in some quarters, but I figured I could get her sorted out for less than half of that.

"I don't have that kind of money," Taylor said. "I can't even imagine hitting my parents up for that."

She sat up and started to put her clothes back on. With her clothes back on, you could hardly notice the tattoos, except for the masks on the backs of her hands, and on her palms.

"I was stupid to even come here," she said. "For thinking that you'd be able to help me. People said you were really a good guy, that you helped people out."

"I am," I said. "But this kind of a job is monumental. It'll be time-consuming and will require a lot of work. I'm a business, not a charity."

"Maybe that attitude will save your life," Taylor said. "If you tried to remove them, it'd probably kill you."

I didn't believe that, but all the same, thought I'd see if anybody at Ink, Inc. or Backpedals had died. Then again, maybe they'd balked at the job, or she'd been price-shopping, was trying to see if she could get a better deal. I was sure those guys would have scaled the removal costs appropriately.

"What you should do is track down that Tio guy," I said.

"Oh, I did," Taylor said. "I went to Las Brujas and I asked around, like if anybody knew this guy Tio. The workers there were scared to death, just looked at me and told me that they didn't speak English, but I knew that they were bullshitting me. I left my number and told them if they saw Tio, to have him call me."

"And did he?"

"No," Taylor said. "Look, Mr. Rossi, I'm running out of skin, here. I'm terrified as to what'll happen next, when it'll strike next, who it'll kill. I've counted the masks on my body, and there are hundreds of masks on me right now. I'm running out of space, and I think it knows it, too. I don't know what's going to happen to me once it's through with me."

"What if I helped you find Tio?" I asked. I didn't really want to get involved in this, but felt like if I could find the guy who maybe did this to her, maybe it'd be alright. Then again, part of me thought I should leave well enough alone, and whoever or whatever this Tio guy was, maybe he was someone I didn't want to mess around with.

"That'd be great, but you really don't have to," Taylor said.

"I want to," I said. "It's the least I can do. Consider it part of my tattoo removal service."

"Yeah, but it's, like, not going to cost me, is it?" Taylor asked, giving me a sidelong glance beneath long lashes.

That was an interesting question. I didn't know this woman, although I did mention that she was ridiculously hot, and I'd never offered this kind of service to any of my other clients.

"No," I said, part of me almost kicking me in the nuts for even saying it. "This one's on me. I'll find this Tio and see what the story is."

Taylor then reached out and hugged me. "Thank you, Mr. Rossi."

Hearing the relief in her voice, I knew that whatever the deal was that led to her predicament, I knew I'd done the right thing.

FOUR

Taylor had taken me up on my offer to track down Tio, which was pretty generous of me, I have to admit, because I normally wouldn't do something like that for a prospective client, but seeing how upset and afraid she was, I felt like there was some kind of moral obligation, there.

What did I think about all of this? I thought at first that maybe Taylor was out of her mind. Some people got addicted to ink, would just cover themselves in tattoos. But to do what Taylor had done was beyond crazy.

We took her car, which was a yellow Dodge Challenger with a black racing stripe, a beautiful, low-slung muscle car that growled as it grabbed the ground.

"Nice car," I said, while she drove, smoothly working the stick shift.

"Nice enough," she said.

"What do you do for a living, anyway?" I asked, watching the city speed by.

"I'm between jobs," Taylor said. "I used to be a beverage girl for Black Star Distillery, but that got old pretty quickly. I mostly just hit my folks up for money."

Rich kid life. Not something I ever had to worry about. I knew Black Star Distillery, though, as they got around, and more than a few kids got their catchy logo emblazoned on their bodies.

"You ever heard of *The King in Yellow?*" I asked. I figured it couldn't hurt. Taylor shrugged.

"I know all about that," she said. "When things got crazy with me, I did some searching on the Net. I know allll about that."

"Okay," I said. "All those masks are representations of the Pallid Mask."

"I know all of that," Taylor said. "Your point?"

I thought I'd just wade into the flaky space, figuring she wouldn't mind, given where she was at.

"You've been turned into some kind of living billboard for the Yellow King, I think," I said.

"But why?"

She cut through traffic like she owned it, while I just hung on and tried to enjoy the ride.

"Only the King knows for sure," I said.

"Meaning?"

That was the big thing, when you got down to it. What the hell did it mean? Every time a person died, my guess being something tied to the King in some fashion, she became adorned by a mask. They slowly were covering her whole body. Once they got to her face, what was left? The last mask would be for her, I was fairly certain.

Again, not like I knew how the King thought, but having dealt with enough of those tats, I could kind of glimpse the terrain.

"The problem isn't all the masks," I said. "It's the Inkling. That thing's the source of the trouble. The masks are just symptoms of the overall ailment. The Inkling's like the lens for it, or the conduit."

"Yeah, okay, Dr. Kyle," Taylor said, gripping the steering wheel a bit tightly. I could taste her impatience, frustration, and hopelessness.

"This Tio Amarillo guy, he just licked the tattoo onto you," I said. "Maybe if we do something like that, it'll work.

I'm thinking it has to be passed from person to person that way."

Taylor gave another half-assed laugh.

"That doesn't help me," Taylor said. "I mean, I can't give this to somebody else."

"We could give it back to Tio," I said. "Maybe he gets all your masks, too. Look, I'm just brainstorming, here. Trying to think outside of the box."

"I appreciate it, I really do," Taylor said, and I thought maybe I believed her.

"I mean, was this Tio guy a wizard? Do you think that?"

Taylor shook her head, slipped us through some traffic with some deft turns of the wheel and some downshifting.

"Alright," I said. "Maybe we just do what he did, only in reverse."

Taylor glanced at me, eyebrow raised.

"You just want to lick your hand and touch it to the small of my back and it'll be all better?" Taylor asked.

I know how it sounded. It sounded stupid and crazy, but that's how things got sometimes. Sometimes stupid and crazy was exactly the way you had to go.

"All I'm saying is that we saw how he transferred the Inkling to you," I said. "Maybe it works both ways."

Taylor scoffed, shaking her head, biting her lip.

"I'm willing to try anything, to be honest," she said. "I feel like I don't have much time."

"Okay," I said. "Let's try that, then. Assuming we can find Tio."

We rolled on up to Las Brujas, which was pretty quiet this time of day. Taylor's muscle car certainly drew attention from the locals, however, and I was both pleased and alarmed to see people crossing themselves and moving away from us when we got out.

Fortunately, Tio came storming out, wearing a black shirt and yellow pants and a matching yellow vest. His eyes were wild, and he was flailing his arms even as he was talking.

"Oh, no you don't," Tio said. "You get out of here!"

I could see he had a pistol in the waistband of his pants, and he gestured to it, looking at us both.

"You infected me," Taylor said. "Poisoned me with your creepy little tat."

"The King goes where HE wills," Tio said, looking me over. "Who's this, your goon?"

"I'm her friend," I said, throwing a punch to his jaw before he could even draw, one of those kickass crosses you picked up from a misspent youth. Sometimes, I found that worked best, because I was able to drop him to the ground in front of Las Brujas and zip-tied his wrists behind his back before he knew what was going on. I worked as a bouncer before I did ink, so I knew how to handle people in a pinch. I took his pistol and then hoisted him over my shoulder while I had Taylor pop the trunk. I had to tell her twice because she was flabbergasted.

In he went, and off we drove.

FIVE

We'd gotten to a quiet place in the city, one of the abandoned lots where you could park if there wasn't anything remotely valuable being guarded by security. This was an old worn-out factory of some sort that was reduced to a husk of a building. I couldn't even tell what was made there, that's how long it had been. Maybe paint or concrete or plaster. It didn't matter anymore, whatever it was.

I'd talked Taylor off the kidnapping ledge when we'd gotten out of there with our illicit cargo.

"Those people who saw us aren't going to snitch," I said. "Mr. Amarillo strikes me as the type likely to be at great risk for being spirited away in an automobile out of the blue one day."

"I'm not going to jail for kidnapping," Taylor said.

"I think if the Inkling has its way with you, jail's going to be just about the least of your worries," I said.

I'll admit that I was spitballing more than a little at this point, but I felt that there could be an internal logic at work, here, some sense amid the insanity. Tio was raging when we got him out of the trunk, thrashing like an angry alligator. I mean, he was pissed. But more than that, I could see he was afraid.

"You thought, what? You'd pass on your curse to this woman and that would be that?" I asked.

"Yeah," Tio said. "Exactly what I thought."

He was straining against his bonds, and I thought it best to keep things moving, just in case some attentive cops appeared.

"How'd you get the Inkling?" I asked.

"The what?"

"What I call it," I said. He glared at Taylor.

"Ex-girlfriend," Tio said. "I mean, not ex, yet. Not then. She gave it to me."

Taylor rolled up a sleeve, showing all the masks adorning her arm.

"Did you have all of these?" she asked.

"Not as many as that," Tio said. "I mean, I got rid of it fast, once I saw what was going on. Damn, grrl. You're covered. You get fully covered and you get to go to Carcosa, all expenses paid. You'll live like a queen with that much ink on you. You been doing the King all sorts of solids."

"I don't want to go there," Taylor said, baring her teeth at him. But I tried to stay on-task, like the mechanics of tattoo removal, even under these circumstances.

"What happened to the tats you had when you passed on the Inkling to Taylor?" I asked.

"Gone to Carcosa," Tio said. "Where they all end up. That's what you are. You're like a Courier to Carcosa, now, dig? You deliver them to HIM."

That made my head kind of spin, the idea that all of those masks on her were a life/soul/whatever, ready to be passed on to the Yellow King, to do with whatever the Yellow King did with souls. Not my jam to dwell on that too much.

"It's why you put it on her back," I said. "Where she couldn't reach it. Not like your palm."

"She shook my hand. My ex, I mean," Tio said. "No harm, no foul. That's how she left it with me, and she gave me that thing when we shook hands, like parting ways, no hard feelings. What she told me at the time."

"Where'd she get it?" I asked.

"I don't know," Tio said. "We weren't on speaking terms after that, once I realized what was going on. She lit out of town, and I never saw her again."

"I'll bet. Alright," I said. "Taylor, turn around, let me see the Inkling."

She leaned on her car, while Tio struggled harder to free himself. The Inkling was just smiling deadly at me, still pretty happy with itself, whatever the hell it truly was. I licked the palm of my hand, then slapped it against Taylor's tat, and was pleasantly surprised when the thing came right off of her back and latched onto my hand.

Now, when I tell you that I could see, feel, smell, hear, and taste Carcosa in those moments that the Inkling and I shared space on my skin, I was grateful that I was stone sober, because it was trippy, like the visions I had, the sky a veil, the dimness hanging like a shroud, the lifeless streets and grey grasses growing through cracked and broken pavestones by the shores of the Lake of Hali, beneath a sky that burned like an ember, throwing off sparks of black stars while moons and dark suns danced, and doubled shadows walked in the darkness, the forlorn feeling crushing my spirit, driving the air from my lungs.

I slapped my wet palm onto Tio's forehead while he wailed, trying to evade me. But the Inkling stuck fast to him, and I felt the relief of the transfer, the visions of Carcosa passing, even as Taylor cried out, her back arching as all that ink she'd accumulated passed from her to Tio, to the Inkling, to Carcosa, in a whitish plume that carried with it the cries of the everlasting damned, not set free by any means, but passing from this world to HIS, whatever that precisely was.

In moments, it was over, and Taylor cried out, screaming.

"I'm clean!" she said, flashing her arms at me, opening her blouse and gazing down at her pristine skin. I was happy for her and was happier that the Inkling was gone from my palm, and the visions it had thrown into me in our moments together.

Tio was less than happy, as he cursed me out, the Inkling frowning on his forehead.

"You son of a bitch," Tio said, clawing at his forehead. "This isn't fair. I can't be cursed twice, man!"

"Returned to sender," I said, drawing a pocketknife and cutting the zip-tie. He got to his feet, looked ready to have a go at me, but I pointed his own pistol at him, which held him back. Twice-cursed he may have been, but he wasn't stupid.

"I don't deserve this," Tio said. "I'm the victim, here. You've damned me."

"Take it up with the King," I said, and didn't have to tell Taylor we needed to get out of there. She hopped to her car, and I joined her, while Tio snarled at us, his furious face mangled by despair and desperation. As she drove off, I emptied Tio's revolver and tossed it out the window. Tio grabbed the pistol and emptied all six empty chambers at us as we got out of there, the Challenger growling.

"I can't believe it," Taylor said. "Cannot believe you pulled that off."

"Hey, it's why I'm the best," I said.

"Clearly," Taylor said, gunning the engine as she got us into third gear without barely blinking. "I don't know how I'm going to pay you back."

"Hmmm, well, this car's a good start," I said, enjoying hearing the sound of her scoffing, which felt almost like hope, crazily enough, as she floored it and we sped right through a yellow light.

Devoid.

WAN.

"That little girl is a greater work of art than anything in this place," Nina Torres said, sucking her teeth. She nodded in the direction of the little girl holding her father's hand. She was holding a cup of coffee, Anton LaFontaine was holding onto the railing.

They were overlooking the milling crowds at the Art Institute of Chicago in the little coffee bar. The light was right, neither day nor night, from where they stood, blond wood and white walls. The little girl was giggling, holding onto a yellow balloon, the string wrapped around her tiny fist. Nina sipped her coffee, nursed the lid with her lips.

The little girl snorted at her dad. She had red bangs and pigtails tied with purple ribbons.

"You're kidding, right?" Anton asked.

Nina was tall, with a thick head of dyed black hair she'd tied back in a ponytail tucked through a blue baseball cap he'd gotten her at a Chicago Fire game a few years ago. She was amply curved, wore scuffed blue jeans and black clogs, like she was a chef. Only she wasn't a chef. She wore an undyed peasant blouse that showed off her tattooed shoulders.

"Nope," she said. "Just look at her."

"She's just a kid," Anton said. "There are literally billions of kids in the world. Anybody can have kids."

The girl disappeared around a corner with her dad, the balloon trailing after her.

"But only one like her," Nina said. Nina was a musician. A classical one. She played flute in the Chicago Symphony Orchestra. Anton would sometimes go see her play. He loved to watch her on the stage. He always marveled how she could see him when she was onstage, despite the lights. She would smile down on him when she'd see him, her dark eyes aglitter with prideful triumph that he was in the audience, while she was on the stage.

"People aren't paintings," Anton said. "Not the same thing. You might find hundreds of kids who are as good or better than that little girl, but you're not going to find work like this anywhere. Nothing exactly like it, anyway; it's different."

Anton stood eye-to-eye with Nina, broad-shouldered, lightly tanned. He still had all of his hair, even though he was pushing 30, which felt, to him, like he was getting old.

Too old to remain undiscovered.

"You try to make a copy of somebody else's work, and it's a forgery," Anton said.

"I heard that some forgeries these days are as good as the originals," Nina said. She gave her coffee another exploratory sip, rolling her eyes at him, like he'd said something obvious or stupid. She did that often, obviously.

"Are we done here?" she asked.

"We just got here," Anton said.

"I know, but how about we just see, I dunno, the Impressionists, and maybe the Modernists, and then call it a day," she said.

"We can be here all day," he said. "It takes at least a day to do it right."

He could tell from her expression that it wasn't sitting well with her. A musician, to Anton's mind, was kind of like being an artistic athlete. The musician, to be fully who they were creatively, required the presence of their instrument and a performance. The problem a musician faced was what they did when they weren't playing music.

Anton had known enough of her compatriots, peers, friends, and rivals to know that you could have somebody who was a superb musician be a complete lunkhead, a crazy, a flake, an asshole, and even an out-and-out loser. But you'd never know it to watch them play. In performance, there was synergy between performer and their instrument of choice. Without it, there was a diminishment. It's not like they were nothing without their instruments; but they were incomplete without them.

As a painter, Anton had a different relationship with his art—he created paintings, which lived as artifacts apart from him. But for Nina, what art she made was purely tied to her musical performance, and as part of an ensemble, or an orchestra. She was a link in a chain, a cog or a gear in a larger mechanism, and her art was performance, as fleeting as a song.

Nina was like that. She was a wonderful musician, but she was no art critic. Visual art was abstract, alien, and cold to her, all but incomprehensible beyond the ruthlessly practical dictates of her mind. Anton felt confident that she could be transported when she played, but where she went when she performed, only she knew. And when she was not performing, she was almost painfully ordinary.

"You really only want to see a couple spots?" Anton asked. She nodded.

"There are better things we could do with our time, don't you think?" She playfully walked her fingers up his forearm.

"Sure," he said.

"Sure," she said, imitating him. Her eyes were mossy brown but trended far darker in the light.

"Let's go check out some stuff," he said.

They spent about an hour at the Art Institute before Nina again got impatient. She'd taken a phone call from somebody Anton didn't know, turning on her chunky, cloggy heel and pacing while he tried to study the paintings. She was always fielding calls from various friends, people she'd casually mention, assorted intimate acquaintances that were apparently integral to the life of a practicing musician.

"I'm saying why should anybody even paint anything anymore?" Nina asked, as they were leaving. "With photography being what it is, what's the point?"

They walked out in front of the Art Institute, intending to hit someplace for a late lunch. It was sunny, a mix of indirect light and clouds of grey, lead, dove, and slate overhead, massive puffs like a herd of cumulus cattle. A storm was on its way.

"I don't paint for any reason but because I enjoy it," Anton said.

"Right, but that's what I'm saying," Nina said. "Painting's been done absolutely to death. You can paint something that looks realistic; you can paint something that looks insane. You can go somewhere in the middle—the point is that everybody's already done it before. There's no new ground. There's nothing new to see."

Anton laughed, took her hand in his, walked her up the street with him. She had long legs but walked slowly, so he would slow his pace to accommodate her. Her hands were strong. Musician's hands, nails carefully pared.

"That's like saying 'Why play Mozart or Beethoven?'" Anton said. "It's all been done before, right?"

She cocked her head and gave him a long-suffering grimace. "It's not the same. Audiences *expect* to hear Mozart and Beethoven—we have to honor the patrons. They want to hear that stuff. You play some modern classical and you'll have them running for the doors."

"Cynic," Anton said.

"Idealist," Nina said.

She gave his hand a squeeze. "Let's go home. I'm tired of walking."

"I thought we were going to get something to eat," Anton said.

"Meh," Nina said. "I'm tired. Food feels like work to me."

"Alright," Anton said. They caught a bus and savored the air conditioning. She sat close to him, laying her head on his shoulder, still gripping his hand.

"I just think maybe you should do something else," Nina said. "The painting is a dead end."

"I like it," Anton said. "I enjoy it. It makes me happy."

"But, well, forgive me, but you're never going to make it as a painter," she said. "You have to throw in the towel sometime. It's like me; I made it to the CSO, and I'm content with that. I've reached my level. I'm comfortable with that."

"I'm not you," Anton said.

She put her hand on his forearm, looked him over down the end of her long nose.

"I know you're not me, Doll. But I'm saying that it's almost impossible to make an impression as a painter. I mean, you're doing better painting houses than you ever will painting paintings."

Nina made a ton of money as a musician. Anton didn't understand it all, but it was like once you were in the club, you were in. You won your seat, and then you became a professional musician. She cleared six figures as easily as breathing. And, sure, she worked hard at it, playing her flute endlessly, working odd hours, working weekends and nights, working every holiday so the withered patrons could come downtown and feel cultured for a few hours, chasing down ensemble gigs for hosted events. She made a lot of money from that work. Her artistic contribution to society was valued.

Unlike his. Anton painted houses when he wasn't busy painting pictures. It was unglamorous and exhausting work, but he needed that work to support himself. Especially when his paintings failed to sell.

"I enjoy painting," he said. "I can't help that I'm a painter. It's my medium. It's how I express myself."

"But there's no future in it," Nina said. "Nothing. You see it at those art fairs you drag me to. You always hate the work you see there."

They reached their stop. He tugged on the chain, and they got off the bus. They could've walked it; they lived in the Gold Coast, thanks to Nina's faultless sense of decorum and entitlement. She'd wanted to live in the best neighborhood in Chicago, so there they were, just a hop, skip, and a jump from downtown.

They lived in the Bierce Building, a building built in 1903 that had been gut-rehabbed at some point into *sotto voce* loft condos in the late '90s that Nina had been more than happy to scoop up when the opportunity presented itself. They had a gorgeous view of the lake and a slice of skyline. Every morning, the sun rose and shined in their place.

Nina liked it because it wasn't attached to any of the other units, and was well-insulated, so she could practice and nobody could hear it, there were no complaints. It had been a celebratory purchase when she'd gotten into the CSO.

Anton had covered the walls with his paintings, all carefully framed. He didn't like the sun coming in and baking the pieces, so he'd often have the blinds down to cover things, while Nina would often open the blinds to let the light in. After morning, it didn't really matter—the place would have indirect light from that point on.

Anton kept a corner of it for himself, his studio. Nina was adamant about it remaining confined to one end, that it didn't get out of control. So, he piled it all in this one end of their unit, the south end, where it could be blocked from view with some fold-out ornamental screens Nina had insisted he put up.

They keyed into the unit and Anton could smell the paint. Just a hint of it, an oil painting he was working on. He'd been giving it ample dry time.

"We need to open a window," Nina said. "You're suffocating poor Widget."

Their little dog, an Italian Greyhound, came bounding up. Nina's face broke into a great big smile at the sight of the dog.

"Baby baby baby baby baby!" she said. "Did you miss us, Baby?"

Widget was all aquiver.

"Why don't you get some food going, while I walk Widget?" she said.

"Alright," Anton said, tossing his keys into a brass bowl by the door, while Nina leashed Widget.

Anton could paint, and Anton could cook. He had a few other talents Nina may have appreciated, but she particularly loved his cooking. He went into their kitchen, their sea of stainless steel and granite, and he put together some Spaghetti alla Puttanesca, just started whipping that up in a few pans, filling the condo with savory scents.

He glanced at the piece he was working on right now, at the far end of the place. It was visible to him from the kitchen. He called it *Mellow Yellow Fellow*. It was a monochromatic painting in yellow. A self-portrait. Anton had been pleased by it, although Nina hadn't understood why in the hell he'd done a self-portrait.

"'If you have to ask, you'll never know.'" Anton had said.

"What's that mean?"

"Louis Armstrong said it," Anton said. "About jazz."

"Clever," Nina said, wagging a finger at him. "One of our trumpet players, Joseph Clarke, he thinks Louis Armstrong was overrated. Or, more precisely, that he was more about personality than technique."

"I don't think Joe Clarke's qualified to judge Louis Armstrong," Anton said. Clarke was this worm-lipped, rubber-faced oldster who most definitely had the hots for Nina. Clarke was always turning up at CSO functions with his meandering stories that invariably framed how impressive he was. He was a Johnny One-Note, but he was one of Nina's many oldest and dearest friends, with whom she'd spend inordinate amounts of time after shows, as the musicians would let off post-performance steam.

"Why is it yellow?" Nina had asked.

"I was inspired," Anton said.

Nina frowned, tilted her head in that way when she was critiquing something.

"But why yellow? It's a terrible color for you. You look embalmed or something."

"I like it," Anton said.

"Why are you wearing a crown?"

"Because I'm the King in Yellow," Anton said. Nina snorted.

"It's not you," Nina had said. "You are blue. Not yellow. And not remotely kingly."

Nina opened the door and Widget came running in, already off the leash. He was all excited to see Anton, did a figure eight between his legs, until Anton petted him. Widget was a cute dog, full of life and spunk.

"Mmmmm," Nina said, sauntering into the kitchen. "That smells heavenly, Doll."

"Yeah?"

"My mom would always say that the way to a woman's heart was through her stomach," Nina said. "You're gonna make me fat one of these days."

"One of these days," Anton said.

She gave him a questing look. "Meaning?"

"Nothing," Anton said. "Let the artist work in peace."

"Sure," Nina said, mocking his favorite word with her own intonation. "I'm going to shower. Is it going to take long?"

"It's fine," Anton said. She trotted off while he cooked. While he didn't liken his painting to his cooking, he felt there was a savory synergy with the culinary arts that was comprehensible to him, the creation of sensation, the interplay of flavor and color that led to something greater than the sum of its parts, which, to him, was the essence of all creation. He became lost in his cooking while she showered, and Widget ambled about, unsure where to settle, until deciding on the sofa.

When it was ready, Anton plated it and poured some wine, while Nina came out in a tee shirt, one of his—the techno-darkwave band he enjoyed in years past, Pallid Mask, a dead-white mask with black stars in its empty eyes, gazing at him upon a field of yellow, flanked by a pair of suns against a distant alien skyline.

"Is it done? Seriously?" she asked.

"Yep," Anton said.

"Show-off," she said. "Jack of all trades."

"That's me," he said, pouring her some wine. Nina loved her wine.

"Marvelous," she said, then twirled herself some of the pasta, popping it into her mouth. She chewed and savored. "Oh my god. I can't believe you, Tone."

She swilled her wine and took her time with the spaghetti. As far as compositions went, it was one of his better ones.

"Do you work tonight?"

She nodded. "Mussorgsky."

"Which one is that?" She was always naming composers, and he could never remember them.

Nina held up her hands, like they were claws, over her head, and began to intone something doom-laden. "'Night on Bald Mountain'? You know it. Everybody knows it, thanks to, what, *Fantasia?*"

He couldn't remember much of *Fantasia,* but the melody she hummed was memorable enough.

"Sounds fun," Anton said.

"Well, you know, Fall, Halloween, all of that stuff," Nina said.

"It's September," Anton said.

"Close enough for the patrons," Nina said. "They don't care. Nobody cares."

Her evening services would have her out until around midnight, maybe later if she hung out with her special friends, which she most often did. Threw back a few drinks. Even classical musicians kept odd hours. It didn't bother him too much because it freed him up to paint. Painting took time and craved solitude.

Nina pushed the plate away, patted her tummy. "That was incredible, Tone. Hello, food baby."

"Aw, thanks."

She got up and picked up the plate and planted a proprietary kiss on his nose. "You're incredible, Tony. The way you cook, you'll never be a starving artist."

She rinsed and popped the plate into the dishwasher, then came back and wrapped her arms around his chest from behind, resting her chin atop his head.

"I'm going to be home late tonight, Tone," she said. "I'm thinking 1-ish. Hope you don't mind."

"Going out drinking?" he asked.

"Yeah," she said. "Olivia's having us all get together at Sonata's after the service."

Olivia Brandt was one of Nina's many orchestra pals. She was Principal Bassoonist for the CSO. Tall and leonine in countenance, overfond of seasonally tanning herself in the midday sun, Olivia could have been a sister of Nina's, and they found much in common with each other, judging from what Nina would say about her.

"I won't wait up," Anton said. "How about that?"

"I'll wake you up when I get in," she said, giving his chest a grab. "I'm gonna go get ready, Doll."

He watched her strut into the bathroom, where she began primping, while he did the rest of the dishes. As so often when he was doing something mundane, his mind wandered, and he thought about what she'd said about painting.

She didn't know what she was talking about.
Painting wasn't dead.

Night fell and Anton paced around the loft. As he gazed out the windows of the condo, over the park, over the lake, he saw only darkness.

Nina had left around 7 p.m., dressed in yet another of her endless black outfits. She had a whole closetful of black stage clothes.

"C'mon, Widge," he said, leashing the dog. "Let's go for a walk."

He went out into the night air, feeling the crisp kick of fall in his face, the cinnamon whiff of rotting leaves, and let Widget go do his thing in the park. They passed a yellow sign urging people to pick up after their dogs. It was a graphic showing a grinning rat, saying something like how rats could eat dogshit. It didn't say it just like that, but Anton knew what they were implying with those signs He shrugged, walked Widget into the comforting darkness of the park.

The Drake loomed near where they lived, as did the Hancock Building and Oak Street Beach. He walked Widget toward Olive Park, near Navy Pier, where the Ferris Wheel was brightly, mindlessly turning. The infernal fireworks hadn't begun, yet; the pointless, nightly festivities that he could often see from their vantage point in the condo.

He found his eyes drawn to the empty celebrations of the Pier, listening to the noise of the milling people, the hustle of cabs, the laughter of girls and the braying of boys, everybody backlit by the gaudy displays. It was hard to believe the country was currently fighting not one, but two wars. There was no sign of war at Navy Pier, only the breathless promise of free fireworks.

In the shadows of the trees, he walked the little dog back into the neighborhood. He'd heard some sirens when he was in the park and saw that there was a fire truck in front of their place, lights flashing.

And a police cruiser.

And an ambulance.

And a crowd.

"What the hell?"

Anton walked up, where people were murmuring. There was a body on the sidewalk, leaking blood. A young man, blondly bloody, ruined glasses a few feet away. He was wearing a blue Oxford cloth shirt, splashed with blood. And grey slacks. He looked like he was sleeping on his stomach, except one leg was bent the wrong way, and his eyes were open, his mouth agape, some broken teeth on the sidewalk, scattered and shattered. Blood had poured from his ears, down his face, in a river delta of death.

"What happened?" he asked one of the onlookers, a fat guy with a silvery beard.

"Jumper," he said. "That kid jumped off the building, here."

It was their building. Anton could clearly see. He tried to steal another glance of the kid, saw people taking pictures with their cell phones. An EMT put a sheet over the kid's body. Anton hadn't recognized him. He and Nina lived on the 14th floor of the building, which was six floors below the rooftop deck, which he presumed the kid had jumped from.

"Such a shame," an older woman said, elegant in yellow-hued costume jewelry. "Such a waste."

Anton pushed past the crowd and walked toward the building. A chubby policeman held up a hand.

"I live here," Anton said. The cop nodded, let him past. Anton gave Widget a tug on his leash, as the dog was curious about the body.

He went inside, where Deke the Doorman was waiting. "Damn tragic, Mr. LaFontaine. I didn't even see it.

Miss Spenser just came in and said somebody had jumped. She was beside herself."

Deke was a burly old cuss, freckled, lantern-jawed and gimlet-eyed. Anton thought of him more as a building bouncer than as a doorman.

"Sucks to be him," Anton said, shaking his head. "Who was he?"

"Alec Simmons," Deke said. "Investment banker. Bright kid. I think he lived right next to you and Nina."

"Yeah?"

Deke nodded. "I think he went to the deck and just leaped."

"Christ," Anton said. "That's messed up."

"You said it," Deke said.

Anton went to the elevator and pushed the button for their floor. It bugged him that Deke knew (and referred to) Nina by her first name, but that's how Nina was. She was always talking to strangers. She was many things, but "shy" certainly wasn't one of them, being only a wineglass away from discovering new best friends wherever she went.

It also bugged him that their neighbor had offed himself. Anton tried to remember the guy and couldn't. He must've seen him a time or two, but all he could see was the kid's dead eyes gazing at the sidewalk, blood all over the place. Dead eyes, pupils wide. An almost surprised expression. What could have been so wrong in his life to drive him to that?

Anton leaned against the mirrored side of the elevator, seeing himself reflected to infinity. He could see that man's face in his myriad reflections. The graceless way the sidewalk had deformed it, like a rough uncle grabbing your face in his meaty hands and holding you there in a paternalistic pincer grip, loudly commenting how big you've gotten, the stink of cigars and scotch on his breath.

Alec Simmons. Investment banker. Next-door neighbor. Suicide.

The elevator opened and Anton got out, saw police down the hall, at the unit. Widget glanced up at him, then pertly trotted ahead on his leash, while Anton fished out his keys. One of the policemen, the fat guy with a fatter mustache, looked Anton over.

"Did he jump from his unit, Officer?" Anton asked.

"Yep," the cop said. "Took a glass cutter and opened the window. A big circle, cuz your building's windows don't open wide enough, right? He just cuts the glass and—"

Another cop appeared at the door, a pale Black cop, maybe Creole. "Reese, get in here."

"Sorry, Wallace," Officer Reese said, shrugging his shoulders. Officer Wallace stared stonily at Anton, who didn't understand why he was getting the stinkeye. He had been out walking his goddamned dog. He didn't even know Mr. Simmons.

He keyed into the loft and shut the door, loosing Widget from his leash. The dog bounded happily away, while Anton took off his shoes, paced around the condo. He went to the window, touched the glass. It was thick. The windows were large. It was one of the appeals of the place, part of the design. Big windows. Anton found himself tracing a circle with his arm.

Simmons' unit shared a wall with them. He walked over to his studio. The place was masterfully soundproofed; you couldn't hear a thing. There was still the flashing of the fire trucks and police cars down below, a blend of red and blue lights peppering the trees, painting the ceiling in contrasting color, like some Public Safety rave going on down there. And shadows of bystanders and onlookers, too, backlit by the lights. A spectral crowd.

It had made Anton uncomfortable. He saw that face again. Bewildered. Empty. Dead. Lifeless. Black eyes.

That big circle in the window, the leap.

He wondered what was going on in Simmons' head to make him do this thing.

What had it been?

To go out and buy a glass cutter, to Anton's mind, made him think it wasn't some spur of the moment suicide. Simmons had thought it out. He'd thought exactly about what he was going to do. Maybe he talked to the clerk about it, got his advice. Who used glass cutters anymore? Not investment bankers, for sure.

Something ineffable inspired Anton. The images elbowed each other inside his head, made his hands itch. Inspiration. A dreadful inspiration, like a tumor in his mind, a splotch on his soul.

The eyes.
The dead eyes.
The window.
The face.

Blank.
Lifeless.
Empty.
Devoid.

Yes.

Anton dug out some canvas, rolled it out. He drew a circle on it, following the length of his arms, so the thing was roughly six feet in diameter when he finished tracing it. He stepped back, looked down at it, hands on his hips.

He made a circular canvas for it, because a square or rectangle was not right for such a thing. He knew this intuitively, stretched the canvas over the circular frame, tested it. Then he set the frame aside and proceeded to affix the canvas to the easel.

Then he went to work on the color. The concept was simple, so the execution had to be perfect. He went through his paints and hunted. He had his Mars Black, held it in his hand, looked at it, frowned.

Not nearly dark enough.

He'd not been able to get the color right. Not with the stash he had. He'd worked on it for a few hours, mixing everything he could think of, and it still wasn't right. He'd polished off that bottle of wine he'd decanted for their early dinner, and that had put him right to sleep, where he'd dreamed about that color, trying to get that perfectly black color for the painting. He'd tried it while awake, and he'd tried it in his sleep.

Then he woke up to a freshly-showered Nina spooning him, poking him.

"Hi, there," she said. "You fell asleep, Old Man."

"Yeah," he said. "You woke me right up, though."

"Mmm hmm," she said, kissing him. "You looked so peaceful there, I just had to disrupt it somehow."

It was 1:23 in the morning.

"Early night?" he asked.

"I just had one glass. Olivia was going on and on about Barcelona, and you know how she gets," she said. "Did I miss anything?"

"Did you know our neighbor?"

"Which one? Alec?"

"Yeah, him," Anton said.

"Not well," Nina said. "I'd see him in the exercise room once in a while. Always doing crunches and planks. He was ripped."

"Yeah?"

"Mmm hmm," Nina said, with entirely too much favor for his liking. She had a drink of water, always kept a glass by the nightstand. "Why?"

Anton saw his face again, against the sidewalk. In his mind's eye.

"He killed himself tonight," Anton said.

Nina coughed on her water. "What?"

"Jumped."

She gasped, startling Widget, who'd been dozing at the foot of the bed. "Oh, that's horrible! Did you see?"

Anton nodded. "I mean, I didn't see him jump; only after. I had taken Widge out for a walk, and when I got back, there he was."

"Wow," Nina said. "Just, wow."

"I know, right? Wow," Anton said. "Right next door."

Nina fidgeted next to Anton. "It's horrible. How about we don't talk about it?"

"Okay," Anton said.

But he couldn't stop thinking about it. It just rattled around in his head, that image of Alec Simmons jumping to his death. He just replayed it in his head, over and over again.

Nina gradually dozed off in her quiet way. She slept like the dead: just inert, motionless, on her side or on her back, and nearly silent. He could hardly even hear her breathing. When he was sure she was asleep, he got up, went over to his canvas, stared at it, the circle. He went back to his pigments and mixed them, tried again to get something dark enough, just stared at the color he'd mixed.

Not dark enough. This was just black. He needed something far darker. He remembered a trip one time, a cave he and Nina had visited in North Carolina, this close, confined little thing, not like the expansive caverns in, say, Kentucky.

It was Linville Cavern. He remembered the Chuck Taylor-wearing tour guide, looking like a Sonic Youth-worshipping refugee from Chapel Hill or Asheville, drawling about the darkness of the caves, of them being 700 feet underground, and the guide turning off the electric lights that illuminated that section of cave, and Nina holding tight to his hand in the absolute dark, the darkest dark that he'd ever seen.

He'd held his hand up in front of his face and had not been able to see it. He'd heard a little kid in the group whimpering, but otherwise, everybody had been silent, and the kid told a story of these two boys who'd cut school and sojourned into these caverns back in 1916, without telling anybody where they were going.

And back then, the cold caves had about four feet of water in them, like chest high, and only one of the boys had brought a lantern, one of those kerosene ones, and the lantern had been dropped in the water, and the boys had been deep in the caves in the pitch black. It had taken them two days to escape the caves, and they'd nearly frozen to death in the terrible cold and wet of the cave, where they'd managed to scrape their way out of the dark when one realized that they could follow the flow of water out of the damnable place.

That was the black Anton needed. He revisited his sense memory of that darkness, that absolute, numbing blackness of that cave. He knew what he wanted but had to find some way of getting it.

He went to the kitchen and poured himself some wine, then thought better of it and just took the bottle and drank from it, pacing around the condominium. He rested his forehead against the window, watched the traffic flow down and up Lake Shore Drive. Even this late, cars still made their way. Chicago slept, but things moved in the dark. Blood flowed. Lives began and ended. It all marched on.

Anton drank and mixed paints, glancing at his self-portrait, which merely looked on.

Dark.

Darker.

Darkest.

He kept going at it for hours, even pouring some of his wine into the paint pot he was mixing. On a whim, he cut his hand and put his blood in there, too. He wanted it dark. He stirred it, gazed into the pot, looked for what he knew was right.

"Art is a sacrifice," he whispered to his self-portrait, almost apologetically. It only looked back at him, wordlessly.

He wanted a black so absolute that it would suck away light itself.

He wanted a black that was the death of dreams.

A black that was darkened city pavement rushing into the face of an impetuously well-planned suicide. A black that was the negation of all that was light and life and truth and holy and hopeful.

A black as final as everlasting death itself.

This must be LaFontaine Black, as he thought with amusement, mixing, mixing, adding, stirring.

Darkening.

Darkling.

Darkness.

And something beyond "darkness." There were no words for it, because when it got to that point, people ran from it.

St. Augustine spoke of Good as the candleflame, and Evil as the darkness, the shadow of that flame, which was, in itself, existing only because of the flame itself, but lacked its own substance.

That was LaFontaine Black.

That was his goal.

Absolute negation.

Anton mixed and mixed, wishing he could break a window and hold the pot out into the night itself, drawing it into the mix.

He remembered lying on a yellow-flowered field with Nina, out in the countryside, far, far away from the city, and staring at the night's sky. Even that was too bright, the stars dazzling chips of incandescence on a velvety sea. It was darker than the sky he saw over the city. But gazing out over the lake, that was inky dark. He half-wished he could stroll out there and steal some of that darkness.

The lake was alive by day and a void by night. It reminded Anton of the ocean. That was dark. A trip to Hawaii when Nina had been on an orchestra tour there a few years back, on the Big Island, and they'd trekked out on those black flats where the volcano had gobbled up the community, where the ground was newly made, a scalding sea of sunbaked lava. Black like that.

Anton went rooting in his closet for a piece of that volcanic rock he'd snagged and kept, found it, felt the stony hardness of it, yet its brittleness, too. He mashed it up with a mortar and pestle, ground it into a fine grain, and poured that into the pot, thinking of them watching the sun set in Hawaii, and how dark it got in that lonely place, with nothing but thousands of miles of ocean between them and true land. She'd held him close, and they'd stared out at that darkness.

Although it wasn't silent. You still heard the waves, the endless crash of them, working to erode the island, one watery lick at a time, endlessly. That agreeable noise offered some tonic to the darkness of the view.

He went to Nina's closet and opened it. He knew there was nothing but black in there.

Black gowns, black dresses, black slacks, black blouses. Tops, bottoms, belts.

Everything black.

A sartorial symphony in black.

Anton wanted to take one of her velvet blouses and dice it up, add it to his alchemical paint pot. He restrained himself, but he stared at that closet of black clothing in the dark, looking over at his studio, where the lone lamp shone, a signal beacon. He blinked away black stars, seeing them illuminating a lampblack sky over a dark and distant city over a lifeless lake. A ghost metropolis, like a hallucination, reflected in the lake.

Carcosa.

The crashing waves of the Big Island still in his ears, Anton closed the closet carefully, walking back to his studio, thinking of that noise. It was louder than their condominium, where Anton worked in near-silence, mixing, trying to get the feel of it right. At last, shining his light into the pot, and finding a lot of nothing, he felt like he'd done it. There was a breath stolen from his lips as he gazed into that pot of paint and saw the absolute darkness he'd created.

There was black and there was black.

Anton LaFontaine had made the deepest, darkest black he'd ever seen.

The creation of the perfect pigment, the black to end all black, it was an accident of cataclysmic proportions. He glanced at his self-portrait, and thought it approved.

As an experiment, and being more artist than scientist, he did not scrupulously log his creation, did not write down the formula. This was an omission more significant than the accident of his creation itself, for it was the ultimate negation, the void-within-the-void, this black hole in his mind that was itself darker than what he had created.

But this knowledge came only later, only after the fact, for what he held in his hands, in a little pot of paint, was the ultimate elixir, a bucket of absolute darkness that stared up at him like a shark's eye, sucking in all of the light around him, making him want to reach out and touch it, just to be sure that it was actually there.

It was blacker than a raven's feather at a funeral, blacker than the ink of a kraken in the ocean's depths on a moonless night, darker than the empty belly of Leviathan, rumbling forlornly at the bottom of the deepest trench in the darkest ocean, on the shortest day of the longest night, during an eclipse.

There was an ineffable quality to the darkness that captivated him, compelled him to do something with it. It was not enough to craft the pigment and let the thing stand unused in its container. He already had the use in mind.

It was staring him in the face, that pallid canvas disc.

Anton opened another bottle of wine and drank, careful not to wake Nina, who was a motionless lump in their bed, softly breathing. Anton drank and thought of his plan of attack, because once he began, he knew he'd have to finish it. He would not profane the pigment he'd just created with half-steps; no, he would begin, and he would reach the end. Anton set the bottle down, half-full (or half-empty, he thought with a laugh, as he gazed upon that abyssal pigment he'd made), and he paced back and forth in front of the canvas. He would get it ready.

He gessoed the canvas, carefully priming it in smooth, ready strokes of his priming brush. Then he let it dry, and rinsed out his gesso brush, setting it aside. He waited in the dark for it to dry, his mind awash with images, as he finished his wine. Then he applied a second coat of gesso, and, again, waited in the dark, glancing at the clock. He wanted to have it painted before sunrise. He had to.

Having prepared the canvas, Anton selected a brush—something strong, firm, and broad, and went back to the pot of paint, pausing for a moment, for the color was truly beyond anything he'd made before. He imagined painting a room with it, or the inside of a box. It would own whatever it touched. He wondered what a bracelet made of this tint would do to the hand that wore it.

Taking a deep breath, Anton dipped his brush into the bucket, watched it take up the paint, watched the tint drop thickly from the brush, watched it take control of the bristles, rendering them mute, obscure, opaque. Then he took the brush and touched it to the canvas with a steady hand.

The first stroke of the brush looked like it wounded the canvas, like it had savaged the material, cut some hole in the very fabric of reality. The contrast could not be sharper between figure and ground, like he had, with one stroke, birthed two worlds.

He dipped the brush again and joined more of this ultimate darkness to itself, again and again. The rhythm of his work took a life of its own, a clockwork dip and click of the brush with a soothing scrape against the canvas, until the wound had widened and had become something more like a jagged mouth, and wider still, until the mouth had become a great eye, and wider still, with careful moves of his arm, until the canvas was painted, a great circle in the center, a hole gaping at him from the confines of the easel. And around it, a smattering of black stars, like an infernal nimbus upon the coronal canvas.

The majesty of his creation was not lost on him. He just stared at this disc of emptiest black that seemed to stare back at him, and wondered aloud:

"What have I done?"

The thing was done with one coat of this blackest paint. One coat had been all he'd needed, for it had laid claim to the canvas the moment it had touched it. The black stars danced around the perfect circle of black, like fitful ash thrown from a diabolical fire.

Anton set down the brush, which itself looked like it had been consumed by the pigment. He could barely see the bristles, though they were just inches away from him.

The great black disc stood on the easel, complete like nothing Anton had ever done was complete before. He got chills looking at it.

Here was absolute darkness, a sublime emptiness in front of him. His creation, this utter void, with only a dozen black stars to accompany it, like handmaidens to a ghastly, monstrous monarch. He gazed on it with awe and even a trace of horror. It was cold.

The sun rose and Anton didn't even notice.

TOO.

"What the hell is that?" Nina asked, startling Anton awake. He hadn't realized he'd passed out in front of his painting, on the old sofa he kept in the studio. The sun was up, the day was on, and Nina was standing there, one arm tucked under the other, drinking coffee, gazing with scornful eyes at the great black circle Anton had painted.

"It's my new painting," he said. "Do you like it?"

"What's it called?" she asked.

Even in the sun-bathed condominium, the painting was powerfully dark. It ate up the light around it. The sun shone everywhere but on his painting.

"It's untitled," he said.

"Untitled," Nina said, scoffing. "Why do you painters always do that—'Untitled (Splendid Grass No. 3)?'"

Anton laughed. "Sometimes it just happens."

"It's weird," she said. "You should name it. It needs a name."

"I'll think of something," he said.

She just stared at it, and, from where Anton sat, he felt like the painting was staring at him, too. One great, big, unblinking eye. It was as marvelous as it was terrible.

"Do you like it?" he asked.

"No," she said. "I hate it."

Anton turned and looked up at her. Since he was sitting, and she was standing, she could look down the end of her nose at him.

"You painted this last night?" she asked. "You should've been sleeping."

"I couldn't sleep," he said. "I kept thinking about our neighbor."

"Mmm," she said, sipping her coffee. "It's horrible."

Anton laughed. "What don't you like about it?"

Nina turned her head this way and that, squinting at it. She didn't have her contacts in, yet; had on her black-rimmed glasses. She hated her glasses.

"I can't look at it," she said. "Not directly. There's something wrong with it. It hurts my eyes."

"It's the paint," Anton said. "I made it very dark."

"I can see that," Nina said. She walked up to it, her willowy frame dwarfed by the great black dot. "You painted a hole on canvas, Tony. And what's the deal with the little black stars?"

"They're part of it," Anton said. "The Hyades."

"The what?"

"Nothing," Anton said.

She reached for it, but Anton stopped her. "It's drying. Don't mess with it. I got it perfect. Look how smooth it is. One coat. One perfect coat."

"You should frame it and sell it," Nina said. "Get it out of here. I woke up to have this thing staring right at me, from across the room."

"Yeah?"

"Yep," she said. "You should've been in the bed next to me. Now we have this…thing in the room with us. I really, really hate it, Tone."

Anton was disappointed at her reaction to it. It was a masterpiece. She just couldn't see it. She didn't know. The tint was sublime. The thought of it seemed to call up a hangover, as he had pain in his temple at trying to recollect how he'd made the stuff.

"I love it," Anton said. "It's perfect. You have no idea."

"No," Nina said. "I don't."

Anton didn't want to part with the piece, but he thought it would make him. He imagined taking it to the 321 Gallery, imagined Josephine Reardon seeing the piece and wanting to put it front and center in her gallery, with a nice price tag on it.

Nina sat down next to him, gave him a kiss on his nose. Her lips were coffee-warmed and wet. "If *you* think it's great, that's what really matters. What's next for it?"

"I was thinking of framing it," he said. "Once it's dry, of course. Maybe a round frame if I can find the right one. Odds are I'll have to make one for it. Then I'll call Jo and see if she'll take it."

Nina squinted at the piece again. It really was hard to look at. There wasn't much to actually see. It just ate the light. It gobbled up her gaze.

"What do you think you'd ask for something like that?" she asked.

"I don't know," he said. "I'll let Jo come up with a good number for it."

"The sooner it's out the door, the better," Nina said.

She yawned, stretching against him.

"How about we go into the kitchen and have some breakfast?" Nina asked.

"Sure," Anton said.

He got up with her and they went into the kitchen, sat down. She played footsies with him a bit, while he drank his own coffee, black. Looking into the white mug, the dark coffee, he thought of his painting and smiled.

"What? What's funny?" Nina asked.

"Nothing," he said. "Life."

Nina smiled and ran a hand through her hair, tousling it. She whipped her head around, her hair getting in her eyes a moment. She parted her hair with a hand.

"Hey, where's Widget?" she asked.

"I thought he was on the bed with you," Anton asked.

"Widget? Baby, where are you?" Nina asked, calling the dog in the pet owner sing-song tone everybody seemed to use. "Widget? Widget?"

Anton drank his coffee while Nina got up and walked around, searching under the bed, opening closet doors, calling to the little dog.

"Tony, get up and help me, would you? Find Widge," she said.

Anton got up and walked around the condo, calling for the dog. They went back and forth in there, top to bottom, front to back, and didn't find him.

Nina cocked a hand on her hip, piqued. "Did you leave the door open or something?"

Anton laughed. "What, our front door? No."

She went over to the front door, and it was triple-locked. Nina was always cautious about that, since she didn't want anybody waltzing in and stealing her $20,000 flute.

"Where's our goddamned dog, Tony?" Nina asked.

"I don't know," Anton said. "It's your goddamned dog, anyway."

Nina gave him a stern look, cocked her head to the side, and Anton laughed nervously, gave her what he hoped was a reassuring kiss. "We'll find him."

"Correction," Nina said. "*You* will find him. I have three services today."

"Sucks," he said. "What, during the day?"

"Yeah," she said. "A wedding and two at the Children's Museum."

Even though she didn't need the money, Nina was always taking on extra work, was always keen to bring in extra cash, working on her performance chops in various settings. She liked performing, loved having all eyes on her, listening to the music she made.

"I'll find the dog," he said.

"Please do that," Nina said. "Make yourself useful. Maybe run the vacuum, too, while you're at it."

"Anything else, Ma'am?" Anton asked.

Nina winced at the "Ma'am"—"Hey, I'm a 'Miss,' not a 'Ma'am.' Not yet, anyway."

She looked young for her age, probably always would. Something about the angles of her face, the kind of cartoonish caricature of attractiveness she possessed.

Nina walked over and moved a couple of the screens used to block Anton's makeshift studio from the rest of the dwelling. She blocked the painting with the screens.

"Hey, what're you doing?" he asked.

"I don't like that thing staring at me," she said. "It really sucks the life out of the loft."

It annoyed Anton a bit to see her doing that. He liked having the thing in the corner of his gaze as he walked about the condo. It kept drawing his eyes, for that matter. No matter where he went in the place, he saw it, that absolute black. Now Nina had blocked his view of it with a couple of beige and tan Shoji screens.

"Oh, very nice," he said.

"I think so," Nina said.

She walked off to the shower, while Anton half-heartedly called for Widget. Stupid dog. Probably got himself wedged somewhere. Although if that were the case, Anton assumed he'd be able to hear him whining or whimpering. He couldn't hear a thing, only the shower water running and Nina humming while she bathed.

He sat back down in his studio, mindful of the Shoji screens, and drank his coffee, looked up at his painting.

"A frame won't do for you, will it?" he asked the painting. "It won't look right. Okay, so I'll just hang you as you are, once you're ready for it."

He glanced at his phone, saw the time. It had been drying for several hours. He'd give it all day, see how it was at day's end.

Setting down his coffee, he walked over to the paint pot he'd used to mix the stuff, looked for the brush. The brush wasn't in the pot, where he thought he'd left it. He picked up the pot and peeked into it, into that utter black. There was still some paint left. Not much, but something he could use. He put a lid on that pot so the stuff wouldn't dry, and put it on his shelf, with his other concoctions.

Then he went up to his painting and looked closely at it. It loomed over him on its easel.

"I really don't want to sell you," he said. "I want to keep you."

But it was a masterpiece, he knew. It was his masterpiece, anyway. His. People would see it and know, unmistakably, that it was his.

Except for one thing. And another thing.

He painted a DO NOT TOUCH sign and put it near the painting, where Nina was sure to see it.

Then he went back to his shelf and took out some yellow paint, found a fresh brush. He had to sign it, but looking at the thing, he knew any signature would mar the piece, would mar the perfect emptiness he'd put on the canvas.

And yet, he wanted people to know it was his.

So, he went to the edge of the thing, and he signed the work. Here, it would not be seen, unless someone specifically tucked their head and looked for it along the bottom edge.

But it was his. He wanted everybody to know that. Then he went out to look for Widget, in case the dog had gotten out into the building somehow.

THEE.

While Nina was preparing for her services, he searched all of the floors, checked with Deke, who hadn't seen the dog. He told the doorman to call if he saw Widget, and Deke said he would do that.

Satisfied and a bit bewildered, Anton called Nina from the lobby, got her voicemail.

"Heyyyy, I'm not here right now. Leave a message, though, and I promise I'll call you back."

Nina always answered the phone with a semi-apologetic "Heyyyy."

"I just checked the whole building, nobody's seen Widget. I think he's stuck in the loft somewhere," Anton said. "I'll be up in a sec."

He hung up and pocketed the phone, hopped into the Art Deco elevator that fed the building tenants daily.

Anton rode the elevator up, thinking about his painting. Whoever would be bold enough to buy the piece would need a grand place for it. He had this vision of a white marble palace, absolutely pristine—classical, columnar, with the painting on display, this phenomenal black holding all that white marble thrall to it, the crown of black stars alternately radiating outward from it and also seeming to spiral inward into the abyss.

He had enjoyed some workmanlike success with his art, but he felt this piece would raise his reputation considerably. He would have to have a party, get people to see it. It would speak for itself.

Anton rapped on the door with a knuckle.

"Nina, you in there?"

Nobody answered. He had a vision of her in bed, naked, music on and candles lit, waiting for him with an opened bottle of pinot noir, already half-emptied.

Anton keyed in.

"Nina?" Anton said.

There, in front of the painting, was Nina. She was on the floor, face-first, her body splayed out, one arm ahead of her. His handwritten "DO NOT TOUCH" sign was on the floor beside her, near her clogs, one of which had fallen off her foot. She was wearing flared blue jeans and a grey boucle blouse, over which she'd put an olive-green jacket and finished with a scarf the color of burnt yellow.

"Funny, Nina," he said. "Very dramatic."

Then Anton could see that her upraised arm, the one stretched above her, didn't have a hand.

"What the hell?" Anton said, and he reached for it, pulled it up, and gasped—her hand had vanished, was gone in an angular slide like she'd reached into a guillotine. "Holy shit."

There was no blood; Nina's arm just stopped in that jagged point. He rolled her over and cried out when he saw that she had no face, her skin was blue. Her head simply ceased at a point just past her hairline and terminated at her chin. There was nothing there. There were no words for it. There was no blood, was no cross-section of bone and tissue he could see—there was just a blankness, an absolute negation of her, like she'd been erased.

"Nina," Anton said, his legs getting weak at the sight of her nonexistent face.

He tried to make sense of it, looked around him. Then he saw it, the roll in the carpet. Nina, always kind of clumsy, had stumbled, and she'd tumbled forward. The outstretched arm, her hand with her phone, catching herself.

But she'd hit his painting face-first.

FORE.

Anton looked at the painting, which, of course, just sat there, inscrutable. He looked at lifeless Nina, and he took a long paintbrush and he walked carefully up to the painting, extending the brush out ahead of him. He pressed the brush into the canvas, seeing that the brush simply vanished when pressed against the canvas. No fire, no noise, just nothing—one second, there was the brush. Another second, the brush was vanishing in the black.

He pulled the brush back and saw the brush had been completely severed. Negated. It was just a wooden stick. He tossed it at the painting, and the thing disappeared the moment it touched the canvas. No sound—no snaps, crackles, or pops. It just vanished.

"My God," Anton said. Poor Nina. He looked at her face, her blank, half-erased face, her body not even fully comprehending what had happened to it—it was a trauma completely beyond the familiar confines of biology. There was no way he would be able to explain it to anybody.

Anton took his cell phone and, perversely, took a photograph of Nina's ruined face. It didn't even look real, her body dying, blue from the lack of oxygen from the lack of a mouth and a nose to breathe with. Her freshly-shampooed hair still scented the air.

He could scarcely believe his eyes, and he was sitting right there.

Looking at the painting, then at Nina, Anton thought of what he should do. He could not imagine bringing the police in there, honestly: "I just came in here and her face was erased."

No way was he going to do that.

Anton wiped his sweaty brow and set down his phone, then picked Nina's body up, and fed the rest of her to the painting. He just hoisted her up with a grunt, marveling at how her lean self was far heavier than he imagined when rendered as dead weight, and he carefully delivered her to the painting, watching her pass silently into the void, watched the load he carried get progressively lighter as he got more of her in there, watched her simply vanish from existence, as if she'd never been.

He tossed her feet in, and then fell on his backside, letting out a gasp. Nina was gone. Anton cried awhile, and then he thought about slashing the painting. He felt like Nina needed to be avenged, somehow. Anton drew a palette knife and took a half-hearted swing at the painting, only to see the palette knife get clipped clean where the metal touched the inky pigment. He lobbed the palette knife at the painting, only to see it disappear.

Then he carefully took it off the easel and hung it on his wall, feeling the psychological chill of the thing as it passed close to him. It somehow seemed safer being hung on the wall, versus out in his way on the easel, where he might trip against it the way Nina had.

And he noticed something else—the circle had gotten somewhat bigger. It was crowding the black stars he'd painted. Maybe it had consumed some of them. He thought there were fewer of them, now, and that the void was bigger.

"I'm not selling you, now," Anton said. "I'm keeping you here."

FAVE.

Anton took photographs of his painting, unsure how the painting had gotten bigger. It definitely seemed larger. He measured it, and thought that, yes, maybe it had grown a bit.

"Maybe feeding you Nina fattened you up," Anton said. "Is that what it is?"

It didn't answer him, so Anton carefully looked at the painting, and it looked to him like the thing had crept ever-so-slightly beyond the boundaries of his canvas. It took him a couple of careful inspections to determine this, but, as he looked upon it, he agreed that, yes, it was now part of his wall.

"Hell," Anton said. "Hell and damnation."

It had gone from being a painting to becoming an installation piece. Anton poked at the edges of it with a putty knife, watched the knife vanish when it touched the painting. He tossed the knife into the canvas, watched it go, watched the painting seem to grow, just a tiny bit.

This would not do. He tried to gauge the depth of the painting, to see how far it had leached into the wall. It looked to be about an inch deep, which he determined by carefully cutting out a section of wall with a saw and removing it, so he could peer at the painting from the side. There was no discernable temperature emanating from the thing, beyond a faint chill.

He looked at the pot he'd originally mixed the stuff in, saw only unfathomable emptiness. He decided to take another brush, stuck that in the pot, and watched the paintbrush vanish in the depths of the thing. He fed an entire brush to the bucket of paint.

Anton was sure it wasn't a portal, judging from what had happened to Nina. Then he went to the fridge and took out a trio of Portland's Pride, a microbrewed lager distributed by the Happy Gnome Brewing Company, and he cracked one and drank it down, threw the can at the painting, watched the can vanish.

He sat down on his sofa, looked at the gaping darkness, drank another beer, crunched that can and lobbed it at the painting, watched that can vanish, too. Just nothing. It just went away.

"That is so messed up," Anton said.

Absurdly, he had this vision of running right for the painting, doing a swan-dive into it. It was a bizarre compulsion, one he felt just the same. What would annihilation feel like? Had Nina felt any pain?

He got up, toting his beer, went to a fruit basket he had on his kitchen table, then took out an orange, walked it over to the painting, pressed the orange against the surface of it. The orange stood out in sharp contrast to the absolute darkness of the painting. Anton pressed half the orange into it, his fingers coming perilously close to the edge of the canvas, and then he backed away, holding the halved piece of fruit.

The orange was not ruptured; it was simply half-annihilated, half-negated. Anton turned it over in his hands, brought the half to his nose, sniffed it. He quartered the orange and tasted it. It tasted like an orange.

Then he got an idea, took an old camcorder he had lying around, duct-taped it to the end of a broom handle, turned it on, and then thrust it into the void. Of course, the moment the camera came in touch with it, it was gone. The whole thing vanished as soon as it was in touch with the surface.

"Damn," Anton said. "What am I supposed to do with you?"

Anton started cleaning up the condo, throwing stuff he didn't want into the void. In like an hour, he had his place all spiffed up. And the painting was a little bigger.

"The more you eat, the bigger you get," he said. "I get it."

He walked up to it, dead center, stared up at it, this thing he'd made. Then he held out his hand, pointed his left pinky finger at it, slowly moved it toward the painting, pressed it against it.

There was no pain. There was a moment of tingling cold, utter cold, but there was not even a sting. There was just nothing. That momentary tingle and then he pulled his finger back and saw that the tip of his pinky finger was gone.

"Christ," Anton said, wiggling it. It was gone like it had never existed. If anything, he'd held his hand too steady, the line was too sharp. Anton held out his finger again, carefully turning it this way and that, rolling it like he was working dough, until he managed to give his fingertip a rounded end. He turned his finger this way and that.

It was insane. Anton understood this. He'd been an idiot to stick his finger into the thing to begin with, but he had to know what it felt like, had to understand what Nina had felt when she faceplanted into it.

Nonexistence would really piss her off. He knew she would be miffed about that, being blotted out of existence.

He took the original pot that had contained the stuff and looked at it again, turned it in his hands. Why had it not eaten through the pot? The pot felt cold in his hand. Anton wondered if the adjoining wall on the other side of the painting, whether it felt cold, too.

Anton tossed the pot into the painting, and it vanished, like everything else had.

"So, now what?" Anton asked. "Am I stuck being the Keeper of the Void? Or do I try to pry you off this wall and get you shown somewhere?"

The painting didn't answer him.

"Talking to a damned painting," Anton said, shaking his head. His self-portrait looked on in jaundiced understanding.

He imagined taking a chisel and hacking away around the painting, so he could pry it loose of its moorings. After that, it was anybody's guess. He couldn't imagine moving it, was sure as hell not walking down the hall with it. And there was no way the landlord would let him lower it through the windows.

Anton looked at it and sighed.

"What am I going to do with you?" he asked. The painting didn't answer.

SEX.

Anton chiseled away at the wall, working up a sweat as he completed the circuit around the thing, unsure if it would even work.

"Now, I'm going to take you out of here," Anton said. "To someplace bigger. A storage space."

The painting didn't answer him, nor did he expect it to. Instead, he took a pry bar and worked around the area he'd cleared with the chisel, until the painting was almost like some kind of surreal flower, the edges bent and buckling.

He pried harder, only to have the painting fly free of the plaster in a rumpled mass, landing on Anton from the knees down, taking everything south of his knees with it as it fell in a flat circle.

To be negated was not something Anton had planned for his day, the icy chill of it, the tingle of affronted neurons as what was him was no more in the blink of an eye.

Anton had managed a gasp as it had happened, and the painting fell in on itself, regaining its perfectly circular shape on the floor, now, having erased everything it had touched, including much of the sofa, the coffee table, in addition to nearly one-third of Anton.

"Oh, God," Anton said, from his perch on the floor, propped by his arms and the stumps of his legs. "I was trying to move you somewhere safer, you Asshole."

The painting was larger, now, of course, having feasted on Anton and the furniture, and now embedded in the wood.

The shock of losing his legs was getting to Anton, as his body and brain went through the horrible realization that what had been there wasn't there, anymore. He imagined his own blood pooling in his legs with every heartbeat, the careful conduits of arteries and veins callously cauterized by the void.

He dragged himself to his work area, taking a bottle of solvent, then spent the better part of an hour pouring it on the painting, tears in his eyes.

The painting drank it down without so much as a single bit of the painting dissolving. Anton hurled the bottle into the void, watching it vanish, like everything else.

And, worse, the painting was eating through the floor. It was unmistakable—when it had been flush with the floor at the moment it had fallen, it was now at least an inch into the wood, maybe more.

Anton crawled to the lip of the painting, peering into it.

"You damned thing," he said. "Do you burn?"

He crawled to the fireplace, where he and Nina had spent more than a few cozy evenings over the years and took the long matches that were in a cylindrical tube and crawled them over to the painting.

Striking one of the yellow-tipped matches, he tossed it at the painting, only to see the fire vanish as quickly as the match.

The painting had eaten its way a foot through the floor, the combination of wood, cement and steel apparently very agreeable to it, because it went right through, and dropped on the tenants below, people Anton didn't even know.

He heard them squawk, muffled, and saw the painting drop flat on their floor, as surely as it had done on his, a perfect, larger circle, perfectly flat, having negated another sofa, and toppling an end table, which, deprived of its legs as surely as Anton had been, toppled forward, dropping into the emptiness of the painting.

The neighbors had been watching television, which was still on, chattering pointlessly on some show Anton didn't watch.

"I'm sorry," Anton said to his negated neighbors, peering at the great hole in the floor. "I'm so sorry."

It was already twice the size of what he'd originally painted. And it had eaten through the back of its own canvas. It existed freely, somehow, unbounded.

The painting was already eating through the floor below, and Anton did the math. The passage from his floor to the one below had doubled the painting's size as it had consumed that matter. It would be over 3000 feet in diameter by the time it reached ground level. In about four more floors, it would be bigger than any single apartment unit in the building, and by the time it cleared eight floors, it would be bigger than the city block they lived on.

And that wasn't factoring in the additional matter falling into it. Anton doubted the building itself could live with an ever-growing hole forming in its old heart. The building would die. Everything would.

He could only imagine what would happen when it reached the ground, how big it would get.

Anton wasn't going to stay around. Grabbing an umbrella, he hooked the door to his place and yanked down on it. Anton pulled himself down the hallway to the elevators, drenched in sweat. His legs were throbbing, swelling from edema. Anton wondered if he'd burst, or whether the void would just eliminate the swelling.

It was easier to just dive into the painting, which was probably what the painting wanted him to do, but Anton wasn't going to do that, refused to give the thing the satisfaction. Instead, he worked his way to the elevator, crawl-dragging himself down the hall, jabbed the call button with the point of the umbrella, and waited for it to come, wondered how long he'd have until the building fell in on itself and fed the monster he had made.

The doors opened and he crawled in. Then Anton hit the button for the lobby, rode the thing down, wondering how much time they had.

It opened into the lobby and there was a young attractive couple there, towering over him, both blond and tan, a matched set of preppy human bookends, mouths open as they gaped unapologetically at what remained of Anton, crawling past them with the umbrella in hand, clacking on the ground.

"If you're smart, you'll get the hell out of this building," Anton said, crawling past them, ignoring them. "Deke? Deke!"

The doorman saw Anton and sized him up with a sweep of his gaze that might as well have been a brush-stroke.

"What happened to you, Mr. LaFontaine?" Deke asked.

"I've got to catch a cab, Deke," Anton said, hearing the elevator doors shut, and seeing the lights flicker a moment. "We've got to get out of this building."

"What happened to your legs, Mr. LaFontaine?" Deke asked.

"An accident," Anton said. "A really big, bad accident."

Deke had turned the knob on the wall that flashed the light that would draw a cab.

"Where are you going, Mr. LaFontaine? Do you need an ambulance?"

"I need a taxi," Anton said. "I need you to hold the door for me, Deke. And I need you to help me to the curb."

Deke, in a moment of inspired doormanship, took one of the brass luggage haulers in the lobby, a wheeled thing, and helped Anton get on it.

Then he wheeled Anton through the service door. The lights had gone out in the building as they'd cleared the threshold.

"A power outage?" Deke asked, turning, pausing, distracted.

"Worse," Anton said, tumbling out of the luggage caddy, not caring that his palms were getting cut on the mica-flecked sidewalk. "Don't go back into the building, Deke, if you want to live."

Deke looked at Anton a moment, not understanding, shook his head.

"I have to, Mr. LaFontaine. It's my job."

And he turned his back on the artist and went back into the building, while Anton pawed his way across the driveway to the curb, to the chemical grass of the boulevard, praying that the cab would get there soon enough.

The human bookends were already dead, he knew. He imagined Chad and Trixie stuck in the darkness of the elevator, not comprehending what had cut the power, only to have themselves blanked out of existence as the painting fell on them like an ebony curtain, smoothing out the wrinkles they would never have, their lives erased in half-a-heartbeat.

The cab approached, Leadfoot Cabs, the logo nearly at Anton's face level as he fumbled with the door, unable to open it.

The cabbie was a young, bald African man, got out and walked around the car. "Where you heading?"

"Airport," Anton said. "Midway. O'Hare. Whichever's closest."

The man opened the door and Anton crawled in, even as his building came down in a tumble of brick and dust that bizarrely ate itself, or appeared to, for someone without a notion of what they were seeing.

Anton gazed at it through the back window, moaning, watching his painting gobble the brick and stone and glass and steel as it fell in upon it, and saw the great circle grow immense, covering the city block, eating the buildings around it, covering the street, claiming cars, which simply drove into the inky abyss, the drivers not knowing what had happened.

"What in heaven?" The cabbie said.

The edge of the painting, bloated and massive as it was, had claimed the rear of the cab, had taken the cabbie, and Anton felt the seat behind him give way as the car was consumed by the great mass of ultimate darkness he'd created with his own two hands, now bloodied and torn.

Anton threw the door open and dropped to the road, crawling away from it.

The lip of the painting was so close to him, now, it was in arm's reach, and across the thousands of feet of the thing, the great inky void, cars were crashing into each other as some drove into it, not guessing their danger, while other cars slammed on the brakes and people sought to avoid the great void. Cars were honking their horns, and police sirens sounded somewhere, but what the authorities could hope to do was nothing at all.

Anton watched the painting eat its way into the ground—first an inch, then a foot, then five feet, then ten, and saw it grow as it fed, undercutting the ground beneath him. He saw the asphalt bend and buckle, like a cake drawn carelessly from a pan, dimpling and cracking, until it dumped him screaming madly into the everlasting depths of his greatest creation.

Of course, the title came to him right before he plummeted into his own self-made annihilation, less than half of an epitaph—

FINIS

A NOTE ON THE TYPE

The text of this book is set in Minion Pro, an Adobe Original typeface designed by Robert Slimbach. The first version of Minion was released in 1990 and is inspired by classical, old style typefaces of the late Renaissance, a period of elegant, beautiful, and highly readable type designs. Minion Pro combines the aesthetic and functional qualities that make text type highly readable with the versatility of OpenType digital technology, yielding unprecedented flexibility and typographic control, whether for lengthy text or display settings.

Robert Slimbach, who joined Adobe in 1987, began working seriously on type and calligraphy four years earlier in the type drawing department of Autologic in Newbury Park, California. Since then, he has concentrated primarily on designing text faces for digital technology, drawing inspiration from classical sources. In 1991, he received the Prix Charles Peignot from Association Typographique Internationale for excellence in type design. Slimbach now directs Adobe's type design program.

The story titles of this book are set in Haltrix, designed by Daniel Sabino for his digital type foundry, Blackletra, which is currently based in São Paulo, Brazil.

The subheads are set in Lydian, a calligraphic humanist sans-serif typeface designed by Warren Chappell for American Type Founders in 1938. It was named after the designer's wife.

Composed by Clever Crow Consulting and Design
Pittsburgh Pennsylvania

ACKNOWLEDGMENTS

I would like to thank Christine Marie Scott of Clever Crow Consulting and Design in Pittsburgh for her wonderful cover art and her invaluable assistance with the layout and design of these pages.

ABOUT THE AUTHOR

Born in Missouri, growing up in Ohio, and settling in Chicago, D. T. Neal has always written fiction, but only got really serious about it in the late 90s. He brings a strong Rust Belt perspective to his writing, a kind of "Northern Gothic" aesthetic reflective of his background.

Writing his first novel at 29, he then devoted time to his craft and worked on short stories, occupying a space between genre and literary fiction, with an emphasis on horror, science fiction, and fantasy. He has seen some of his short stories published in "Albedo 1," Ireland's premier magazine of speculative fiction, and he won second place in their Aeon Award in 2008 for his short story, "Aegis." He has lived in Chicago since 1993, and is a passionate fan of music, a student of pop culture, an avid photographer and bicycler, and enjoys cooking.

He has published secen novels, *Saamaanthaa*, *The Happening*, and *Norm*—collectively known as The Wolfshadow Trilogy—*Chosen*, *Suckage*, *The Cursed Earth*, and *Return to Summerville*. He has also published three novellas—*Relict*, *Summerville*, and *The Day of the Nightfish*.

ALSO BY D.T. NEAL

THE WOLFSHADOW TRILOGY
Saamaanthaa
The Happening
Norm

Lupinia:
The Selected Poems
of Polly Drinkwater, 2007–2015
A Wolfshadow Book

NOVELS
Chosen
Suckage
The Cursed Earth
Return to Summerville

NOVELLAS
Relict
Summerville
The Day of the Nightfish

Nosetouch Press is an independent book publisher
tandemly based in Chicago and Pittsburgh.
We are dedicated to bringing some of today's most
energizing fiction to readers around the world.

Our commitment to classic book design in a digital
environment brings an innovative and authentic
approach to the traditions of literary excellence.

*We're Out There™

NOSETOUCHPRESS.COM

Horror | Science Fiction | Fantasy | Mystery
Supernatural | Gothic | Weird

"Fun, strange, weird…"
—Sasha, Netgalley review